YUMA COUNTY
LIBRARY DISTRICT
2951 S. 21st Dr. Yuma, AZ 85364
(928) 782-1871
www.yumalibrary.org

LOOK

LOOK

ZAN ROMANOFF

Dial Books

DIAL BOOKS
An imprint of Penguin Random House LLC, New York

Visit us online at penguinrandomhouse.com

Printed in the United States of America

Library of Congress Cataloging-in-Publication Data
Names: Romanoff, Alexandra, author. Title: Look / Alexandra Romanoff.
Description: New York : Dial Books, [2020] | Summary: "While falling in love with the mysterious Cass, Lulu sheds her carefully crafted social media persona and takes ownership of who she is in this feminist, queer coming-of-age story"— Provided by publisher.
Identifiers: LCCN 2019021278 (print) | LCCN 2019022312 (ebook) | ISBN 9780525554264 (hardcover)
Subjects: CYAC: Identity—Fiction. | Bisexuality—Fiction. | Feminism—Fiction. | Social media—Fiction. | Love—Fiction.
Classification: LCC PZ7.1.R6682 Loo 2020 (print) | LCC PZ7.1.R6682 (ebook) | DDC [Fic]—dc23
LC record available at https://lccn.loc.gov/2019021278
LC ebook record available at https://lccn.loc.gov/2019022312

10 9 8 7 6 5 4 3 2 1

Design by Cerise Steel
Text set in Winchester New ITC

FOR THE WOMEN WHOSE WRITING GOT ME HERE

● ● ● ●

Beauty is always something you can lose. Women's beauty is seen as something separate from us, something we owe but never own . . . We tend it like a garden where we do not live.

—Jess Zimmerman, "What If We Cultivated Our Ugliness?"

Pretty girls don't know the things that I know.

—"Magnets," Disclosure, ft. Lorde

CHAPTER ONE

● ● ● ●

LULU ARRANGES THE image before she turns the camera on herself. Patrick's mother is kind of a monster, but at least she's the kind who makes sure all of the lighting in her house is flattering, even in rarely used guest bathrooms. *You have to give her credit for that,* Lulu thinks.

The light in here is so even that it almost seems sourceless. The shell pink of the wall is suede-soft, and it makes Lulu's hard-earned winter tan glow golden in contrast. Everyone who's not at the party will wonder where the hell she is when they see this.

So will the people who are here, actually. She didn't tell anyone that she was going upstairs, and most of them don't know the house well enough to recognize this room without context. The image will pop up on their screens at some point tonight, and they won't be able to identify where she was when she took it.

They won't ask. That's a thirsty move, and they're all supposed to be better than that. The idea of parties like this one is that you only get invited if you act like the invitation doesn't matter to you.

Lulu explained this to her older sister once.

"Doesn't it gross you out?" Naomi asked. "Treating your life like it's a game?"

"Don't you like to know the rules?" Lulu asked her in return.

Lulu was fifteen then, spending her afternoons riding around in Kingsley Adams's BMW, learning how to smoke weed and how to drive stick, and how to tell if a boy liked you or just liked the way you looked next to him, stoned and pliant, riding shotgun.

She was wrong about how much King liked her, as it turned out, but right about the rules in general. There were rewards for knowing what they were and following them carefully. Rewards like when Lulu leaves a party to be alone for a little while, people assume that it's because there's something wrong with the party, instead of thinking there's something wrong with her.

Lulu is pleased when her image blinks onto the screen. It looks like she imagined it: Her long dark hair is caught up in a messy topknot, pinned in place by a slash of gold. Bea made her laugh so hard she cried earlier, when the sun was still up and the world still seemed interesting, so her eye makeup is a little smudged in a way that suggests she's been having too much fun to bother fixing it. She gave Owen his ring back but kept the chain she wore it on. Its empty curve dangles below the frame, where it won't give too much away.

Lulu closes her eyes, opens them, and snaps herself in the act of looking up, so that the picture looks like it's been taken by someone standing over her, catching the edge of her attention.

Then she takes a movie: her looking at the camera, and then laughing, and then looking away. She thinks maybe she should be embarrassed—it's kind of cheap, just her flirting with herself—but whatever, because it will also work.

She posts the files and then settles on the stool at the edge of the bathtub to thumb through the rest of her Flash timeline. She can probably kill at least another fifteen minutes before anyone thinks to come looking for her, and hopefully that someone will be Owen or Bea. If it's Bea, she can talk her into leaving—going home and going to sleep.

If it's Owen, she won't have to work very hard to give everyone something new to wonder about.

When the bathroom door opens, though, Lulu doesn't recognize the girl who walks through it.

"Shit," the girl says, even though Lulu is fully clothed and sitting like four feet from the toilet. "I'm so sorry. Shit, shit, shit, sorry."

Her hair is curly and copper red, and she's milk pale, freckle-sprinkled, very thin. She flushes pink and takes a step backward, knocking into the open door. "Ow," she says, and then, again, "Sorry."

Lulu can't help but be charmed. "It's fine," she says. "I mean, I'm not, like, using it. The room. I'm just taking a break. You can—" She starts to stand.

"No!" the girl says. "No, honestly, I'm—I was going to do the same thing."

She's still flushed, but smiling now too. Lulu, who endured years of middle school orthodontia, admires the almost aggressive evenness of her teeth.

"Kind of sucks down there, huh," Lulu says. She sits again. "But Patrick's parties are always like this, don't you think? He likes getting shit-faced so much that he forgets there are other things we could be doing. Like, anything else. I'd play cards right now. Boggle. Anything but sitting around doing shots."

"This is my first," the girl says. "Party. Here, I mean. Not, like, my first party ever."

"Thank god," Lulu says. "I would hate for this one to ruin your opinion of them."

The girl laughs. "I'm Cass," she says. "By the way."

"Lulu," Lulu says. She doesn't offer her hand, and Cass doesn't either. Lulu can't decide if Cass recognizes her or not, and it would be way too narcissistic to ask.

It seems like she probably doesn't; she isn't watchful around Lulu the way girls who know her from the internet sometimes are. They usually don't say anything, but their eyes jitter across her body restlessly, trying and failing to look away.

Cass slumps down to sit with her back against the counter, stretching her legs out on the fluffy rug in front of her.

No one cares that much about you, Lulu reminds herself. She's the one who cares way too much about everyone else.

Speaking of caring, she can't stop herself from doing her usual assessment: Cass is wearing slightly too much mascara, a thin white T-shirt, and tight black jeans Lulu doesn't recognize the brand of. The soles of her flats are scuffed with patterns of wear. Lulu can't decide whether Cass is trying and kind of failing, or if maybe she doesn't even know she should be trying.

When Cass pulls an iPhone with a cracked screen and no cover out of her pocket, a third possibility occurs to Lulu.

Is it possible that Cass just doesn't care about trying either way?

"Do you and Patrick go to school together?" Lulu asks, trying to triangulate.

"Yeah," Cass says. She frowns at something on the phone and swipes it away dismissively. Then she looks up at Lulu, her face glowing faintly blue from its light. "How do you know our host?"

"Elementary," Lulu says. "JTD."

So Cass goes to Lowell. She doesn't look like the Lowell girls Lulu's met. There's usually a particular put-together sheen to them, she thinks. Something about Cass strikes her as raw. She's not undone on purpose, like Lulu's own carefully careless bun. But there's something about her that's just—

"I didn't grow up here," Cass says.

—*what it is,* Lulu thinks. She asks, "When did you move?"

"To LA? When I was twelve. I transferred to Lowell when I was a freshman."

Lulu gets distracted by her phone, which is lighting up with notifications: people liking her post, and replying to it, and sending her videos of their own. She's getting to the point, follower-wise, where she's going to have to turn notifications off soon. Every time she posts anything, there's a flood of this, just nonsense—girls she doesn't know asking her where she got her jewelry and makeup and boys sending her snaps of themselves shirtless in their bathrooms, trying to look hard-eyed and distant.

If Naomi were here, she'd be asking Lulu about this too probably: *Why do you keep doing it, Lu?*

Lulu wouldn't have a good answer for her.

She puts her phone down. "Do you like it?" she asks Cass. "Los Angeles?"

"Not really."

Lulu doesn't catch herself in time to not roll her eyes.

"Oh," Cass says. She leans forward just slightly. "So it's like that."

"It's not like anything," Lulu says. She lolls her head against the wall behind her, to make sure they're both clear on how much space there is between them. "Whatever. Why would I care?"

"Oh." After a beat, Cass leans back too.

Lulu should leave it at that. She should go downstairs and be social and stop sitting alone like a weirdo. She should go back and pretend everything is normal, so that at some point, everything will *be* normal again.

Instead, she says, "I think you have to give it a chance."

"Oh?"

"I mean, I don't know. It's just such a big city, and it's so weird. I feel like it takes a while to figure it out. And people always come in with these ideas about what it is, or what it should be. It's so exhausting. Like, just because you've seen it on TV doesn't mean you *know* anything about it, I guess. Is all."

"I guess. Is all," Cass says, imitating the fall of Lulu's voice at the end of her monologue. She nudges the toe of her shoe against Lulu's ankle, to let her know she's only teasing.

Despite herself, Lulu laughs a little bit. She tries to mask it with a shrug.

"But no, I get that," Cass continues. "That seems fair. I guess I just haven't found the parts of it that I love yet, really."

"Nothing?" Lulu asks.

She risks looking up. Cass is leaning forward again, intent, unembarrassed.

"There's this one spot," Cass says. "It's sort of amazing, actually. I could take you, if you want."

Lulu's phone flashes with a message from Bea.

> Where the hell are you girl??
> Don't make me wander through this whole
> horrible fake castle on a search. Come
> back!!!!!

And then: O says he might be leaving soon.

Lulu knows exactly how the rest of her night will go if she leaves Cass here and walks back downstairs to the living room.

Owen will be drunk; probably a little sloppy. Maybe he'll try to talk to her, or kiss her or something, and she knows perfectly well that she should let him. She should. That would be a big step toward normal: bringing Owen back into her life.

Lulu knows how to follow the rules, and she knows what happens when she does.

She feels the first edge of a hangover coming on: the throb of a headache, the curdle of nausea in her gut. It's silly to think that leaving with Cass will allow her to escape her own body, much less her life.

But if she leaves, people really will have to wonder about her. They'll ask questions, and they won't know where to look for answers.

"Okay," she says. "Why not? Let's go."

CHAPTER TWO

• • • •

CASS'S CAR IS a few blocks away from Patrick's house, taking up half of the street behind the bend of a blind turn and sitting directly under a NO PARKING ANYTIME sign. "Whoops," she says as she unlocks it. The car is a boxy Volvo, not ancient but definitely not new. Cass grabs an armful of stuff off the passenger seat and gestures for Lulu to sit.

She doesn't consult her phone's GPS, which impresses Lulu. "You know your way around this neighborhood?" she asks.

Cass shrugs. "Reception sucks in the hills," she says. "And I have a pretty good sense of direction."

"Oh," Lulu says. And then, to have something else to say: "I don't."

"You seemed to know your way around that house pretty well."

Lulu steered them down the way she'd come up, taking a back staircase and then a side door, slipping them out the front gate without anyone seeing them go. She messaged Bea: hey feeling weird heading out talk tmrw? Though Cass is right about reception: When she looks down now, she sees that it didn't send. She hits RETRY.

"I've spent a lot of time exploring at Patrick's," Lulu says. "And houses are different, anyway. There are walls."

"Yes, there are," Cass agrees.

Lulu knows that was dumb, and she moves to explain, to defend herself—there are *limits* is what she means, there are borders to guide you—but Cass doesn't seem to be dwelling on it. Instead she keeps driving, fast and certain, taking them up and up and up.

She says, "We're not far from where we're going, by the way. I didn't just, like, lure you into my car on false pretenses." She keeps her gaze on the road but raises an eyebrow suggestively. "I'm not that kind of girl."

"Me neither," Lulu says. Which—whatever. Whatever. *That* isn't a conversation she needs to have with Cass right now, especially if Cass doesn't already know.

"See," Cass says. "Look, we're here."

Here is a dark gate so tangled in vines that at first Lulu isn't even sure that there's anything underneath them. Someone has cut away a patch, though, to allow for the swing of the hinge, and the metal glints faintly in the car's headlights. Cass leaps out to tap a code into the keypad. The gate swings open at her command.

Beyond the gate is a long, tree-lined drive. Unkempt branches laced together overhead turn the night's darkness dense with shadow. It should look menacing, but instead it's dreamy. Cass gets back in and eases the car forward, her foot light on the gas.

The gate swings closed behind them.

"So this is the hotel," Cass says.

"The Hotel? Is that, like, its proper name?"

"For now. Do you want to hear a story?"

"Sure." Lulu settles back in her seat and cranes her head up so she can look out the window at the trees. She can't tell whether the flashes of light she sometimes catches through them are lights that have been woven through the branches, or if she's high enough up that somehow, she can see the stars.

"Avery Riggs built this place around the turn of the century," Cass says. "You know the name, right? As in Lowell's Riggs Science Center, or—"

"It's the Riggs Library," Lulu says. "At St. Amelia's."

Every private school child in Los Angeles knows the Riggs name; over the course of a handful of generations of increasingly lawless progeny, the family has donated a wing or at least a building to almost every campus improvement project in the city. Plus, one of the Riggs heirs, Roman, was in her sister Naomi's class in high school—at least until he dropped out at the beginning of their senior year to run a start-up that became Flash.

"Exactly," Cass says. "Avery was the one who made all of that money in the first place. He came out here at the very beginning of Hollywood to try to be a king of cinema. Movies didn't end up working out for him, but real estate did. This place was his first big success."

They come out of the tree canopy and all of a sudden Lulu

sees it: The Hotel. Its white face is lit by the car's headlights and Los Angeles' ambient glow, and it looks almost luminous, gleaming, against the black of the hillside at its back. Floor-to-ceiling glass enclosing the first story shimmers. The floor above it is punctuated by the iron railings of balconies, dark against radiant white.

Cass doesn't exactly park. She just pulls the car to a stop and turns it off. A black Range Rover is sitting right next to the front door, but no one's in it. Since there doesn't appear to be anyone else here, Lulu figures it doesn't really matter where they leave the car.

"Is it . . . open?" Lulu asks.

"For us," Cass says. She unbuckles her seat belt and opens her door. She stands and stretches into the night, raising her long, bony arms to the full white moon, which is sweet and heavy overhead. Her shirt pulls up so that Lulu can mark the points of her hipbones, and imagine the shadow at the curve of her waist.

Cass notices that Lulu hasn't moved. "We aren't going to get in trouble," she says. "I promise."

"I don't know what kind of girl you are," Lulu says. "But breaking and entering, that's really not—"

"You aren't going to get in trouble," Cass repeats.

"How can you be so sure?"

Cass rolls her eyes. "We're not breaking to enter. I had that code, didn't I?"

Lulu gets out of the car.

This is what she's been craving: something completely new.

The night air is cold on her skin, sharp and shivery, and even with the moon it's surprisingly dark. She's out here alone in a place she's never been with a girl she doesn't know.

Anything could happen. Anything at all.

Lulu turns to Cass. "This is your favorite place in Los Angeles?"

"Shhh," Cass says. She holds an actual finger to her lips.

Lulu pauses.

"Hear that?" Cass asks.

Lulu shakes her head.

"Exactly."

"You like that it's quiet?"

"I like that it's *private*," Cass corrects. She takes a step forward and starts to say "Look—" but that's as far as she gets before a light on one of the balconies flips on, flooding them both in buzzing fluorescent bright. Lulu's heart spasms in her chest. She ducks instinctively.

When she looks up, Cass is still standing, an arm thrown over her eyes. "Ryan!" she yells. "Fuck! That light!"

On the balcony there's a figure in silhouette—a boy, Lulu thinks. He drags something heavy into place and stands on it, fiddling with the base of the lamp that's hung there. "Sorry," he calls down. "Sorry, Cass, I forgot about the motion sensors."

"I thought you were going to turn those off!"

"I did in Three," the boy—Ryan—says. "But then I fell asleep in Four."

"Why don't you turn all of them off?"

"Then what if some random creeps came sniffing around?"

"Are you just hoping to blind them to death?"

"The security cameras, Cass. Can't record a creep you can't see."

The light finally flicks off, and the dark that follows seems to swallow them all.

"You still there?" Ryan calls.

Cass scuffs the toe of one of her flats in the dirt. "Be hospitable, you asshole," she says. "I brought someone with me. Come meet your first real guest."

"Come up," Ryan says. "It's fucking freezing out."

Cass looks at Lulu. She's shy, suddenly, for the first time all night. "We don't have to," she says. "I just wanted to show you— I didn't mean to— You don't have to—"

"What kind of boy is Ryan?" Lulu asks.

"Nice," Cass says. A smile steals across her face: small, secret. *Oh*, Lulu thinks. "A nice one."

"I like nice boys," Lulu says. "And, whatever. What else am I doing tonight?"

"Good point."

Ryan must be Ryan Riggs, Lulu realizes as they head inside and up the stairs. Roman's little brother. He goes to Lowell too, so it makes sense that he and Cass know each other.

Lulu doesn't know anything else about him, though, which is

sort of unusual. Private schools in LA are a very incestuous little ecosystem: Colonies from elementary school spread and mutate into middle and high schools, so that everyone knows someone who knows someone else. But Ryan had a private tutor until his freshman year, and he hasn't been around much since then. She doesn't really see him out at parties, anyway.

The room Ryan fell asleep in is still heavy with the scent of his body, a warm, animal funk that makes Lulu think of Owen, and then makes her wish she hadn't. The rest of the space is very teenage boy too: There's a twin bed pushed against one wall, the mattress covered by a tangle of white sheets and a white comforter; a coffee table with a vape pen, a handful of empty cartridges, and a collection of lighters on it; then, on the floor, a stack of books and a stack of external hard drives, plus an enormous Mac desktop with a pair of nice speakers plugged into it. Not much else.

Ryan doesn't flick on the lights when they come in. Instead he goes out to the balcony, brings in an armful of candles, sets them on the table, and lights them.

"You're getting very witchy, Ry," Cass says.

"I'm learning about atmosphere," he returns.

Cass sits on the floor like she did in the bathroom, this time with her back against the bed frame. Ryan settles himself next to her. He doesn't touch her, but he could.

Lulu knows that distance well. It's a suggestive positioning of bodies—close enough for warmth, but far enough that contact has to be intentional. It occurs to her that she's definitely the third wheel in this extremely weird situation.

She sits facing them, cross-legged on the floor. Lulu is relieved when Cass pulls the vape off the table and charges it up before taking a hit. She inhales deeply, and exhales a curtain of white that obscures her face as it drifts toward the ceiling.

Lulu's not usually much of a smoker—doesn't like the heady, uncertain way it makes her feel, the unpredictable nature of her own self when she's high—but at least soon they'll all be messed up, and she can stop wondering if she should have left before they came up the stairs.

"I told you that party was going to suck," Ryan says to Cass. Then, to Lulu, he says, "Oh, I mean, sorry, it was your friend's thing, yeah?" In the candles' flickering, forgiving light, Ryan looks searingly romantic. He's dark haired and handsome, with high, finely cut cheekbones and a wide slash of a mouth.

"I thought it sucked too," Lulu says. She reaches across the table and plucks the pen from Cass's hand. She may not exactly know what's going on here, but that doesn't mean she can't act like she does. That's one of the rules: Behave like you belong. "And he's not really my friend."

"Why did you go, then?" Cass asks.

They've only known each other for half an hour, and once again, Lulu can't seem to keep herself from telling Cass the truth. "Saturday night," she says. "I don't know, it was something to do."

"Why did *you* go, Cass?" Ryan asks. "Because as I recall, you don't think much of Paisley—"

"*Patrick*," she corrects.

"Or parties in general."

"Broadening my horizons," Cass says. "And hey, look, I made a friend."

Lulu's phone buzzes in her bag. She pulls it out and finds that her message to Bea still hasn't gone through. Instead, Bea sent her: not funny srsly where the hell are you.

Left on an adventure but got a little stranded. Can you come get me? Lulu writes back, relieved to see the delivery confirmation pop up almost as soon as she's hit SEND.

"Hey," Ryan says. "No phones up here. There's only one rule at The Hotel—"

"I didn't tell her," Cass says apologetically. "Sorry, Lulu, this is Ryan's, like, *thing*."

"My friend was just saying she's leaving the party," Lulu explains. "I think she's going to come get me. Give me a ride home."

"You sure?" Cass says. "I got you here. I mean, I can—"

"Thanks," Lulu says. "But I'm good, really. Can you give me the address to give to her?"

"What the hell was that?" Bea asks. Lulu watches Cass disappear as the gate slides closed behind them. Cass is so pale she looks like a ghost against the driveway's dim. "Did you get a good Flash or two out of it, at least?"

Lulu blinks at her own reflection where it appears in the windowpane, shimmering under a passing streetlight. She realizes that The Hotel is the first place she's been in a year, at least, where she didn't take a picture or a video. Even before Ryan told her she couldn't use her phone, it didn't even occur to her to try.

"Wasn't anything worth seeing," she says to Bea. She doesn't feel like getting into it right now—even though if anyone has gossip on Ryan and Cass, it would be Bea, who has gossip on everyone. Everyone who matters, anyway.

"Oh, you know you're always worth seeing, baby," Bea says. She reaches out a hand across the space between them, and Lulu leans gratefully into her touch.

CHAPTER THREE

● ● ● ●

BEA MAKES THEM both breakfast in the morning. It's nothing complicated: scrambled egg whites, avocado toast. Lulu squeezes juice from oranges from one of the trees in the backyard. They eat at the little table in the kitchen, where the light is good.

"You look like a religious figure," Bea says, her eyes fixed on Lulu's image in her phone. "Like the Madonna bathed in God's holiness or something. I think my aunt has this photo as a painting in her bathroom, actually."

Bea's parents emigrated from the Philippines; they're pretty agnostic, but her extended family includes some of the most Catholic people Lulu has ever met. Which isn't saying *that* much, but still. Lulu secretly loves the art in Bea's family's houses—she's probably talking about her aunt Tereza, who lives in the Valley, in a sea of gold-leafed crosses—but Bea thinks it's tacky.

"You would know, Beatriz," Lulu says. "And, I mean, Jesus' mom was a Jew too, right?" She tilts her head. "Wait, are you filming?"

"I was," Bea says. She tap, tap, taps at the screen and puts the phone down. "Now I'm not."

"Can I see?"

Bea rolls her eyes. "I muted the audio," she says. "And you look great. You know I wouldn't put up anything that made you look bad."

"We don't always agree on what that is, though."

Bea scoots her phone across the table to Lulu. "You can delete it if you really want."

Lulu flicks it back. She knows she's been a little too sensitive about stuff like this lately. Who cares if there's another unflattering video of her on the internet for a day? Wouldn't be the first time. And Bea doesn't even have as many followers as she does, which is sort of a shitty thing to think about, maybe, but it's also true.

When she looks up, Bea is touching her fingertips to the faint violet of a bruise blooming just above her collarbone. Apparently the reason it took her so long to notice that Lulu had actually disappeared last night was that she and Rich, her on-again, off-again, were getting it on. Again.

Gross.

"Has he texted you?" Lulu asks.

"Not yet," Bea says. "But I'd bet I hear something about that Flash in, like, the next five—"

As if on cue, her phone vibrates on the table. She and Lulu both break into peals of laughter.

"He's *so* predictable," Lulu says.

Bea nods like, *Well, yeah*. There's value in predictable, and they both know what it is. Rich is definitely someone who follows the rules.

"He says they all passed out at Patrick's last night," Bea reports, and she doesn't have to clarify who *we* is for Lulu to know who she means. Rich, their friend Jules, and probably Owen too. "They're thinking about breakfast. Would it be, like, way too weird if I invited them over?"

Lulu shrugs.

Bea puts her phone down more decisively this time. "You know this is up to you, Lu. I'm not bringing people to your house if you don't want them here. I just thought, I don't know. You might want to." There's a phrase that's left unsaid in Bea's sentence: *You might want to see people again, be social, pretend things are fine, talk to Owen*. Stop being such a recluse.

Lulu knows she's being unfair by not giving a straight answer. Bea's trying to be a good friend. It's not her fault that Lulu just wants someone else to make this decision for her so that she won't have to be responsible for whatever the consequences turn out to be.

She doesn't think she's wrong that Owen's been looking for a way to un–break up with her for the last few weeks. He's definitely been trying to talk to her about something, and what else could it be?

It's just that at no point, in all of those days and nights, has she been able to figure out if she wants to let him or not.

It seems like the right thing to do.

She liked dating Owen the first time. Why wouldn't she like doing it again?

She would definitely like how much easier it would make her life.

"No one will think less of you," Bea says, a little softer. "It's not like he— Everyone knows you guys were in love. I don't think you should be embarrassed to take him back."

Again, Lulu knows what Bea isn't saying: *It's not like* he *embarrassed* you. Of course it wasn't. It was Lulu who hurt and embarrassed Owen, so badly that he ended things.

But maybe he's over that, and now he wants things back the way they were.

"He was knocking on doors looking for you last night," Bea says. "He was the one who found me, and told me you were, like, actually gone."

"Found you—"

"I don't want to talk about it," Bea says. "We had not considered that we might want to make sure we'd actually locked the door of the room we were using."

"I don't want to think about it either," Lulu says. "Anyway, of course it's fine. Invite them over. It's always fun to have them here."

The boys used to come over a lot back when she and Owen were still together. Lulu and O would make out in the grass while everyone else kicked a soccer ball around the backyard.

"I really need to shower before they get here, though," Lulu says.

Bea is looking at her phone again. "Rich wants to know if you're the kind of Jews who eat bacon."

They are in theory, but Lulu knows her stepmom's shopping habits and her dad's cholesterol. There's no way there's any bacon in the house right now.

"Tell Rich that beggars can't be choosers," she advises. "But he's welcome to bring his own."

The boys take up so much space. Jules had to go home, but Patrick comes with, so it's him, Rich, and Owen in the kitchen, sitting on the countertops and heckling Bea while she scrambles more eggs, these ones with their yolks.

Lulu swats Patrick's calf and says, "Get down."

"What, are your parents home?" he asks.

When have her parents ever been home? "They're probably at Olivia's soccer game," Lulu says, which, now that she thinks about it can't be true, because it's a Sunday, but whatever.

"It's so weird that you have a sister who's twenty-one and a sister who's five," Patrick says. God, he has no tact.

"Six," Lulu says, and then, "Half sister," like either of these things matters to anyone but her. As if to prove her point, Patrick's already turned away, in the process of doing something weird and violent to Rich's upper thigh.

So she's surprised to hear Owen pick up that piece of the conversation after her. "Half sister, Patrick," he repeats. "You know that."

Patrick nods. "Right," he says. "Half sister. And your step-mom is hot."

"Isn't that the point of stepmoms?" Lulu asks.

Bea turns around from the stove. "You want to make more OJ, Lu?" she asks.

Lulu hates that Bea can tell she needs an out.

"I can get it," Rich says. He's moved so he's standing next to Bea at the stove, like she might need his help scrambling eggs. It would be sweet if Lulu were in a better mood.

"We have to pick more oranges," Lulu explains to him. "I've got it. I'll be right back."

It's early afternoon already, and outside, the sun is warm through her clothes. Lulu thinks of stepping out of the car at The Hotel last night in her impractical outfit—a thin dress, no jacket—and the bite of the air against her skin. The way she felt exposed to some darker kind of night. Now the world seems tender again, offering up soft ground, green grass, sweet fruit.

The orchard isn't really big enough to be an orchard, technically—it's just a loose cluster of a half dozen or so trees (oranges, lemons, and a lone avocado) and stone benches that sit, quiet and solid, under their branches.

Lulu hears Owen before she sees him. He's quiet too, bare-foot like she is, but Lulu has spent years and years in this space when it was truly empty. She knows what it sounds like the moment someone else arrives.

He's carrying a bowl. "I didn't know if you needed some-thing for the oranges," he says. "To put them in."

24

"Oh," Lulu says. "Yeah. That's smart, actually. Thanks."

Owen places the bowl on one of the benches, and Lulu puts the oranges she's already picked into it.

"It was also a good excuse," Owen says. "To. Um. Talk to you."

How long have they known each other? Lulu watches the way the light filters through the trees' leaves, falling on the mess of his sandy hair, and does the math: since the first day of seventh grade. It was five years in September, then. Like, basically a third of her life so far.

"About what?"

"I'm sorry," he says, "to start with. The way I ended things . . . I'm not proud of it."

Owen didn't ghost her, but he came close. He told her he didn't want to talk about what had happened on the phone, and then he didn't try to make plans with her when he got back to LA. Finally, desperate, she called him the night before school started.

He said, "I can't do this anymore, Lu." He probably said other things too, but that's what Lulu remembers: the word *can't*, and how tired his voice sounded, and how much her heart ached, like it was exhausted, like all it wanted was to be allowed to quit beating for a while.

Now he says, "You were, like, really important to me, and I hope I didn't make you feel, just because it ended badly, that I hadn't—that I didn't—that—that wasn't true."

This does not sound like a prelude to an offer of the two of them starting over again. Lulu feels her defenses rising as surely as if they were physical walls going up, locking firmly into place.

"You don't have to apologize to me," she says. "I mean, since you're here and everything. I feel like it's obvious that I'm okay with you. Don't worry, O. We're good."

"I'm glad," Owen says. "But I also—I know there's no good way to break up with someone, but I wish I hadn't gone dark on you like that. I just needed some time, you know? I needed a minute to figure things out. But lately I've really been missing you, Lu. And I want us to try being friends again, if you're interested in that."

Lulu doesn't know what to say.

"I get that I can't, like, ask you for anything. So I'm not. I'm just saying: If that's something you want, that's something I want."

Lulu nods. She turns back to the trees. It's their season, and there are so many ripe oranges that she doesn't even have to go looking for them. When she reaches, they fall right into her hand.

Owen is offering her something. It's not what she imagined or guessed, but it's *something*.

The problem is that it's something new. Lulu has no idea what it would be like, what it would mean for them, to be friends. She could probably figure out the best way to play this, but she needs much, much more time. She feels undone by the scope of possibility, the idea that there's some halfway point between being nothing to each other and being *them* again. The idea that he could want her, but not like that.

She doesn't want to lose him, though. She knows that much.

She says, "You can help me with this, for starters."

"Sure," Owen says.

If they were—when they were—he would have razzed her about not answering questions, about being evasive, the same way Bea was giving her shit earlier.

Lulu thinks, *Serves him right*, that he can't be familiar with her anymore. He can't ask for more than she decides to give him.

On the other hand, now he's just another person she has to keep a wall up with. And she already has so many of those.

CHAPTER FOUR

• • • •

LULU DOESN'T TELL anyone about the specifics of her conversation with Owen. Bea is too distracted by Rich to ask on Sunday; by Monday, all anyone's thinking about is finals, which start next week.

But the sense of detente between them seems to filter through their friends, and resettle some of the fracture their breakup caused in September. Lulu finds herself sitting at tables with the boys during lunch again. On Wednesday, Rich asks her to share her calc notes. On Friday sixth period, Jules texts her that they're going up to the lookout to get drunk if she wants to come.

She doesn't.

It would be easy to sneak off campus—technically she's got Cinema Studies this period, but Mr. Winters is giving them "research time" to work on their midterm projects, so it's not like anyone would notice if she left. The projects aren't due until the beginning of next semester, which Mr. Winters thinks makes their lives easier but actually just extends their stress for another few weeks after finals are supposed to be over.

But Lulu doesn't want to go hang out with her friends right

now. What she wants, instead, is quiet. And she knows where to find it: Recently she's claimed herself kind of a spot in a corner on the top floor of the library. She can go up there and post something to Flash, the way she did at Patrick's party, so that on the internet it doesn't look like she's hiding out.

The space isn't ideal for taking pictures, but she's figured out how to make it work. The overheads are horrible fluorescents, but the windows are big enough to let some actual sunlight in, and the camera's eye is so easy to trick once you know it. All she has to do is hide most of her face in shadow and she looks okay.

"One of my nannies taught me a game when I was little," Lulu whispers to her phone. "Literary prophet, she called it. You ask a question, pull a book off the shelf, and let it fall open to a page that will have the answer you need on it." The app blinks at her: *full*. Okay. They can only be like ten seconds long.

Lulu uploads that video fragment and starts another. She films her feet, clad in a pair of new boots, walking across the library's industrial carpet floor. She asks her question before she chooses the book. "Why am I so fucking bored?"

Of course, she's up in the science section, surrounded by textbooks. "Because it's my biological destiny, apparently," Lulu says, and slams the book closed. She snaps a few stills of the illustrated dissection diagrams and then a last black frame over which she adds the text: I GUESS JUST DONATE MY BODY TO SCIENCE WHEN IT WITHERS AND GOES OKAY.

It occurs to her then that, probably for the first time in her life, she actually has something she wants to look up in a book. There's a small section on the first floor of the library dedicated to Los Angeles' past, with a display table encouraging kids to read up on the history of St. Amelia's Studio City campus and farming and water rights and whatever.

Of course, there's also a couple of books about the library's namesake: Avery Riggs.

Lulu did some cursory googling about Avery after her visit to The Hotel, to see if she could find more information about him and its history, but most of what she turned up was loose threads and weirdness: conspiracy theorists claiming he was illuminati, or that his wife was a vampire, or that if you draw a line between every building with his name on it in the city of Los Angeles you'll come up with a pentagram or a map to a portal to hell.

Normally she would have left it at that—Lulu isn't really that into history, even when it's cult-conspiracy history. But the supernatural bent to people's theories made her curious. She wants to know how Avery, who seemed basically kind of normal when he was alive, has a legacy that got so warped after he died.

The first book she pulls is called *The Men Who Built Los Angeles*, which only has one chapter on Riggs. Apparently his dad had a very big trust fund and an even bigger gambling problem; Avery was raised to believe he'd never have to work, and then, when he came of age, discovered that he if he didn't, he and his mother and sisters might starve. He left the East Coast for Hollywood, hoping to remake the family name out there in the wilderness. But he wasn't really a very good director, and after a while, no one would hire him.

He got lucky when he begged his way into a screening of a film called *Bluebeard,* an adaptation of the fairy tale starring a young actress named Constance Wilmott. She was still a teenager, and aside from her studio contract she had nothing. He married her even though it wouldn't do anything for his "prospects": a true love story, very touching. Except that it turned out she was a good investment, because it was the money she'd earned on that film—her first and last—that he took and used to buy his first property.

Lulu recognizes the outline of the story, if not the specifics. Her dad was still a junior associate at his firm, not a failed director, and her mom didn't choose to stop being a serious actress, she stopped getting good roles, but other than that, yeah, she pretty much knows how this one goes. An older man and a younger woman; two people with almost no power, and yet, somehow, one of them has more.

The book says: *Wilmott may not be a star that many remember today, but in fact her single role changed Los Angeles irrevocably. The intangible forces of her beauty and talent became the seeds for a real estate empire that would materially reshape the hills and valleys of Los Angeles. It was her image that allowed Avery Riggs to begin to create the city according to his singular vision.*

It makes Lulu feel shivery to imagine it: these two people,

small and ordinary, falling in love and changing the course of an entire city's history. Connie playacting in a movie, and her acting turning into money that turned into land and business and a legacy. Maybe that's why people are so obsessed with Avery Riggs: He made something out of nothing. He married a much younger woman and turned her into an empire.

If only her dad had figured out how to do *that*, Lulu thinks, instead of the extremely boring regular thing he did, which was to dump her mom when her career never took off, and marry someone younger, and then someone younger again.

She almost misses Rich's response to her Flash amid all the stuff from people she doesn't know. He went up to the lookout with Jules, apparently, and Bea, and a smallish bottle of vodka. In the video he sent her he's holding his phone at arm's length and filming the two of them, Bea's dark head huddled close at his side. "You think that just because you have—what, two thousand—"

"Five thousand!" Bea chirps. She's definitely drunk.

"*Five* thousand Flash followers," Rich corrects himself, "you're too cool to hang out with us now?"

"You're bored 'cause you're boring," Jules says, somewhere off camera.

"Julian Powell!" Bea yells. Rich swerves to turn toward Jules and Lulu catches a glimpse—barely that—of Owen.

Someone is standing next to him. Someone shorter.

Some girl.

Then the video cuts out.

Lulu thought her heart froze the day Owen broke up with her; she thought she put it in deep freeze and left it there to just—well, not rot. Ice. Whatever. So it surprises her to feel it kicking in her chest, the gasp of a spasm where she was supposed to be numb. She wasn't sure she wanted Owen back, but she definitely didn't want him to move on first.

She's sure her face will give her away if she tries to send a picture back.

Instead she messages Bea, I hope you're defending my honor up there.

OBVSSSSSSSSS, Bea replies. BUttt shouldn't you be here defending it yourself?

Lulu types, I have English eighth.

Come out with us after, Bea says. We'll be at R's house for a while and then I think going to some party? Someone Patrick knows?

Lulu weighs her options. It's nice to have something to do, first of all, and if Owen is—whatever—with whoever—and who would he even be—she should assert her claim to her place in the group. She belongs there with them. She has belonged there for years, in ways that have nothing to do with being or not being Owen's girlfriend.

But also: ugh.

Then a second thought occurs to her. If the party is being thrown by someone Patrick knows, he might know Cass too.

She said she never went to those parties. It's totally a long shot. But last time Lulu disappeared, Owen went looking for her, and everyone knew it.

Okay fine, Lulu sends Bea. I guess I'm in.

CHAPTER FIVE

• • • •

THE GIRL FROM Rich's Flash, the one who was standing with Owen, comes to the party too. Kiley Rathbone. Some *sophomore*.

The worst part is that Lulu knows her a little bit: They're in Cinema Studies together. Kiley doesn't talk much, but when she does, she usually says smart-seeming things. She sits with a girl named Maija, who Lulu knows because she knew Maija's older sister, Sam, when she was a senior last year, and also because Maija is probably the prettiest girl in the sophomore class. Not the most popular, but the prettiest, which means Kiley isn't afraid of pretty girls. Which probably means Kiley has some sense that she's very, very pretty too.

The only other thing Lulu knows about Kiley is that she dances, or at least she was in an assembly teaser for a dance theater show last year. That was the first time Lulu noticed her, up on stage, but to be fair, it was hard not to: She was the only black girl up there.

Also, she was, like, *good*.

Lulu ignores her and tries to look cheerful about it.

Luckily, there's plenty to distract her. In the kitchen, Jules turns a TV on so he can watch the Lakers, but it's part of an art installation that shows looped clips from news reports about missing and murdered girls spliced in with scenes from cop shows about the same thing. Whoever's house they're at—Isabel, maybe, someone said her name was?—her parents have truly atrocious taste, and an amazingly huge collection of stuff that demonstrates this fact. There are ugly "modern" sculptures and garish abstract paintings everywhere, and after the television incident, Lulu is afraid to sit on or really touch anything in case it turns out to be art.

At least the booze is stashed out back near the pool, where it's obvious what it's supposed to be.

Lulu scans the crowd for Cass and doesn't see her. Something goes tight in her throat at the idea of spending the whole night standing around and making, like, small talk. Trying to get or keep Owen's attention. Everyone looking at her, and looking at Kiley, and Owen and Kiley, and Owen and her, and thinking whatever they're thinking.

Bea nudges her shoulder. "If this stuff is what these people think is appropriate for company, can you even imagine what they keep in their bedrooms?"

"Ooooh," Lulu says. "Are you suggesting we find out?"

Bea widens her eyes like, *Who, me?*

"C'mon," Lulu says. She and Bea lope away giggling. She hopes Kiley is watching them disappear and wondering what they're up to. Imagining that it's something super exclusive and cool.

Isabel's parents' bedroom is on the second floor, and Bea was right to guess that it would be weird. It looks like a vampire's lair: Their round bed sits on a mirrored pedestal, covered in pristine white sheets, and everything else in the room is glass or crystal or bone, except the curtains, which are deep, purple velvet.

"Oh my god," Bea says, turning in a circle. "Oh my *fucking* god." She dashes over to the window and wraps herself in a curtain, fashioning it into a heavy-draped dress. "This is glamour," she announces in a husky voice.

"Daaahling," Lulu intones. "You are *everything* right now. You are the earth. You are the moon. You are a moondrop dancing with a god in the night."

Bea laughs and lets the curtain drop. "What are you even talking about," she says. "You're a nut, Lu." Before Lulu can answer, she goes on. "This is so wild. Can you imagine having parents who live like this?"

Lulu shudders at the thought.

"Oh no. Oh *no,*" Bea says. She points, and when Lulu turns around she sees it: a sculpture of a naked woman, but she has two rows of teeth where her legs should be.

"Gross!"

"Tell me about it."

Lulu goes over to inspect the thing. The woman is arranged in one of those improbable comic book poses, boobs thrust forward, waist turned at an angle. Lulu tries to mimic it with her own body, but it's basically impossible.

"No," Bea says. "It's like this, see?" She tries to out-pose

Lulu, but her legs get tangled as she tries to step around the curtain. She windmills her arms, teetering, before toppling over. From her crash landing on the ground, Bea sticks her tits up as far as she can. "Closer?" she asks. "This looks hot, right?"

Lulu is laughing too hard to reply. She pulls out her phone and takes a video of Bea squirming.

"You animal!" Bea yells.

Lulu writes *@beatrizzzo is art* over it and presses SEND with a flourish. Bea has her phone out now, and she's taking a picture from the floor, which has to be a hideously unflattering angle.

"You!" Lulu reaches to grab Bea's phone, but Bea pulls her down too. Lulu thumps next to her ungracefully, still laughing.

She looks up and sees Kiley in the open doorway, staring at them.

"Hey," Kiley says. "I thought I heard voices. I was just going to get something from Isa's room."

Bea leaps to her feet. "Oh, yeah, us too," she says. "We uh . . . didn't know if this was it."

It's a bad lie, but Kiley is too drunk to notice. They've only been there an hour or so, but she's already looking pretty sloshy, the alcohol loose and glistening under her skin. "No," she says. "It's over here."

"Great!"

Now there's nothing to do but brush themselves off and follow her.

Kiley looks at the phone still in Lulu's hand. "Is it true that you have, like, five thousand Flash followers?" she asks.

Lulu says, "Whoa. Um. Yeah."

She doesn't know how to feel about that number. It's sort of a lot, and sort of not, really. It's not like anyone's offering her sponsored content deals or auditions for television shows on the strength of it, anyway. She's definitely not a Kardashian, or some famous heiress or Instagram model. Mostly it's just that Owen's dad is famous, like seriously famous, like eventually-definitely-gonna-be-in-the-rock-and-roll-hall-of-fame famous, and so people care about Owen, and then, for a while, people cared about her.

And then there was that other thing.

As if on cue, Kiley says, "You always do such cool stuff. It's not surprising. I didn't see the one with Sloane—"

"We've gotten some pretty good stuff here tonight," Bea says, cutting her off. "With the, um, we were posing with some of the art. I think maybe this is Lu's finest work yet."

Lulu shoots her a death glare, and Bea smiles sweetly.

"Sorry," Kiley says. "Am I asking too many questions? Am I too drunk?" She leans in conspiratorially. "I'm still figuring out getting—ummm—drinking—how to get drunk right."

"You're fine," Bea says. She puts a hand on Kiley's arm. Lulu wishes she were less annoyed by that. The part of her that can't bring herself to be rude to Kiley wants Bea to do it for her. "How do you know Isabel?"

Kiley opens a door that leads into a much more normal-looking bedroom. "From, uh, we used to go to the same ballet studio," she says. "When I did ballet. Oh, look, there's the vodka."

Bea and Lulu are still in the hallway. Bea knocks her shoulder against Lulu's. "Whatever," she murmurs. "She's a baby."

It doesn't matter if Kiley is cool or not, Lulu thinks. She's really just very pretty, and she doesn't have a history with anyone here, which means she has what Lulu wants: the ability to get drunk unself-consciously, and meet someone new, and feel like she belongs places. To be excited, and exciting.

The stuff they're drinking downstairs is cheap shit—Romanoff or something—but a bottle of Grey Goose is sitting on Isabel's desk with a Post-it next to it, a smiling face drawn in Sharpie. Kiley dumps her cup in the sink of the en suite bathroom; as Bea and Lulu walk into the room, she returns with it empty, and fills it back up. She grimaces when she takes a sip of straight vodka. "Ugh," she says. "Blech."

Lulu gives Bea her cup to deal with and wanders around, pretending to be casual. It's easy to find what she's looking for, though: A stack of Lowell yearbooks is crammed onto the bottom shelf of Isabel's bookcase. She recognizes Cass right away. Cassandra Velloro, third from last in the junior class, looks as flat and uncomfortable as every other kid in the surrounding pictures. Lulu tried to find Cass online, but it was hard without a last name. This will definitely help.

Bea peers over Lulu's shoulder. Lulu flips the page quickly, so she can pretend she's just skimming.

"Looking for your next boyfriend?" Bea asks.

Lulu shrugs and snaps the book shut. From the corner of her eye she sees Kiley's head tilt minutely toward them. She'll do whatever she wants to with Owen, Lulu knows—an older girl with some social seniority just isn't enough to deter you when a cute older boy is dangling himself in front of you. But if Lulu is moving on, that gives Kiley permission to go after Owen without worrying what it looks like.

"I wanted to see if Patrick's hair looked as dumb as I remember when he was trying to do that faux-hawk thing," Lulu says.

Bea rolls her eyes. "God," she says. "That was the worst."

No wonder she was hard to find. Cassandra Velloro doesn't have a Facebook profile, an Instagram, a Tumblr, or a Twitter. Lulu almost doesn't bother searching Flash—why would someone who's so obviously opposed to social media make an exception?

But then, the whole thing about Flash is that it's there and then gone again—videos disappear a day after you post them, and there's a private messaging system too. She thinks that Flash actually might appeal to Cass, whose favorite place in Los Angeles is a spot where no one can hear or see her. Plus, she's BFFs with the founder's brother.

And, in fact, there she is. Lulu follows her.

A few minutes later, Cass follows her back.

Lulu and Bea did Grey Goose shots in Isabel's room, and they went to Lulu's head too fast. Now she's in the middle of the kind of expansive, tipsy feeling that makes everything in the world seem like a good idea. Lulu sends Cass a picture of herself standing still, surrounded by her friends dancing. I keep expecting someone to show up and rescue me, it says.

In the seconds after the message goes she feels incredibly, supremely dumb. She shouldn't have gotten so fancy about it, all #aesthetic and stupid. Simpler would have been better. She should have just—

Cass breaks every messaging protocol Lulu has ever known and chats her back right away. I was just thinking about heading to The Hotel, she says. The picture shows her sitting in a room so dark that her body is mostly just a shadow on the screen.

And then: Come with?

Lulu slips out of the room before anyone can see her typing and ask who she's talking to. She finds a couch to sit on and writes back

I'm in Brentwood

I don't have my car here

I'll pick you up

You sure?

I'm coming from Silver Lake.

Technically, all of this is out of my way.

Silver Lake. That makes sense, Lulu thinks, or she thinks it makes sense—she doesn't know Cass or the neighborhood very well at all.

If you don't mind, she says, and sends Cass a pin of the house's location.

She's concentrating so hard on not making any typos that she doesn't notice Owen coming to sit down next to her.

"Hey," he says.

"Hi."

"Are you causing trouble?" he asks, gesturing at her phone.

Lulu blanches.

Owen catches himself. "That's not—you know that's not what I meant," he says.

It probably wasn't, really. That stupid Sloane Flash. Lulu hates that she can't think of it without feeling two distinct, unbearable sensations: the warm, thrilled moment of taking it, and the sharp, hot shame when she realized who she'd sent it to.

"Sorry," Owen says.

They're definitely not going to talk about this now. Or ever, hopefully, but especially not now, on a night when Owen has some new girl hanging around, on which Lulu is drunk, on which Lulu is leaving, anyway, so—

"I'm heading out in a bit, I think," she says.

"Is it because of me?"

"Don't flatter yourself, O."

"Sorry," he says again. He means it. This is the problem with Owen, the reason she can't—that no one can—stay mad at him for too long.

"I know you are."

A cry goes up from another room, and Lulu hears the distinctive rumble of Jules bellowing "Party fouuuuul!"

"How can you leave such a super-cool party?" Owen asks. "So sophisticated. So mature."

"I know, right?"

Quiet falls between them. Lulu holds herself very still to keep from doing what she wants to do instinctively, which is lean her head against his shoulder. Her body is so convinced that it knows how to be with him.

"Are you just going home?" Owen asks.

"No." Lulu doesn't want to tell him about Cass, but she wants him to know that he's not the only thing going on in her life anymore.

"Found a cooler scene?"

"Wasn't hard to do." Lulu smirks.

Owen laughs at her.

Lulu laughs at herself.

"I know I can't, but I sort of wish I could go with you," Owen says.

Impulsively, Lulu asks: "Why can't you?"

"Oh," Owen says. "I mean, I guess I figured you wouldn't want me to."

Lulu wants to ask about Kiley and can't.

"It would be pretty weird," she says. She can't quite picture Owen—solid, comfortable, easygoing Owen—in the dark, strange space of The Hotel.

But it would also be a place she could show him. That the two of them could have together. One last secret, even if they aren't going to be together like that anymore.

One more thing no Kiley can ever take from her.

"I should be getting back," Owen says.

"You can," Lulu agrees. "You should. But you can also come with me if you want."

CHAPTER SIX

••••

IF CASS IS pissed about Lulu inviting someone to join them, she doesn't act like it. Lulu figures she's relieved, probably. This way there's no third-wheeling worries: just two girls, two boys, an abandoned building, and the night. Exactly the way it's supposed to be.

Right?

The Hotel seems darker than it did last time. The fairy lights strung through the trees along the entryway aren't on, and the moon is waning, turning thin in the sky. Owen makes a joke about being a kidnapping victim and Cass laughs politely.

"Lulu made it out okay," she says.

"Lulu was the bait," Owen says, straight-faced. "I'm the real prize."

Cass throws a look over her shoulder at him in the back seat. For just an instant she's razor sharp, as if a mask has fallen away, leaving the slice of her judgment raking over him. "No you're not," she says. And then, just as fast, she's smiling again. "I mean, I hear Lulu's the one with five thousand Flash followers."

"That does seem to be the fact of the day," Lulu says. "Also, currently, five thousand and one."

Since last time they were here someone has spray-painted actual lines for parking spaces directly in front of The Hotel, which makes it feel less magical. Lulu is pleased that Cass pointedly ignores them, pulling her car in so that it straddles two spots. The same black Range Rover, presumably Ryan's, is parked sideways to take up the remaining three. "Full for the night," Cass observes as they step out.

Lulu inhales lungfuls of cold, clean air. Last time she was here she was so caught up in the strangeness of it that she couldn't see details, but now smaller things come into focus: the spray of pink jasmine being trained to grow along The Hotel's second story, and the soft rustle of its leaves and blooms in the night. She listens to their small sounds and breathes that blank winter air and feels something go loose across her chest.

The lobby is brightly lit, and from outside Lulu can see a reality TV show playing on a flat-screen installed on a wall. A piece of printer paper tacked underneath it reads WARNING: THESE PREMISES ARE BEING MONITORED BY CAMERAS. Aside from the TV and the sign, the room is mostly bare.

Ryan is alone inside. He's pacing around, smoking a clove cigarette and looking broody. Lulu wishes Bea were here so that they could make fun of him for being such a pretentious hipster together.

Instead, Cass greets Ryan with a kiss on the cheek. He slings a proprietary arm around her shoulders. "Ryan, you remember Lulu," Cass says. "And this is Owen."

"Owen Lewis, right?" Ryan asks. "I know your dad."

Lulu glances at Owen. He hates talking about his dad. They get along—they're pretty close, actually—but people get kind of weird about it.

"He played my dad's seventieth last year," Ryan goes on. "He's a cool guy."

"Oh," Owen says. "Yeah. I remember that party." His dad's band isn't usually the type to do that kind of thing. Lulu wonders how much money Riggs Senior had to spend to get them to agree.

But it's a good thing, maybe, because the dick-measuring tension that was in the air feels like it deflates, then disappears. They both have dads people sometimes get weird about; tonight, at least, no one is going to make it weird.

Ryan turns to Cass. "So what are we getting up to?" he asks.

"Aren't you supposed to be hosting us?" she returns.

"Fuck, you're right, I am!" Ryan laughs. He detaches himself from Cass and looks around the space, frowning at its emptiness. "Hope you weren't expecting a cool party or anything."

"Lulu's been here before," Cass reminds him.

"We just left a cool party," Owen says. "Wasn't that fun, turns out. So we're definitely open to other ideas."

Ryan takes them up to his room and instructs them to gather supplies: blankets and pillows and candles, plus a big canvas bag and a bottle of vodka. The space doesn't look much more fully inhabited than last time Lulu was here. She wonders where Ryan actually lives.

She doesn't ask, though, out of habit. She's so used to pretending to know more than she does that she's almost forgotten how to let someone know she's curious. Plus, Ryan and Owen are deep in a conversation she doesn't want to join or interrupt. Something about the Dodgers' spring training prospects.

Instead, she grabs the bag—it's annoyingly heavy—and drapes herself in a blanket. She follows Cass back down the stairs. "You guys do this often?" she asks.

"Sort of," Cass says.

"Usually without two randos along for the ride?"

"The Hotel is always changing," Cass explains. "A year ago it was too dangerous to go inside any of the buildings, and six months ago it wasn't wired for electricity yet. We got running water last week."

"The parking spaces," Lulu says.

"What you can do with it changes," Cass says. "Every week it's a different adventure. A different project."

Lulu thinks of sneaking around that house with Bea, taking their dumb, funny Flashes, making each other laugh. She thinks of the way they find fun together wherever they go, and she thinks she understands.

Lulu and Cass walk out past the cars and through a small gate to a flat stretch of patio, which surrounds a gigantic empty pool. Cass picks her way around the perimeter to the shallowest point and descends the steps there, her footfalls echoing as she heads toward the deep end. Watching her walk is surreal: Lulu can't help imagining the water that's supposed to surround her, and how quiet it would be as she disappeared underneath it.

She half expects the air to feel different on her skin when she follows.

It doesn't, though. It's a little darker with the building's lights blocked by the pool's rim, but otherwise the same. Cass takes the bag from Lulu and unzips it to reveal a bunch of poles and more canvas. "Can I . . . help?" Lulu asks. She has no idea what Cass is doing.

"Nah," Cass says. "Ryan and I have a two-man tent setup pretty figured out." She starts piling the poles up by size.

Lulu makes herself useful by taking a swig of vodka. Her buzz from earlier dissipated on the drive, and now she's just feeling anxious. She tries to drown the butterflies in her stomach with booze.

"From the bottle," Cass says. "Bold."

"I can handle myself," Lulu says.

"I can see that."

Cass is still focused on the task at hand, but the clarity of her assessment—the same sharp certainty she used to put Owen in his place in the car—feels surprisingly familiar. It's a distinct echo of the unapologetic, unadorned voice that has presided in the back of Lulu's own head as long as she can remember. The one she always listens to, but never lets speak for her.

I like you, she thinks at Cass's back, and then takes another swallow.

The boys are carrying less, but they make more noise coming out through the parking lot and down into the pool. Ryan makes a big deal out of helping Cass with the tent. He stands behind her, accidentally-on-purpose pressing his body against hers, making a point of how small she is, and how neatly she fits against him.

Owen drifts over to Lulu and she hands him the bottle, wordless. Their fingers brush in the exchange and Lulu has a flash of the two of them a little over a year ago, at the beginning: sitting on someone's couch, comparing the size of their hands. Owen's palm was bigger, of course, and warm. He folded her hands into fists and wrapped his around them, fingers on the backs of her wrists. Lulu knew it was stupid to like that he made her feel small, and liked it anyway.

Now she says, "You and Ryan seem to be getting along."

Owen makes a face about the burn of the vodka going down. "Like a house on fire," he replies.

"Let's hope not."

The tent is standing now. Lulu has never been camping, not really, but a few years ago Deirdre had them glamp in yurts up near Big Sur, and that's sort of what this looks like: round and white, although much smaller than those ones were. Lulu picks up one of the pillows at her feet and hands it off to Cass, who tosses it inside and reaches for more. As soon as she's done with the cushioning, Ryan disappears inside, and Cass follows him. Lulu moves to do the same, but Owen grabs her sleeve.

"What are we doing here, Lu?" he asks.

Lulu doesn't know how to explain that it's been months and months since she felt comfortable with anyone besides Bea. That she hasn't wanted to go anywhere since the Sloane Flash, but this is different—it isn't exactly going *out*, even though it's definitely not staying in.

Lulu used to be comfortable with Owen too. Always, without question. Maybe she still is: She finds herself telling him the truth, or at least part of it.

"I don't know," she says.

Owen nods. He's not like Lulu: always weighing and measuring, trying to see all of the angles and come at it from the best one. He just likes to know his own mind, to make sure he's right with himself. He knows how to keep his balance better than almost anyone else Lulu knows.

"That makes two of us," he says, and slips between the canvas flaps.

Lulu looks up at the darkness of the sky above her: all of that limitless black. In the context of infinity, it's easy to think that there's no right thing to do, at least not right now, at least not tonight.

She follows Owen in.

● ● ● ●

Once they're settled, Owen takes out his phone to try to play music, but Ryan makes him put it away again—"No phones at The Hotel," he says, and Cass echoes him. *No phones at The Hotel.*

At first the quiet that surrounds their conversation unnerves Lulu. You can hear each of them tuning in and out again. The moments in which no one has anything to say stand out, stark and unmissable.

Eventually, though, in the later, woozier hours, she starts to find it comforting. *There's a rhythm to this,* she thinks. *What we're doing here together.* The way conversation falls away and then finds itself again, if you let it.

Lulu wraps herself in a blanket; she tips sideways into Owen's lap. His hands tangle in her hair. She remembers digging her fingers into his thighs, his back, the back of his head.

"Are you guys together?" she hears Ryan ask. The words sound like they're being spoken somewhere very far away.

"Nah," Owen says. "We were."

"You look so pretty like this, though," Cass says.

"Lulu and I love each other," Owen says. "That's all."

Lulu hears bodies shifting, rearranging themselves.

Cass asks, "That's all, huh?"

Lulu wishes she were awake enough to read Cass's tone.

"That's all," Owen says. "That's all there is, right?"

CHAPTER SEVEN

• • • •

LULU WAKES UP because her face is too warm. She blinks and blinks. She must have fallen asleep in the tent last night. Now the sun is falling over the lip of the pool's edge, streaming through the thin canvas. Owen is next to her. Ryan and Cass are gone.

She stumbles outside, only barely managing not to step on Owen. The day is beautiful: clear sky, clear air, exactly the kind of fresh, sweet a.m. hour that makes having a hangover feel especially depraved. Lulu wishes she had her sunglasses, at least.

The lobby has a bathroom, but its fixtures haven't been installed yet: Three toilets sit, attached to nothing, in the stalls. Lulu heads upstairs and then hesitates. Ryan said something the first time she was here about spending time in room Three, but she's only ever seen him in Four. He's probably still there, right? And it probably has a functioning bathroom, right? Cass said there was running water now.

Lulu is in luck: Three is deserted and the toilet works. There's toilet paper, but no soap to wash her hands with, which is better than it could have been, at least. She doesn't even think about the sound of the flush in the otherwise silent morning until she emerges back into the hallway and finds Cass there.

Cass is wrapped in a blanket, and above its woven fabric, her pale shoulders are bare except for one dark tank top strap.

Oh, Lulu thinks. Well, that makes sense. Good for them.

"Sorry," Cass says. "I know we kind of abandoned you guys out there last night. You were very insistent about sleeping under the stars, and—"

"It's fine," Lulu says, though she has only the vaguest memory of this part of the conversation. She definitely overdid it on the vodka. "I'm good."

"You found the bathroom okay?"

"Yeah."

Ryan appears over Cass's shoulder. He's dressed, or at least wearing sweats and a T-shirt.

"You gonna invite her in?" he asks.

Cass looks flustered.

Lulu doesn't want to make her feel weird. "I should probably," she says, "go."

"Don't be silly." Ryan steps back and gestures for Lulu to join them. "Come on."

Ryan's bed is unmade. An enormous digital camera is sitting in the nest of its sheets.

"I was just taking advantage of the light," he says.

"Ryan's a photographer." Cass flops onto the bed and lets the blanket fall from her grasp. She's wearing a pair of sweats that look identical to Ryan's except they're enormous on her, fabric pooling shapelessly between her waist and where she's scrunched them up on her calves.

Cass grabs the camera and aims it at Lulu and Ryan. "Click!" she announces.

Ryan isn't interested. "Cass. C'mon."

She rolls her eyes and hands it to him.

Light is streaming in through the windows. Cass's face falls in shadow, and her hair, still sleep-mussed, is an electric halo of crimson and gold. Lulu looks at the camera in Ryan's hand and understands the instinct to capture her, and all of this: to pin down the strangeness of this space, and the impossibly beautiful girl in it.

Lulu doesn't think of herself as a photographer. She loves taking pictures for her Flash, but that's different. It's not art; it's just easy. She found out the difference when she tried to take a photo class last year and wound up hating it—all the technical talk, f-stops and exposure length and blah blah blah. But she recognizes Ryan's instinct: She knows exactly what it's like to see a moment and want very badly to figure out how to keep it for yourself.

"Cass and I were just talking," Ryan says. He barely looks at the camera as he turns it on and focuses it on Cass. "She says you're big on—"

"I thought we covered that," Lulu says. She tries to sound polite. What planets have fallen into alignment? Why does the universe insist on reminding her, over and over again, of Flash, and then, inevitably, of Sloane, and that night?

"I fucking hate Flash," Ryan says. "Roman was smart to make it, but it's the stupidest thing I've ever seen. Another platform where all anyone does is make themselves look good."

Lulu wants to ask more about Roman, but she knows better than to pry. She remembers the way Ryan and Owen assessed each other last night: the way Ryan said *my dad, your dad,* and that put them on the same terrain. No one here knows who Lulu's dad is, or cares.

"Are you making me look bad?" Cass asks.

Ryan doesn't answer her. He's holding the camera casually, but Lulu can see, in its tiny screen, that he has Cass neatly framed. He says, "No one ever records their hangovers. Their actual first-thing-in-the-morning selves. *I woke up like this* is total fucking bullshit. It's all just, like, filters, and the best fifteen seconds of the party."

"That's not exactly—" Lulu starts, and then stops herself. Does she really want to defend Flash? She likes it, but Ryan's not wrong about how she uses it, especially lately: to make her life look beautiful and interesting, especially when she's lonely, or uncertain, or bored. "So you're doing something different?"

"I don't photograph people, mostly," Ryan says. "That's not what I'm interested in, as subjects. It just feels cheap, you know? It's not hard to take good pictures of hot girls."

"What's this, then?"

Ryan gives Lulu a look she doesn't understand. "Mostly what I'm doing is process shots," he says. "The Hotel as it's being rebuilt. I'm documenting the whole thing so I can have a record of it."

"It's one of our projects," Cass says. "While the space is being made, we make things in it."

Ryan holds the camera up a bit, and it draws Cass's focus. Lulu watches him watch Cass smile.

"You want to come sit with me, Lu?" Cass asks.

Lulu is glad she hasn't seen a mirror this morning. That's probably the reason she's bold enough to do it, she tells herself: to sit down next to Cass, cross-legged, on the bed.

"You want some real morning-after shit, this is it," she says to Ryan. "I bet you let Cass brush her teeth first."

"Nah," Ryan says.

Cass bares them in a grin. "See?"

Lulu leans forward as if to examine Cass's mouth. It's all a joke, just part of the weird elongated prank she's playing on herself by being here, except she's been thinking about Sloane too much, and here she is again, on a bed with a girl, her body inclined forward. She feels the world shifting around her, gravity rearranging itself. Ryan's camera doesn't make noise when the shutter blinks, or maybe he's not even bothering to take pictures.

Lulu thinks, *This is definitely not,* and then nothing else because, thank god, Owen is standing in the doorway, looking pained.

"If I was going to puke somewhere," he says, "do you have a preference about where I do it?"

Once Owen's stomach is empty he feels much better, so Cass takes him and Lulu back to the cars they left outside of Rich's house, their first stop last night. "See you soon," she says, and drives off fast.

Lulu turns to Owen. "So that was . . ." she starts.

"Yeah," Owen says. "That was awesome. I've never done anything like it before. I didn't even know we could do that. How long have you been holding out on me, Lu?"

"Cass and I met last weekend," she says. "So not very long." Lulu feels the weight of a conspiracy—small, inconsequential, but real—forming between them. She looks up at him and says, "It is weird, but I'm, like, into it, you know?"

"I do," he says.

"Cool."

Lulu laughs, and Owen laughs too. It feels warm for a second, and then Lulu thinks, *It's been a while since we*, and hurt slices through her, sharp and merciless. She looks away and starts fumbling through her bag for her keys.

"Hey," Owen says. He looks uncertain, at first, reaching out for her, but then his face breaks into a smile and he's laughing, pulling her tightly against him. He musses her hair and kisses the top of her head a little too roughly, like he can mask the affection of the gesture. "Bring me with you next time too, okay?"

Lulu thinks she knows why he's laughing: Because it's absurd for them to hug and absurd for them not to. It doesn't change all of the easy, intimate ways they used to touch each other, or the fact that they aren't touching each other that way anymore. Because they're trying to find their way to a friendship they never had, which, in the face of what they had instead, feels like nothing much at all.

From inside the circle of his arms, all she can think is that Owen smells so familiar. Lulu knows plenty of people's shampoo, their soap, their perfume or cologne, but Owen she knows all the way down to the salt of his sweaty, sleepless skin.

No one knows what they're doing right now, or where they are. For the next thirty seconds, she thinks, there are no rules. Maybe that means there are no consequences either.

Lulu doesn't think Owen can feel the fleeting kiss she brushes against the cotton of his shirt. She's careful where he was rough; the motion is meant mostly for herself, instead of him. "Of course I will," she says.

CHAPTER EIGHT

● ● ● ●

"OH GOOD," LULU'S dad says when he sees her. He's standing in the kitchen in suit pants and a crisp white button-down. The remnants of a family breakfast are still on the table next to him. "Get dressed. We're going to be late."

"Where are we going?" Lulu asks stupidly. He's always doing this: assuming she just, like, *knows* what his plans are.

"Temple," her dad says.

"Temple?" Lulu repeats. She understands what he means in a literal sense, but she's still confused: They haven't gone to a Saturday morning service at Shaare Tikvah since she turned thirteen, and Olivia's too young for pre–Bat Mitzvah stuff yet.

"Yes, Lulu, temple," he repeats. "Go get dressed."

"I don't feel great—" she starts.

"I'm sure you don't," he says. "You should probably shower if you can do it quickly. Rinse off, at least."

"I really don't—"

"Don't waste time."

Lulu could stand here arguing with him, but she knows from long experience that she'd just end up getting thrown into a dress and packed into the car at the last minute anyway, so she salutes him and turns to head upstairs to her room.

Twenty minutes later Lulu's hair is in a wet knot on top of her head and she's wearing a new sundress with an old cardigan. Her face looks bare without any makeup, but there wasn't time to put any on, and she was almost glad. Something about the idea of crusting herself up again—caking her eyelashes, her cheekbones, her lips—felt extra-nauseating.

She's got one piece of toast and two Advil in her stomach. She throws the whole bottle in her purse and takes one of Olivia's post-soccer Gatorades out of the fridge for good measure. When she gets to the front door, the rest of her family is assembled, waiting for her. Lulu feels the familiar sensation of being the one puzzle piece that's out of place.

"Lu!" Olivia says. "You're coming!"

Lulu returns her little sister's hug gingerly. She loves Olivia's enthusiasm—she does—she just wishes it were coming from a slightly gentler place right now.

"I told you it wouldn't be boring," Deirdre says to Olivia. "Lulu will sit with you, won't you, Lu."

Where will you be? Lulu doesn't ask. Deirdre really isn't that bad of a mother, or a stepmother, as these things go. She just doesn't seem to understand that Lulu isn't always as wild to hang out with Olivia as Olivia is to hang out with her. *You girls,* Deirdre's always saying, like they're both her babies. Olivia is nine; Lulu is seventeen; Deirdre just turned thirty-five. *The math*, Lulu wants to tell her, *doesn't work out quite the way you think it does.*

"Come on," her dad says. "We should have been in the car ten minutes ago."

"If you'd told me last night that I was supposed to be ready—" Lulu starts. She can't resist needling him, even though she knows it doesn't help.

"If you'd been home last night, I would have," he says. His back is to her. The same way that Deirdre assumes Lulu always wants to do what Deirdre wants her to, her dad always assumes that she's scampering behind him, listening intently.

"Don't be nervous, honey," Deirdre says to Lulu's dad. "If he invited you, clearly he thinks you're—"

"He invited the whole firm," her dad says. "I'm the only one he's going to be expecting to know the prayers."

Lulu follows them into the car and slumps gratefully into her seat. Of course this is some business thing of her dad's; some other partner's son turned thirteen and now Lulu's being dragged out of her house on a Saturday morning to illustrate how thoroughly, totally picture-perfect his life is. So what he's on his third marriage? His daughters are growing up beautifully, and his wives are staying young the same way.

Lulu snaps a video of her reflection in the car's window, just the line of her collarbone and the sleeve of her sweater, sound off. She captions it *Will I ever sleep again.*

It's early enough that responses only kind of trickle in, which is why she sees Cass's as soon as it comes. It's a shot of Cass in her own bed, probably, eyes closed, face slack. You get into so many kinds of trouble, her message says.

Enough to know this morning's is the boring kind, Lulu replies.

Midway through the service, Lulu's Advil wears off, and a headache starts to press a barbed-wire crown of pain against her skull. She slips out to take some more and can't make herself go back in. It's been so long since she was at temple. She doesn't remember any of the words.

Instead, she makes her way to the reception hall, where, by the grace of the god Lulu's just been failing to pray to, the Bar Mitzvah boy's parents ordered catering, and a spread is already set. She drinks an entire black coffee while she covers a bagel in cream cheese and lox; she's well into her second cup as she heads for the bridal room, a changing space off the hall that's usually unlocked. Lulu may not know the service well, but she's an expert in every place you can go to get away from it.

The room is empty, nothing but four walls and a mirror, but that doesn't matter. Lulu sinks gratefully to the floor and eats half of the bagel in three or four bites, swallowing throat-sized lumps. She takes another Advil with the last of the coffee.

Glancing up, she catches sight of her reflection: her hair, dry now, down and limp. Her bare face, bare legs, bare arms. The dollop of cream cheese at the corner of her mouth.

Who do you think you are? Lulu asks herself.

She has absolutely no answer.

Lulu rubs a knuckle against the cream cheese, realizing as she does it that she didn't grab any napkins. Her finger hesitates. The door swings open.

Kiley Rathbone walks in.

Of *fucking* course.

"Heyyyy! I thought I saw you earlier with your family," she says, like she expects Lulu wanted to be seen, or acknowledged.

"Yeah," Lulu says.

"I don't usually?"

"No."

Lulu wipes the cream cheese off her finger and onto the carpet.

"I'm here every Saturday, so I know the regulars," Kiley says. "I think my parents make us come to prove a point. Like, *See, look at us. We're real, live black Jews! We're still real Jews!* It's so boring."

Lulu doesn't say anything.

Kiley is undeterred. "I also don't think I've ever seen you eat carbs before," she says.

"I don't—uh. Sorry. But, like, do you watch me eat?"

Kiley looks mortified. "I mean it's not like—I don't—I'm not *creeping* on you," she says. "It's a bad habit from ballet. The monitoring. And I do, you know, see you around, like on the quad, at lunch and stuff. And on Flash, when you post, there's usually, like, not food? I guess it's still weird that I notice."

She let the door close behind her when she came in; Lulu watches her glance back at it, assessing the cost of leaving now, and admitting that she doesn't belong here, versus what she can gain if she stays.

Lulu shouldn't be surprised that Kiley collects herself. She laughs, shrugs, sits. "You know how it is," Kiley says. "I mean, you'd be lying if you said you weren't watching too, right?"

Lulu doesn't know what to say to that. Of course she's watching: what she eats and what everyone else eats. She does it so instinctually that she doesn't even think of it as a thing she *does,* any more than she would think of breathing as, like, a hobby, or a pursuit.

But she doesn't want to find common ground with Kiley. She doesn't want to let Kiley put the two of them on the same level. If Kiley is dumb enough to admit that she's trying—and exactly how—that doesn't obligate Lulu to do the same for her.

It's a good reminder, actually, that Kiley is young; Lulu has been playing this game longer than she has. All Kiley knows is that Lulu disappeared last night and took Owen with her. She probably thinks Lulu has the upper hand. The trick is to act like she's right.

"My mom is gluten-intolerant," Lulu says. Her mom is intolerant of anything that anyone has ever said might make her fat, but Kiley doesn't need that level of detail. "Usually I figure it's better to avoid it too, but, you know. Desperate times." She gestures to herself and laughs, like her hangover is funny, like she doesn't care if she looks like shit.

66

Kiley will figure it out for herself, if she hasn't already: Acting like you take your own good looks for granted is the easiest way to fool people into thinking you're pretty when you aren't. Or maybe that's a trick you only need to know if you aren't that pretty. Lulu has never been entirely sure how much she's faking it in comparison to everyone else. Maybe Kiley never has to think like this.

"Late night?" Kiley asks.

Lulu thinks, *Wouldn't you like to know.*

"Yeah." To be polite, she asks, "How was yours?"

Kiley shrugs. "I don't think we hung around for too long after you peaced," she says. "Wasn't that good of a party."

"Are they ever really that good, though?"

Lulu says it mostly to have something to say, but Kiley shakes her head in earnest agreement.

"*No,*" she says. "No, right? I'm so glad to hear you say that, because I only really started going out in the last, like, little while, so I thought maybe it was just me who didn't understand. Is there something I'm not getting that *makes* a party universally fun? No, right?"

Lulu gives her a placeholder shrug.

Kiley doesn't back down.

"If you asked me about the most fun I've had at a party this year, I'd say it was this one I went to last weekend," she says. "And it was, like, pretty much sophomores only, and not even that big, and mostly it was me and Frida—my friend—hanging out. It was sort of quiet, and we just chilled and did whatever.

And it was *nice*, actually, to not be worrying about who else was *there* and who might be *coming* and just, like, to be there. With who we were with. Which is why it's funny that—" Lulu sees her snag on the words, watches her trying to decide whether she's going to say them or not.

One of us will, she wants to tell Kiley, because now that the first half of the sentence is out there, the second is coming, one way or another.

Kiley says, "It's funny that when I stopped hoping someone cool would turn up, Owen did."

Lulu wishes she hadn't eaten the bagel. She wishes she hadn't eaten anything, ever, so that she would never have lived to experience a lurch of vertigo picturing how it must have happened: Owen looking for her at Patrick's party and not finding her. He was thinking about leaving anyway. Someone had invited—not him, probably. A friend of his from the baseball team. Whatever. He decided there wasn't anything for him at Patrick's, so he left, and found Kiley instead. Someone new. Someone nice.

"He's great, right," Lulu says, forcing the words out.

"Yeah," Kiley says. "I really, um, I really like him."

Lulu nods.

"It's not really anything yet," Kiley says. "It's not even enough of anything to really talk about, obviously, except that you're— I know you—" She squares her shoulders. "I respect you," she says. "I know that sounds like a weird thing to say, but I do. I remember seeing you around last year and thinking you seemed like someone who had your shit together.

"And then when the thing happened with Sloane, the way you handled it—you were so *brazen*. Not everyone could have done that, I think. Handled it well. Handled it at all, even. So, like, not because you're popular, and not because you're older, but because you're you, I wanted to say that I hope that whatever happens with Owen and me—I hope you won't hate me." She laughs. "Let's start there, I guess."

Lulu is breathless. A small piece of her is in awe of Kiley's monologue, the apparent uncalculated *truth* she just put out there, the sort of basic human semi-decency of what she just said.

"I don't hate you," Lulu says. "I don't, um. I don't know how I feel about any of it yet."

"Like I said, maybe there's nothing for you to even be feeling things about," Kiley says. "But I like him. And as long as he keeps liking me—yeah. I don't imagine you're going to want to be friends with me. But I really don't want you as an enemy if I can avoid it."

Lulu forgets, sometimes, that there are people who think she's powerful, that because she has these Flash followers and because she knows how to play by the rules so well, they think she could actually do something to them if she wanted. She gets so obsessed with people liking her that she forgets that she could decide not to like them. She could turn against them. She could probably turn other people against them too.

It doesn't feel good to imagine hurting Kiley, starting a rumor, spreading some little bit of poison. But at least it feels powerful; it fills in the icy, empty pit that opened in her stomach when Kiley said Owen's name like he was someone she *knew*. The idea that Lulu could do something—exact revenge—gives her enough space to feel like she doesn't have to.

Because the real power move is to say "You'd have to do more than hook up with my ex to become my enemy." Like Lulu's got boys and social capital and generosity to spare. Like she isn't dying at the idea that all she can do is be generous, and pretend she's letting Owen go, when really he's the one who doesn't want her back.

CHAPTER NINE

• • • •

THE WHOLE STUPID point of Flash was that it didn't archive anything. That was the idea, anyway. You uploaded pictures or video snippets, either for general public consumption or to a few select friends, who could watch them once, and then never again.

Lulu knows it was stupid to believe that was possible, that anything on the internet could live and then actually die. Or not die, she thinks now, because the dead don't disappear either, do they. They leave corpses too. Traces.

Evidence.

She and Owen had been dating for nine months when she proposed the idea of the girls. At the time it seemed brilliant. Things had been a little quieter between them, almost even sometimes a tiny bit strained, and Lulu had thought that here was a new thing she could offer to keep him interested. It would be sexy and wild, something he wouldn't get from anyone else: Lulu kissing a girl, and him watching.

It would make him look at her all over again, the way maybe sometimes she'd seen him looking at other girls, lately, just for a second, without even knowing he was doing it probably. It would make other girls part of their relationship instead of a threat to it.

It wasn't like he'd never seen her kiss a girl before, before they were together. Owen hadn't seen the beginning of it, how it started in the sixth grade, when it was just lessons, Lulu at sleepovers offering to teach and be taught. But he'd seen the end result, which was that, as a teenager, it had become her party trick.

They would be sitting around drinking and someone would bring it up. Lulu would monitor a girl's reaction: whether she got flustered, or curious. If she was curious it didn't take much coaxing. Lulu just had to be casual about it, laughing, playful, and together they'd watch how much the boys loved it. She would kiss a girl until a boy got up between them, and laid claim to whoever it was he'd decided he wanted to kiss for himself.

It was the kind of behavior, Lulu discovered, that if you didn't explain, people would happily explain for you. If you didn't tell everyone right away that you were questioning, or queer, or bisexual, or any of those other too-clinical, too-certain words, and especially if you were a girl with long hair and a lot of pink in her wardrobe and a lot of followers on social media—well, they already knew what kind of girl she was, so they knew what to think of her. Everyone knew that Lulu Shapiro would do anything for attention.

Lulu always wanted to correct them, to say that, in fact, she did it as a dumb bit of misdirection. It was easy for her to let people know that she liked kissing girls; who wouldn't? Kissing was fun, and easy. Kissing girls made Lulu seem like someone who was fun and easy. Kissing girls in public was a way of showing a side of herself people were interested in seeing, and at the same time making sure they'd never look closely enough to see any of the rest of it.

Which was also why she didn't explain to Owen that, with her, with girls, it went beyond kissing, that his body was not the only kind of body she knew how to want. Lulu didn't want to try to explain something to him that she was still in the process of figuring out for herself.

Even still, he didn't love it at first.

"I need—" he said. "Some time."

"I don't have to do it," she said. It was one of their rare long nights together. His dad was on tour and his mom was away for the weekend at a conference. They'd bribed his younger brothers to stay downstairs and keep their secret. Lulu was naked, she was in his bed, she was *his*, she was so *his*. It felt safe, somehow, like he could give her permission to do this thing and it wouldn't mean the same things as if she did it on her own. And then she would have everything: Owen, and girls, and a life that was safe and exciting and normal and good and *right*.

"It's not like a compulsion or anything," she explained. "I just sort of thought you might be into it. A fun little game." Lulu pouted for good measure. "A lot of guys would want to."

But maybe Owen sensed that Lulu's intentions weren't as pure or selfless as she was making them out to be.

"I just—as long as you don't leave me out of it," he said. He was smiling like he was just kidding around, but Lulu knew him well enough to recognize his serious eyes. "It's not just you making out with random girls at parties and I stumble on it and it's like, oh, cool, there's Lulu doing her thing."

Lulu hated the idea of hurting him. That wasn't what she wanted at all. "It would be for us," she said. "For you and for me, together."

"We could try it out," he said. "We can definitely try."

Owen wasn't at the party where Lulu met Sloane. It was late August and he was on tour with his dad at that point, doing one week of adventuring before he had to start school. He wasn't there when Jules introduced them, when they sat next to each other on the back patio all night, Sloane's thigh warm and soft and so incredibly bare against Lulu's.

The two of them shifted and twisted, moved against each other without ever managing to lose contact. It was sweltering outside, the air refusing to calm and cool even when it was long past dark, but all Lulu could feel was the burn of desire in her belly, in her fingertips. It sparked her. It lit her up. Someone said something to Sloane about her ex, and Sloane said, "Yeah, she was . . ." and Lulu didn't hear anything else for a whole minute.

She chatted Owen on Flash. Might have an adventure in mind for later, she said. That thing we talked about. A girl. I could send you pictures?

No fair, he replied. Stuck on the bus tonight. Can't even really jerk off in peace. A picture of the cramp of a bunk, the bulge in his sweats. Lulu was dizzy, she was drunk, she couldn't be expected to keep track of all the things in the world she wanted to touch and be touched by.

That's going to be tough for you, then, she said. Unless you tell me not to.

Just keep me in the loop, he said.

It wasn't even hard, Lulu kept thinking. It wasn't hard at all, with a girl who wanted what you wanted. With a girl who wanted you.

The party got late, got loose. Lulu went inside to make herself a drink. She lingered in the kitchen.

Sloane followed her in.

"So hot out there," she said. She lifted her hair from her neck and twisted it away from her face. A bead of sweat ran down the side of her neck, traced a lazy pattern across the sheen of her skin.

"I think the AC is on upstairs," Lulu said. "If you want to, like, take a break."

"I feel like I've mostly been talking to you anyway," Sloane said. "I doubt anyone would miss us if we went missing."

"No one's home," Lulu said. "We can—wherever."

She doesn't remember much of the next few minutes—what they talked about, or where they walked. Lulu doesn't remember anything except the fever in her blood and how she knew, she *knew* that soon she would have Sloane's hands on her to soothe it, to draw it out and set it down.

They found a bedroom. Lulu let Sloane kiss her for long, hot minutes before she explained about Owen, and pulled out her phone.

"We can do whatever we want," Lulu said, even though that wasn't the deal exactly. They hadn't really made a deal. "He just wants to know what I get up to."

"I don't like the idea of sharing you," Sloane said. Her hand was on Lulu's hip, palm pressed against her belly, and it was hard to concentrate on anything that wasn't that single, physical fact. "I'm sure he doesn't either."

"There's so much of me," Lulu said, and in that one moment it felt true, and it felt possible. It didn't feel humiliating to be so expansive. To want. To have. "I don't run out, I'm not—"

Sloane kissed her. Lulu untangled one of the hands that was in Sloane's hair. She filmed something. She didn't look before she pressed SEND. Not at what it looked like.

Not at who she was sending it to.

It was Owen's dad's fans who'd started archiving her public videos. They were always looking for evidence: of Owen or his dad or the band, the pieces of their lives that brushed up against hers.

Later, when she emailed one of the big fan sites to ask them to take it down, just this one particular clip, they were adamant that it wasn't porn or anything: just two girls kissing on a bed, fully clothed. It was almost sort of funny to see how chaste it looked if you didn't know how it had felt.

It was painful like nothing else Lulu had ever known to watch the video and see at the last minute how Sloane looked up into the camera, smirking. How it made it look like something they had planned, had talked about, and had meant for everyone to see.

CHAPTER TEN

●●●●

LULU SPENDS THE rest of the weekend studying. She has a B-plus average and every intention of keeping it up. She's not like Bea, who applied early to Brown; Lulu has applications out at a handful of different schools, and they all seem fine to her. She figures the best thing she can do between now and when the letters come in the spring is try to keep her grades up and her options open.

These kinds of study binges are the only time she actively avoids her phone, in part because the post-test reunion with it is such a delicious reward. As soon as she's done checking and rechecking her answers, she hurtles outside and lets her notifications wash over her in waves.

Flash is crammed with content from friends who don't share her strategy: video of Rich flinging his notes into a backyard bonfire, his traditional start-of-finals ritual, and Jules filming Owen passed out, surrounded by highlighters and Red Bull. Bea quizzing their friends Amanda and Gina in super-slow-motion. And Cass and Ryan, hanging out at The Hotel.

It's just a picture, not a video, taken sometime yesterday

evening, probably: Cass's phone camera capturing Ryan's digital one, their lenses aimed at each other, Ryan's hand already reaching out, oddly elongated by perspective, to tell her to stop. It stays on her screen just long enough for Lulu to register that it wasn't a public offering—Cass broke the rules of The Hotel in order to send it directly to her.

Lulu takes a picture of the sky and writes back, Free from finals for the day:) :) :)

Cass gets back to her almost immediately. ME TOO, she says. Want to go to the beach?

Lulu doesn't even really think about it. Yes.

Bea grabs her phone out of her hands. "What's this!" she asks. "What's *that* look about, Lu—" but the Flash has already disappeared. It doesn't matter. Lulu's heart is already kicking against her ribs, and her hands move panic-fast. She tugs her phone from Bea's grasp so hard that it goes flying, landing on one corner of its case before settling, faceup and undamaged, on the ground. Thank god.

"Whoa," Bea says. "Sorry, Lu."

Lulu picks the phone up slowly, all of the hot curdled Sloane shame joining with a rush of new embarrassment: at the idea that Cass was even—that there's something to even be embarrassed—that Lulu's *face* was doing something.

"It's nothing," she tells Bea, because she can't come up with a more convincing lie.

Bea assesses Lulu for a long moment before she says, "Okay."

She lets Lulu put her phone in her bag and rearrange her hair. "Froyo?"

This is their post-finals tradition. For every test, a scoop of vanilla with rainbow sprinkles eaten on the sun-warmed hood of Bea's Audi in a strip-mall parking lot.

"Shit," Lulu says. "I mean, I guess it wasn't nothing. I was making plans with someone."

"Someone who?"

"My friend Cass," Lulu says. "We met at Patrick's party the other night—remember, the girl who took me to that weird hotel? And she was talking about going to the beach, and I said I would. I just wasn't thinking. I'm sorry, B."

"You have to go right now?"

Lulu looks down at her phone. Cass has written back, Meet me in Malibu in 30-45? Point Dume?

She should go get frozen yogurt with Bea and then go home and study for the rest of her finals. She should stick around and say hi to Owen, remind him how much fun they had the other night.

She's not going to, though.

"I'm so sorry," Lulu says again. "Rain check? Double scoop tomorrow?"

CHAPTER ELEVEN

● ● ● ●

SUNLIGHT IS WHITE through the windshield as Lulu drives the 101 through the Valley, passing Sherman Oaks, Encino, Tarzana, and Woodland Hills before she hits the rows of luxury car dealerships that mark the beginning of Calabasas. It's been a dry winter and the land is brown, mostly, occasional patches of green scrub sitting low against the shocking blue of the sky.

As she gets off the freeway and starts to climb the curves of Kanan Dume, she rolls the windows down and lets the clear, dry air rush across her body, tangling her hair and raising goose bumps on her arms. The radio's signal gets lost in the shadows of the canyon and the hush of the wind. From the top of the hill she can see the dark, distant gleam of the ocean.

At the beach, she pays an attendant ten dollars to park, pleased to recognize Cass's Volvo already there as she cruises toward a spot. The day is bright but windy, and even chillier than it was in the Valley, so the sand is mostly empty. Lulu kicks off her Uggs and carries them with her to where Cass is sitting, her hair flame bright against the pale sand and the ocean's darkness.

"Hey," Lulu says, when she's close enough to be heard.

Cass doesn't say anything, but she scoots over, leaving Lulu room to join her on her beach towel. It's faded now, but clearly used to be a bright Barbie pink. It doesn't look like Cass's style at all, which Lulu loves. Cass is maybe the only person she knows who doesn't care if she *matches* all the time.

Lulu drops down to sit at Cass's side. They're close enough that it's awkward to look at each other while they talk, so instead she stares straight ahead at the restless ocean.

"What's up," Cass asks.

"Um," Lulu says. "You know. Just took a final. Tomorrow I take another one."

"How was it?"

"I didn't bomb, I don't think."

"Didn't bomb mine either."

"Nice."

There's a pause before Cass asks, "How's Owen doing?"

"Fine, probably," Lulu says. "I don't know, actually. I haven't really seen him since you dropped us off the other morning."

"Oh."

"We don't usually hang out that much anymore. That night was kind of an exception."

"You guys seemed pretty chill, though."

"We were together for a year," Lulu says. "We've only been broken up for a few months. It's weird, but it's almost— It's actually easier for us to pretend we're still together, kind of, you know? Like, we know how to be nice to each other, and how to be close. It's the being distant thing we haven't figured out yet."

"Yeah," Cass says. "That makes a lot of sense, actually." She's been leaning back, but now she tilts her body forward and wraps her arms around her knees.

"Can I ask about you and Ryan?" As soon as she's said it, Lulu understands just how much she doesn't want to hear the answer.

"We're," Cass says, and then stops. "He's my best friend."

"Just a friend?"

"Nothing *just* about it."

You're hedging, Lulu thinks, but she doesn't want to push the conversation out of the casual zone. She doesn't know Cass well enough for that yet.

"That seems nice," she says. "I've always wanted to have a guy friend who was just—who was only that. Or maybe an older brother, I guess? Best of both worlds, right? Someone who can tell you what the hell dudes are thinking, and also, you can date his friends."

"You clearly don't have an older brother."

"You do?"

"This is his, actually." Cass tugs the sleeve of the oversized plaid flannel she's wearing. "So he is good for that. He would rather eviscerate himself than talk to me about dating, though, and he'd certainly eviscerate his friends for looking at me twice."

"Eviscerate," Lulu says. "That's a good word." She feels self-conscious. Maybe Cass is super smart. Maybe she's about to discover that Lulu's not. St. Amelia's is a good school and everything, but Lowell kids can be kind of on another level.

Cass doesn't dwell on her vocabulary, though. "You have a brother, you learn how to describe all kinds of gross shit," she agrees. "Anyway, Ryan is—I mean, we're not anything. But he can, I guess he can be a little possessive. I understand why people get the wrong idea about us."

"He does seem . . . intense."

"He is," Cass says. "About everything, actually. Not just me. But it's a whole thing with him. His family . . . if I'd grown up with his parents, I'd be intense too."

"What are they like?"

"Ryan's dad was almost kidnapped when he was a kid. You know that story?"

It's one of the things that came up when Lulu was googling the Riggses, Roman Senior's near abduction. He was ten when it happened, old enough to understand, and to have been terrorized by the fear of it happening again ever since.

"It fucked up his whole life," Cass continues. "That's why Ry was homeschooled until he was fifteen. They raised him to believe that he had to always be on the lookout for people who were trying to take things from him. Who were only interested in him because his last name is on a lot of buildings."

It's funny. Lulu has lived her whole life around rich people;

she is rich people, technically, she's pretty sure. But she's not the kind of rich that Ryan is, or even Owen—lasts-you-generations-type money. Famous-last-name-type money.

Growing up around kids like Owen and Ryan has taught her a very particular type of lesson: Lulu has known since she was a child that there are some worlds she can walk into, where she'll look like she belongs, but where she doesn't actually live. She knows the language and she can fake the dress codes, but she's not a native, and her passport might be revoked at any moment. There's no trust fund waiting for her; her parents have taken excellent care of her so far, but eventually, it will be up to her to take care of herself, and she needs to figure out how to be up to that task.

So she understands what Cass means, and at the same time, she doesn't.

Just because your problems are clichés doesn't mean they aren't your problems. But she still wants to say, *Yeah, you know he's not the first rich kid I've ever met,* and *My dad's kind of a whack job too,* and *Maybe Ryan should go out more, and be nicer when he does, if he wants to have real friends.* But then she doesn't want to argue with Cass. Don't get too personal, don't be too prickly: easy rules. Lulu learned them early.

"You definitely don't have to answer this," Lulu says. "But—do you *want* to date him?"

"No," Cass says. "Yeah. No."

She's switched something off; she's hedging again. One of the things Lulu likes about Cass, she thinks, is that Cass isn't opaque on purpose. She's not playing a game. She's just being private. And she's good at it—maintaining a distance between herself and the rest of the world. Not keeping anything out, but not letting much in either.

"It's not the same thing, obviously, but I'm always down for girl talk," Lulu says. "Or, I mean, boy talk, I guess? Whatever. You know what I mean."

"Really?" Cass asks.

Lulu doesn't know what to say. It seemed like such a normal offer—the next thing you say in a conversation like this. But then the whole point of Cass is that she's someone outside of Lulu's so-called normal life: a late-night escape hatch, a secret Flash message, an abandoned hotel and a bunch of projects and everything Lulu usually doesn't let herself think, or want, or say.

"If you want to," Lulu says again, but even she can hear how unsure of herself she sounds. "Isn't that what girls do?"

"Some of them," Cass says. "It's not really my thing."

Lulu thinks of sitting with Bea in her kitchen, gossiping about Rich and Owen. She thinks about the hundreds of hours she's spent poring over screenshots of digital conversations or trying to reconstruct half-remembered Flashes, close-reading much more thoroughly than she's ever done with her English assignments. It's hard for her to imagine a life that doesn't include that. She wasn't being facetious with Cass—isn't that what girls do with each other?

But then, some of the things she wants from Cass aren't things she wants from Bea.

It's too much to think about the idea that Cass might want those kinds of things from Lulu too.

"Let's talk about something else, then," Lulu says.

Cass grins sideways at her and then leans back on her elbows, tilting her face up to the sky.

Lulu can't help thinking about what it would feel like to be allowed to kiss the line of her throat.

The afternoon disappears too fast. Lulu's stomach rumbles; she hasn't eaten anything since the green smoothie Deirdre made her as a special pre-final treat this morning. Cass reaches over and taps her fingers lightly against Lulu's side. "Hungry?"

Lulu doesn't want to disturb the funny little world they've created for themselves, but she really, really is. "Yeah," she admits.

"There's a place across the street," Cass says. "Ryan introduced me to one of the bartenders once. We can probably get in as long as we don't try to order any alcohol—" But as she's saying it she's fumbling her phone out of her pocket.

Lulu feels the first clench of disappointment at its return, and then another, deeper pull when Cass says, "Or actually forget that. Ry's at The Hotel if we want to head there. He won't have food, but he will definitely have weed, and we can get takeout on the way or something."

"Sure," Lulu says. "Totally. Sounds good."

CHAPTER TWELVE

● ● ● ●

LULU BEATS CASS to The Hotel. The gate is already unlocked, so she cruises through it and finds Ryan waiting for them at the building's entrance, camera in one hand.

Standing in line at In-N-Out with Cass, it seemed reckless and bold to order a burger animal style, French fries, and a vanilla shake. Now, holding the paper bag, her fingers slippery with grease from the fries she ate while she drove, Lulu feels exposed and stupid, like she's showing too much of her belly. Here she is, just another hungry girl.

It gets worse when Ryan nods a greeting and turns the camera on her. He doesn't say anything, so Lulu doesn't say anything either. Instead, she takes a defiant sip of her shake. The sugar seems to crystallize in her mouth, and her throat feels full with the slick of the milk fat.

"I thought you said taking pictures of people was cheap," she says when she's swallowed.

"I said *hot girls*." Ryan smirks. "And anyway, you looked so fucking pissed, I had to. I was just shooting these guys." He gestures to the lounge chairs that have been assembled out in front of The Hotel's doors. They make the driveway look like an ersatz pool deck. "They just got delivered."

"So they won't stay here?" Lulu sits down on one and stretches her legs out in front of her.

Ryan, mercifully, puts his camera down.

"Nah, I just haven't gotten them moved yet. I'm kind of into it, though, right? The surreality of it."

Lulu stifles a groan. She knows so many dudes like Ryan. They take one art history class and think it makes them deep.

"I bet you'll be pretty bummed when this place opens for real," Lulu says. "And it isn't yours to play around with anymore."

"If it does," Ryan says. "Cass didn't tell you about the curse?"

Lulu laughs.

Ryan shrugs.

"A curse? For real?"

"I mean, it's not like my ancestors killed a Gypsy woman's child or anything," Ryan says. "But you know, this place has kind of a history."

"I thought we weren't supposed to use that word anymore," Lulu says. "Gypsies." It's one of those things her sister Naomi is always on about.

"Well, listen, don't tell any Gypsies I said it, okay?"

"I don't really think that's the point," Lulu says.

"What's the point?"

"Why not call people what they want to be called?"

"Why should I have to?"

The answer to that is *Because it would at least make you look like less of a dick,* but she can't say that to Ryan, not and have it come out right. Instead, Lulu says, "Maybe if you did, your family wouldn't be cursed."

Ryan laughs. "There are people who actually believe that," he says. "I mean, the people who believe in the curse believe it's our fault. My great-great-grandmother was an actress." Right. Lulu read about Constance Wilmott. "And she was only in one film, and then she stopped acting. Probably because she was busy having kids, but some old conspiracy theorists got obsessed with the idea that it was her husband who made her stop which could be true too. Apparently he was mad possessive."

Lulu does not make fun of him for saying "mad possessive." She hopes Cass shows up soon, before she runs out of self-control.

Ryan gestures to The Hotel. "He took the money she made and bought this place. Feminists always think her ghost is pissed because she had to stop acting, and then he got rich and famous. But"—he looks around, like The Hotel itself is evidence of what he's about to say—"she lived in style. I don't think she gave a shit about a *career.*"

"Why are you rebuilding it, then? If it has all this weird history. Why not demolish it, or sell it off or something? The land's gotta be worth—"

"That's what my dad wanted," Ryan says. "And he would have, but I chose it for my project."

"Project?"

"Riggs family tradition," Ryan explains. He picks up the camera again and starts scrolling through the photos he's taken, like he's bored by his own story. "When we turn eighteen we get a little bit of our trust on the condition that we don't spend it on ourselves. It has to go toward making something. For a while that was improving land, mostly, but recently there have been a lot of nightclub and restaurant investments. You can imagine."

"Oh."

"That's how Roman started Flash—that was his. They want us to learn how our money can work for us," Ryan says. "And how fast it can disappear. Avery—my great-great-grandfather, the guy who built this place—his dad spent a literal fortune gambling. He wanted to make sure we wouldn't be that dumb."

Cass's car appears at the mouth of the driveway.

"So you chose this place?" Lulu asks. "Even though it's maybe-cursed?"

Ryan smiles. This is the face Lulu knows best on him: certain, and pleased with himself about it. "Yeah," he says.

"You believe you can—what, break it?"

Cass parks and gets out of her car.

Ryan says, "I'm not scared of it. I figure, fuck a curse, you know?"

He's all princely arrogance and rich-boy bluster. Ryan is so used to the idea that the rules don't apply to him that even a supernatural one doesn't faze him. Of course he doesn't believe in curses. He probably doesn't even believe in luck. Ryan has a thousand-dollar cell phone in his pocket and a brand-new car in the driveway. He's been given money that could feed a family for years and told to use it to teach himself some lessons. So what if it *is* all a waste? He'll still have the idle afternoons he spent here, king of his castle, high on a hill.

He'll have the pictures too, Lulu thinks. Whatever he says about hot girls and easy subjects, he has them if he wants them. Which means he has the power to make the world think his life is beautiful and enviable and interesting even when all he's doing is wasting it away.

They go down to the tent, which is still in the pool. Cass gets stoned, stretches out on her back, and zones out, rubbing the corner of a thin, gauzy blanket carefully against her cheek.

It turns to the golden hour. Light spills through the canvas, turning her into a creature made of shadow and cream. She's dappled with shocks of color, streaks and splotches of pink and red and yellow. A breeze blows through the tent's unzipped flap. The air is thin and dry, soft with the scent of sage that grows wild around the property, at least where Ryan's gardeners haven't cut it back.

Lulu didn't see Ryan bring the camera in with them, but then he lifts it to his eye. Because it's digital, there's no sound when he takes a picture. Cass doesn't even seem to notice he's doing it. He said he was documenting The Hotel, but Lulu has only ever really seen him take pictures of girls.

"Ryan says there's a curse on this place," she says, mostly to get Cass's attention.

But Cass keeps her eyes closed. "Yeah," she agrees. "He says that."

"You don't believe in it either?"

"No one should believe in it," Cass says. "But Ryan likes talking about it because it makes him sound fearless. As if it's anything to be afraid of. It isn't. It's just— You know how it is."

"I don't," Lulu says.

"Beautiful women and their faces. What aren't they responsible for?"

"I've never said it was anyone's fault," Ryan says.

"If there *is* a curse, she's the one who cursed it. Connie."

"Okay, Cass, fine. Sorry for being the patriarchy."

Lulu bristles on Cass's behalf at Ryan's tone, which has the hint of a sneer. But Cass doesn't seem to hear that, or if she does, it doesn't bother her.

"It's not your fault," she says. "It's just how it is when people tell stories about girls. Like they're unnatural forces or something. Witches. If she was beautiful, of course she had to end up cursed."

Lulu feels like she's lost track of the conversation. She turns to Ryan to see what he's making of it, and catches him in the act of taking a picture of her. Which means that he's noticed it, probably, that she isn't hiding it the way she wanted to—the way Lulu's face looks when she looks at Cass.

CHAPTER THIRTEEN

• • • •

"YOU'RE STILL COMING on Friday, right?"

Lulu was already halfway home from her second final before she realized she'd just ditched Bea again. She sent a Flash apology filmed while driving, her saying "B, I'm risking life and limb and the world's most expensive ticket to apologize, I feel like shit, I'm so sorry," and didn't get anything back.

So she's extra-glad to hear Bea calling for her as they leave their calc final on Wednesday. "Of course!" she says, before she even really registers what the question was. "Yeah, definitely," she adds, reinforcing it for herself.

Bea has a perfect party house—a side entrance that leads onto a huge-ass backyard with high, thick hedges that block any nosy neighbors. Unfortunately, she also usually has parents around who keep them from taking advantage of it. But they headed to Gstaad early this year, trying to beat some of the jet lag, and so on Friday, Bea is throwing her first ever blowout.

"I wouldn't miss it," Lulu says. She and Bea fall into step with each other, heading toward the parking lot. "So, like, ice cream?"

"I'm the one with plans now," Bea says. "Rich." She gestures to where he and Jules are standing, waiting for her to catch up to them.

"Oh." This is pretty standard—Lulu ditched Bea plenty too when she and Owen first got together—but it's been a while since she's been on this end of it, and even longer since Bea had a boyfriend and Lulu didn't. It's one hundred percent Lulu's fault that this is happening right now, but it still sucks.

"Well. Cool," Lulu says. They're still walking; they're closing in on the boys. This conversation is about to end. Lulu doesn't think it's ending on a good note.

Bea says, "I was thinking you should invite your friend Cass to the party."

She doesn't say the word *friend* with any particular inflection, or irony.

"Oh, yeah, totally," Lulu says. "You'll like her. She's great."

"I'm sure," Bea says. "Later, yeah?" She holds out a hand and Lulu fist-bumps her. Then she's gone.

Lulu pulls her phone out of her bag, in a hurry to make it look like she didn't just get ditched. She doesn't even know if anyone is watching; it is, she knows, a ridiculous reflex. But as long as she's just doing things, she messages Cass about the party.

Thinking about Cass reminds Lulu that she has something she's been meaning to do while she's on campus. If she's going to be in the middle of someone's curse, or myth, or—whatever, she wants to know more about Avery Riggs, and she doesn't want to have to comb through the library to do it.

She goes to Mr. Winters's office. He's the Cinema Studies teacher; he should be able to point her in the right direction.

"I'm so glad you're taking an active interest in film history," Mr. Winters says. "Especially this part of it. A lot of students aren't as serious as you are, Lulu. They just want to watch the fun stuff. Not that this isn't fun. It's just not as obvious, I guess, *why* it's fun."

He's always doing this—giving you compliments, like you should be really thrilled that he's noticing you. It gives Lulu a slight but definite case of the creeps.

"Yeah," she says. "Thanks."

"Any particular reason you're interested in the Wilmott story?" he asks. "Do you know Ryan?"

"Do *you* know Ryan?"

"His family," Mr. Winters says. "His older brother, Roman— maybe five years older than you? He was one of my students my first year here. I met his mother at a parent-teacher conference, and we hit it off. They actually hadn't ever seen the Riggs version of *Bluebeard,* and I got to introduce them to it. That was fun. We've been friends ever since. I do Thanksgiving at their house when I don't want to go back home to my parents'. Always a glamorous evening. I love eavesdropping on their other guests."

It's weird hearing a teacher talk about having parents. Lulu knows he wants her to ask who the other guests are and what he's heard, and she should, probably—ingratiate herself with him, why not—but she really doesn't have the patience for it today.

"I don't really know Ryan," she says, which is true as far as it goes. She doesn't, like, *know* him. "I met him the other night. I'm thinking about my midterm project for class, mostly."

"Are you planning on writing a paper? I assumed you'd take the creative project option."

Lulu shrugs and smiles. "We'll see, I guess," she says. "I should get back to studying, but—"

"If you want to learn more about Connie, there's a podcast you should check out," Mr. Winters says. "It's called *Beauty, Power, Danger*, and it's about women in the arts. Have you heard of it?"

Lulu shakes her head.

"They did an episode on Connie and *Bluebeard* at some point. I know the woman who hosts it a little bit—I wrote for her sometimes when she was an editor at the *Weekly*. Christine is . . ."

Lulu taps *beauty, power, danger* into the Notes app on her phone, and tunes out the rest.

Lulu has actually been pretty lazy about updating her Flash story lately, so lazy that she got a couple of messages yesterday asking her what was up. She feels self-conscious and then self-conscious about being self-conscious. She knows she shouldn't care what these people think of her. She doesn't even know most of them.

She can't help it, though. She does care. At first, right after Sloane, it was a reflex to keep doing what she'd always done, to pretend that nothing had changed and everything was fine. Lately she's not sure, but she keeps at it. Treading water. Staying afloat.

So before she gets in her car, Lulu texts Tae Young, who's in her English class, to ask her if she's studying for the final tomorrow. Tae Young invites her over to her house, where she and her friends and Lulu spend the afternoon googling themes and quizzing each other on quotations.

At the end of the afternoon Lulu convinces everyone to jump in the pool fully dressed. She goes with them, and then gets out to film the girls, their hair and their clothes billowing around them like soft flowers in the water. It makes her feel better about everything in her life right now, to know that at least it still looks like she's living the way she always has.

CHAPTER FOURTEEN

• • • •

BEA IS SITTING on Rich's lap, her knees curled to her chest and her head flopped lazily against his shoulder. Jules is sitting next to Rich, and Patrick is sitting next to him. Patrick's girlfriend, Taylor, is perched on the couch's armrest with her feet in Patrick's lap.

They look like a puzzle, Lulu thinks, neatly put together so that everything fits. She's sitting on the floor with the rest of the odds and ends: Emily Williams, who's Bea's best friend from elementary school, and Jason Aguilar, a junior on the baseball team who one of the dudes must have invited.

Lulu never knows what to call the thing that happens before the party—the part where whoever's closest and most *in* comes over to hide valuables and lock bedroom doors and take shots together, to assert their ownership over the house and the night and one another before anyone else is allowed to come inside. Like so many things in her life, it's a ritual she has no language for, because no one ever talks about it. It's just—you get the Flash that says Come over at 8, or you're relegated to some outside circle, and what you hear from a friend of a friend, that *the party starts at like 9ish.*

This hour used to be her favorite part of the night. It was the part that made her feel sure of herself—that she was wanted, that she was okay, that she still knew how to say and not say the passwords that guarded all the doors of her life. Now Bea won't quite look at her and no one wants to talk to her and any minute now, Owen and Kiley are going to walk in, fresh from the dinner they had before coming over, and Lulu's not entirely sure she'll be able to stop herself from crying.

Jules slides off the couch so that he's sitting on the floor too. "Emily," he says. "You go to Beverly, right?"

"Yeah," Emily says. "A real-life public school girl. Have you ever met one before?"

Jules grins. Lulu can tell that he thinks he looks charming. "No," he says. "Is it dangerous? Are there *gangs*?"

Emily laughs. "Persian mafia, maybe," she says.

"I bet you can take 'em. You look tough."

Emily makes a fist and flexes a skinny biceps. Jules reaches out to touch it, and she lets him, flexing even harder before dissolving into giggles under his touch.

That's how it starts. Lulu knows this dance down to her bones: You sit still, and see who's looking at you. If you like it—the way he looks, and the way he looks at you—you make yourself available to be touched, which involves a certain amount of holding still too.

Boys think they're predators. They think they make the moves and the plans. They have no idea how much patience it takes to communicate to them: *Hey, it's safe. Hey, come over here.* You hold still and you let them approach, and you smile when they hold out a hand for you to sniff at. Lick it delicately, maybe; touch your tongue, and let him know you aren't opposed to the taste. Let him touch your arm, and then your back. Hold still while he works up the nerve to come in close, to find out where your teeth are. Wait, and wait, and wait, and then give in.

Lulu has a Solo cup with rum and Coke in it. It's too sweet, but that's what there is to drink. She sits still and watches Bea and Rich, and Patrick and Taylor, and Jules and Emily. Jason glances at her and glances away. She doesn't know if he isn't interested, or if he doesn't even think he could be. She's an older girl. That's not how it happens.

Lulu holds still out of habit, even though no one is looking at her.

CHAPTER FIFTEEN

●●●●

THE RUM DOES its work. Hours later, Lulu is drunk and losing at beer pong. Emily is playing extra-hard to get, or maybe she just really hates pong. Either way, Jules is stuck with Lulu for a partner, and he's pissed about it.

"Keep it together, Shapiro," Jules warns her as Lulu lines up a shot.

"I've *got* it," Lulu says, and promptly misses. The ball arcs over Jenny Price's head and into the darkness beyond.

"You can go get it," Jenny suggests.

Lulu grumbles, but she sets off toward where the ball seems to have disappeared, a loosely populated patch of grass where a group of guys is standing around in a circle talking.

"Lu*lu*," one of them says, and holds up a hand for a high five.

"Hi Oliver," Lulu says.

"You're hittin' 'em *wild* tonight," Oliver says.

"Mmmhmmm."

"Is it going to get wilder?" he asks.

"Might."

"Hell yeah." Oliver turns to high-five Jason, who's standing next to him. "Don't you wish more girls were like Lulu?" he asks.

Lulu imagines the small white ball smacking Oliver right between his wide-set blue eyes.

"What's Lulu like?"

Lulu turns to see Ryan standing at the edge of their circle. He's holding the ball she came to retrieve. Cass is standing slightly behind him. Lulu doesn't know that she's ever seen Cass look so small before, or so uncertain.

Oliver is delighted to see Ryan. "Ryan Riggs!" he exclaims. They give each other a bro-y, backslapping hug. "Dude, in the fucking flesh." He looks between Ryan and Lulu and says, "Oh damn, wait, did you come with Shapiro? Are you guys, like, happening?"

"Nah," Ryan says at the same time Lulu says "*No*."

"We're just friends," Lulu says. She reaches out a hand and Ryan drops the ball into it. "Sorry, I gotta finish this game."

"Riggs, stay and drink with us," Oliver orders. He starts introducing Ryan to his friends. They did AYSO together, apparently. So someone does know Ryan, but of course they do; when it comes down to it, *someone* always knows you in this world.

"Hey," Lulu says to Cass. "I'm almost done if you want to come hang out for a minute?"

"Sure," Cass says, and falls into step with her. "I mean, you don't have to babysit me. I saw Owen on the porch, I can—"

Owen and Kiley have been all over each other all night. Lulu doesn't know why she hates the idea of Cass being a part of that, only that she does. "It's not babysitting," she says. "I invited you to a party where you don't really know anyone. It's my job to be your guide."

"Okay." Cass gives Lulu a small smile. She looks around, taking in the scenery. "Thanks for inviting me, also. This place is kind of amazing."

"I know, right? God, I love Bea's backyard. It's paradise, basically. Or it would be if they had a hot tub."

"Very picky," Cass says.

"We're talking about *paradise*," Lulu reminds her.

When Lulu and Jules have officially lost, she takes Cass to find Bea. That was the whole point of Cass being here, after all. But also, Lulu is curious. She wants to know if they like each other; if they can even get along. She doesn't think Cass will really love anyone else at this party, but she's proud of Bea. She wants Cass to know that if there's anyone worth hanging out with here, it's the girl Lulu has claimed for her best friend.

Bea is, after all, the first person who showed Lulu that you could make your own kinds of rules—that, once you understood how it functioned, you could adjust the optics and control a scene instead of just starring in it.

They were both in ninth grade when they started hanging out together. At first it was convenient: Lulu was dating King, and Bea was with his best friend, Seb. It was at a party like this one where they decided they actually liked each other. Seb was wasted and puking; King was taking care of him; the rest of the boys were ignoring them as off-limits, and the other girls were ignoring them as upstarts and usurpers.

Lulu had been angling for those girls, trying to convince them to take her in—she had a feeling the thing with King wasn't going to last the year, and she didn't want to lose her access to his friends and his parties and the aura of sophistication they lent her, which kept anyone from looking too close and seeing that she wasn't nearly as cool as she was pretending to be.

So she didn't want to be associated too closely with the other freshman at the party. She probably would have ignored Bea if they hadn't ended up in the empty kitchen at the same time, refilling their drinks.

They were at a girl named Jordan Epstein's house; her father was a famous director, and the kitchen windows looked out onto a terraced backyard, a hot tub spilling steaming water into the gleaming aqua of the pool below. It was December then too, another chilly night. In the living room they could both hear the party going on without them. Bea looked at the yard, and down at her cup. Then she cut a glance at Lulu.

"Fuck this," she said, sudden and decisive. "Do you want to go swimming?"

"Now?" Lulu asked.

"Yeah," Bea said. "Seb's going to puke until he passes out; King's going to be with him until that happens. And I can't spend another hour being ignored in there. Why don't we do something fun?"

At first Lulu thought of Jordan coming out and seeing them and thinking, how childish, that they couldn't get along at the party, that they'd snuck off to splash around like babies.

Then, though, another thought occurred to her: one of the boys coming and seeing two girls in their underwear, wet and laughing. What *that* would look like to him.

"Yeah," she said. "Let's do it."

That was the night she started paying attention to Bea. Bea hadn't snared Seb just because she was pretty; Bea would never say so out loud, but she was playing the game just as carefully and strategically as Lulu herself. It was comforting to see that: to know that someone who seemed so natural, so sophisticated and easy, was trying just as hard as Lulu was to stay afloat.

Lulu finds Bea caught up in a thicket of girls dancing in the grass. Her hair is sweat-matted, and her face is flushed pink. She tries to pull Lulu into the dancing with her, but Lulu pulls her back. "Wait," she says. "I want you to meet Cass."

Bea stops moving. She cocks her head and takes Cass in. "Cass," she repeats. "Shit! Nice to meet you."

"Hi," Cass says.

"I sort of bailed on B when we went to the beach the other day," Lulu explains, trying to make the intensity of Bea's interest seem less weird to Cass. "She got curious."

"Everyone's curious about Cass," Bea says. "I mentioned to

Isabel that she was coming, and she like, she didn't seem like she believed me. She said you and your—Ryan, that you guys never come to parties. So, what, you guys are, like, too cool?"

"God, not at all," Cass says. "We just don't really love it, so we don't do it. And then people treat it like it's a crime, not liking what they like."

"Well," Bea says. "I hope this party isn't too painful, then."

Lulu watches the two of them misunderstand each other like a car crash in slow-motion. Bea is trying to be arch, and Cass is trying to be honest, and they're missing each other's points entirely. Lulu wishes she were allowed to set the terms of the conversation, to explain to them, no, you'll like each other if you do it like *this*.

"Um," Cass says. "I— It seems nice. Should we, like, get drinks or something?"

"Sure," Bea says.

So Cass has learned this survival technique, at least: Drink till it stops being awkward. Which tonight may be never.

When they get to the porch, Ryan, Oliver, and Jason are at the table, refilling their cups. Oliver offers the bottle he's been pouring from to Lulu. "Want some?"

"I'm good," Lulu says.

"Shapiro turns down a drink," Jason crows. "When was the last time *that* happened?"

Lulu gives him dagger eyes.

"Have you and Lulu been to a lot of parties together, Jason?"

Bea asks sweetly. God, even when she's being a pain, Lulu loves her. What an exquisite bitch.

But Oliver isn't a junior who can be cowed by Bea's candy-coated rudeness. "Please. Everyone knows the girl is thirsty," he says. "Everyone knows this girl has got the thirst. Speaking of which. Ryan. Is this one your lady?"

"This one's not anyone's anything," Cass says, ducking out from where Oliver is trying to throw an arm around her shoulders.

Don't do that, Lulu wants to tell her. *Don't let them know they're making you uncomfortable,* but it's too late. She understands better than ever why Cass avoids parties: She's sharp enough to understand so much of what's going on at them—and she can't hide the look on her face that broadcasts how dumb she thinks all of it is.

"Oh damn, an independent woman," Oliver says. "A free agent. Got a lot of single women at this party, actually." Lulu sees him realize it, but there's no time for her to stop what comes out of his mouth next. "Got a lot of options for you, Lulu, huh."

Lulu freezes. She and Bea have never talked about the Sloane snap, certainly not in terms of what it meant about her, and she doesn't think Cass or Ryan knows about it at all. So she could just write his comment off as drunk nonsense. If she ignores it, maybe everyone else will too? Or is Oliver going to try to press the point? Will they even really get what he means if he does?

Bea steps up easily. She isn't afraid of them, probably because she knows the boys are too distracted by the girl they think is their prey to see her best friend coming. "Sounds like you're looking," she says to Oliver. She actually physically puts herself between Jason and Oliver and Lulu, making her body available to them as a distraction. "Show me who you've got your eye on."

"Who *don't* I have my eye on, more like," Oliver says, turning away from Lulu and Cass to survey the party. "Okay, see that girl there, in the pink?"

Bea nods.

Thank you, Lulu thinks at her back, *thank you, thank you, thank you, thank you.*

While Lulu was distracted, Cass was conferring with Ryan. Now she steps in close and says, "Hey, um, I think we're gonna take off."

"Shit, really?"

"Yeah." Cass shrugs.

"I'm sorry if Bea—"

"No, no, it's not her fault I can't hang," Cass says. "I'm sorry. I shouldn't have even come, probably. I don't do well in these situations."

"You didn't have to come."

"Oh," Cass says, and Lulu knows she said the wrong thing.

"No," she says. "I didn't mean—I just—I'm sorry if you didn't have fun."

"It was fine," Cass says. "It's fun to see you in your natural habitat."

Lulu looks around. Is this her natural habitat? She's certainly spent a lot of time at parties like this one. It's sort of funny, then, that she still feels so uncomfortable. That it feels like a relief to be invited every time. What has she done tonight except worry that she's screwing everything up?

The answer is, drink to forget that she's screwing everything up.

"You know me," Lulu says. "I'm great at parties."

"You are!" Cass says. She throws up her hands, and somehow Lulu finds herself stepping in toward Cass's body, taking advantage of the movement to wrap herself around Cass in a funny, too-tight hug.

As soon as she does it she realizes they've never touched like this before. Lulu is shorter than Cass, and her head fits against her shoulder, and if she turned her head—casually, it wouldn't even be a thing, really—she could touch her face to the skin of Cass's neck.

Cass, for all she's thin and spare, is also warm and solid. Her arm comes around Lulu's shoulders and Lulu allows herself to stay there, laughing, feeling Cass laugh with her.

"Cass," Ryan says. "You ready? The car's going to be here in, like, two minutes, and I think if I miss another they're going to kick me off of Ryde permanently."

"Yeah."

For a wild moment, Lulu wants to beg her: *Take me with you. Get me out of here.* This party—which she wouldn't have questioned six months ago, which she's spent her whole high school career working to keep getting invited to—is the last place in the world she wants to be.

But instinct holds her back. *Don't ask to go where you haven't been invited. Act like you have somewhere to be even—especially—when you don't. Hold still, hold still, hold still.*

"Bye, Lulu," Cass says.

"Yeah, okay, bye," Lulu says.

CHAPTER SIXTEEN

• • • •

LULU WAKES UP in the wrong bed. It takes her several long minutes to sort that out: *wrong*. It's not unfamiliar, it's just not— But it is hers. It's her bed at her mom's apartment, because she's on winter break now, and that means she's staying with her mom.

Lulu allows herself a self-indulgent groan while one hand gropes for her phone.

Her mom's place is fine, obviously. It's not a hovel or anything, and Lulu's not so spoiled that she can't recognize that having not just one but two places she can live in is nothing to complain about.

It's just that this one has somehow never felt like home. It has a castle vibe, and not in a luxe, royal way—there's something very haunted fairy tale about it. Lulu's mom moved in after the divorce and turned the place into a princess palace, with fresh flowers in the bedrooms and clusters of candles on every side table. Lulu and her elementary school friends loved to hold séances here during sleepovers.

It sometimes feels like they succeeded in bringing down bad luck on the place, or else they sensed that it was destined for a pall of sadness—because ten years later, Lulu's mom is still here, and single, waking up in a canopy bed and cursing her lonely princess fate. A row of her headshots hangs in the hallway where a different type of mother might have family photos.

Her mom's asleep now, and she probably will be for another hour. Lulu has the kitchen to herself as she rifles through the cabinets, trying to find something to eat that isn't some kind of nut or seed. Usually she doesn't mind being on whatever weird diet her mother's gotten obsessed with while she's here, but just now Lulu really, really wants toast with butter on it, or at least real coffee. Fuck.

Instead she makes green tea that smells like old moss; there's some dubious-looking gluten-free "bread" in the fridge that, toasted, tastes like warm cardboard. Lulu nibbles it very miserably. With her free hand, she fumbles for her phone and searches for the podcast Mr. Winters mentioned. She scrolls back to the first episode and presses PLAY, the volume on low.

A woman's voice issues from her phone's speakers. "Every woman owns her own beauty," she intones. "And yet somehow, when it is put up for sale, it is almost always men who see the bulk of the profit. Artist and muse, studio head and actress, prostitute and pimp: All of these relationships function with varying degrees of consent and autonomy. But they all also uphold the same underlying economic structure, which holds that a literal middle*man* should be the person presenting a woman to the world—and taking a hefty cut of the profits in the process.

"If a man paints or photographs a woman, it's art; if a woman paints or photographs herself, it's an act of narcissistic self-indulgence. Women are assumed to be artless until they are put in someone's art; it's only the approval of someone else's eye that makes them worthy of serious consideration.

"Men recognize the power of women's beauty—and the danger in allowing them to harness it for themselves, without permission or intermediary. *Beauty, Power, Danger* is a podcast about the history of beautiful women in the arts, and an examination of the ways the men in their lives have sought to control their bodies, lives, and legacies for their own ends. I'm Christine L. Tompkins, and this is *Beauty, Power, Danger.*"

Lulu hits PAUSE. This seems like a lot for nine a.m., and especially for nine a.m. with a hangover. She's not even sure how much it applies to her: No one is selling Lulu's image but Lulu herself. Or does Flash technically own what she posts? She always forgets to check up on that. Either way, it's not a problem she's going to solve this morning.

She throws away the rest of her breakfast and goes back to sleep.

When she wakes up again, it's early afternoon and someone is hovering uncertainly at the foot of her bed. Naomi looks like she was about to either sit down or sneak out, and Lulu happened to wake up in the middle of it.

So Nao is home from college for winter break.

Lulu's head is so muddled that when she opens her mouth, what comes out is "No."

"That's how you greet your sister after months of separation?" Naomi asks. "No?"

"I'm tired!"

"That's not surprising. This room smells like a distillery," Naomi reports. "It smells like—a grow room. It smells like skunk, and feet, and death, Lu."

"You know what a grow room smells like?"

Naomi ignores her. "I tried to stay up to see you last night. When the hell did you get in?"

Lulu groans and rolls onto her back. "Like, three?" she says. She's really not in the mood for a lecture from her sister. "I'm very tired," she says. "And hungover. And I want to be left alone."

Usually being rude works on Naomi, but today she seems determined. "I bet you're also hungry," she says. "If you get up and take a shower, I can drive us to Nate and Al's for brunch."

Lulu's stomach grumbles, and she remembers her gross, aborted breakfast. How likely is it that the house has grown new food in its cabinets while she was sleeping?

And what are the chances her mom will make anything remotely palatable for dinner?

Lulu sits up. "We should go grocery shopping, after, too," she says.

"Already planning on it."

Naomi is halfway through her junior year at Georgetown; her international relations major is a disappointment to their mother because it's boring ("Like so you can be a diplomat?" she asked, when Nao announced it as a sophomore. "Like because a Jew who cares about the human rights of Palestinians should help negotiate peace in the Middle East," she replied) and to their father because it's unlikely to make her rich.

Lulu doesn't understand it either—it's *way* less sexy than the international-travel-and-intrigue thing she first imagined—but that makes sense: Her sister has never in her life chosen the sexy option. She's steady and straightforward, well suited to the patient unknotting of delicate, complicated problems.

"You're interested in the same things," Bea told Lulu once, in a rare moment of extreme earnestness. "Isn't diplomacy just like high-level social management, when you think about it? Knowing the gossip on everyone? Knowing who you can ask for what?"

"I guess," Lulu said then. She remembers it now, listening to Nao talk through the politics of the office where she's interning this semester. Maybe Bea had a point.

When Naomi goes to the bathroom, Lulu does what she always does: takes out her phone and snaps a Flash of her face washed out by the window's light. You can't see much of anything, but it's kind of cool looking. She's trying to figure out whether she wants to filter it when Naomi slides back into her seat at the table. Lulu automatically clicks her screen dark and puts her phone down.

"Don't let me interrupt," Naomi says.

"No, it's fine, I'm done."

"Are you, um, were you Flashing?"

"Oh my god, no."

"You're not?"

"I mean, I was on Flash, but no one—*no one* says that, Naomi."

"I don't know." There's something in Naomi's tone that sets off warning bells in Lulu's head. "I don't really know anything about it."

"It's not that interesting."

"It is sometimes, though." Naomi has been looking down at her hands in her lap, but when she says this she looks up. She looks Lulu in the eye.

Fuck.

"One of my friends was writing this paper for a feminist studies class," Naomi says. "About the narrative possibilities of young women— Whatever, it doesn't matter. Anyway. She was doing some research. She found this video."

Lulu buries her face in her hands. "Nooooooo," she says.

"I'm not—we don't have to talk about the video it*self*," Naomi says. Lulu imagines forcing her prim, reserved older sister to discuss sex with her, and feels only marginally better. "I just wanted to check in with you about it. First of all—do Mom and Dad know?"

"Know about what?"

"That there's a *sex tape* of you on the internet."

"It's not a sex tape, Naomi, Jesus."

"A make-out tape."

"They don't know that there are any . . . sexual . . . images of me on the internet."

"Not even Deirdre knows?"

"Deirdre isn't that young," Lulu says. "Besides, you know her: She's too cool of a stepmom to go looking for dirt on me."

Naomi makes a face. "Soooooo cool," she says. "What an awesome parenting trend: neglect."

"I'm hardly *neglected*."

"Are you?"

"I'm not making porn, Naomi. It was a mistake."

Naomi nods.

"Oh my god, did you think it was like . . . revenge porn? You think Owen would do that?"

"I've only met Owen once," Naomi says. "And I never pretend to have any sense of what the hell a man might do if he got his feelings hurt."

"*A man*." Now it's Lulu's turn to roll her eyes.

"Seriously, Lu. Can you just—can you tell me, I don't know. Are you okay?"

Lulu hates that question. It's the one she's been trying to avoid by staying home and standing in corners at parties, by plastering a smile on her face and keeping her grades up.

Is she okay? She doesn't know.

She'd like to be okay, because then no one would have to worry about her. But if she's okay about that whole—thing—it seems like no one thinks she *should* be okay, so maybe that's a mistake. She doesn't know how she's supposed to feel about having exposed herself, or having hurt Owen, or having that video of her out there forever.

There are no rules for this situation, because this is a situation you don't find yourself in if you actually remember to play by the fucking rules.

"It was a mistake," Lulu says. "But I posted it myself, okay?" It was her own fault. Lulu knows that much. "And I promise, honestly, I'm totally fine. You can check my grades if you want to. You just watched me house this food, so you know I'm eating. You saw me sleeping." She smiles. "Right?"

Naomi smiles thinly. "Right," she says. "After staying out all night getting drunk."

"It was the end of the semester. There was a party. I'm going to parties. I'm still a regular girl." Naomi seems unconvinced. "We should get the check."

"I want to be here for you," Naomi says. "I want to be a part of your life, Lulu."

So much for getting out of here quickly. "You are," she says. "See? Brunch."

"I want you to be able to call me, if you want to."

"I will, I swear, but this really wasn't—"

"I remember what it was like, you know. The first time I drove down the block, and I made a turn, and I couldn't see the house anymore. And I realized: I could do whatever I wanted."

"You're complaining about that?"

"It was fun," Naomi says. "Don't get me wrong. But it was scary sometimes too. There were nights—" She looks at Lulu, shakes her head, and looks away.

"Nights when what?"

"Bad nights."

Lulu honestly can't imagine what Naomi would consider a "bad night." Did she drink three beers and feel the room spin around her? Get ignored by a guy who she wanted to pay attention to her? Have him pay so much attention to her that all she could think about was escape? Has Naomi ever stood in line for the bathroom and listened to someone retching, helplessly, miserably sick, on the other side of a door? What are the odds that she's ever *been* that person?

Lulu looks at her sister. Naomi is wearing jeans and sneakers and a worn-in Georgetown sweatshirt. Her long, dark hair is loose around her face; thin gold hoop earrings are threaded through each earlobe, but she doesn't have on any other jewelry, or any makeup. She has their father's strong, sharp features, and his seriousness too. For most of their lives, Lulu has felt like Naomi was at least part stranger, someone she's never really known.

Lulu asks, "What do you mean by bad?"

Naomi shrugs.

"You can't ask me about mine if you won't talk about yours."

Naomi twists her mouth. "I know you've probably done it all," she says. "But it makes me feel like an irresponsible older sister to tell you."

Lulu snorts. "I will respect you *so* much more if you tell me you ever broke a rule," she says.

"Lulu, of course I broke rules."

Naomi isn't a stranger at all, and unwillingly, Lulu knows exactly what she means: Lulu breaks dumb rules—about drinking, and kissing boys, and girls too. Naomi broke Lulu's Rules for How to Get By. She breaks them every day.

She's not a stranger, but she and Lulu still don't understand each other at all.

"Whatever your bad nights were, though," Lulu says, "you survived them."

"I did. I did. It's just that—what if *survival* wasn't really what mattered?"

"Huh?"

"Like, yeah, I lived through it. I grew up. I'm fine now. I just think it could have been easier."

"If you'd never been allowed out of the house on your own? To make your own mistakes?"

"If, after I'd made my mistakes, I could have come home and talked to someone about them."

Naomi looks at Lulu, so level and direct that Lulu can't bring herself to look away.

"I'm trying to be someone you can talk to," Naomi says. "That you *want* to talk to, even."

"I'm not one of your projects," Lulu says. "I'm not some kind of self-improvement thing."

"Of course not. You're my sister," Naomi says. She forks a raspberry off of Lulu's plate.

In the spirit of sisterhood, Lulu lets her.

CHAPTER SEVENTEEN

• • • •

LULU STANDS OUTSIDE of The Hotel's gates with empty hands. Cass texted her the code this morning, with an invitation to come hang out. Lulu recited it to herself on the drive over, across the long, hot plane of the freeway, and then as she wound her way through the lush, quiet neighborhoods, up and up into the hills.

She knew it was stupid to be scared, but she worried anyway—that she would get there and the message with the code wouldn't load on her phone, that she wouldn't be able to call Cass and ask to be let in, that she was in some kind of fairy tale where, when you tried to come back in daylight, on your own, you couldn't even find the door.

But The Hotel isn't a fairy tale. It's just a place. Lulu enters the numbers and the gate swings open for her as easily as it does for Cass. Lulu steers her car along its tree-lined driveway with the windows down, one arm stretched out to grab palmfuls of the warm, dry air.

The front door is unlocked, but she can't find Cass or Ryan in the lobby. Upstairs, they aren't in either of the finished rooms. She's about to go back down when she hears Cass call, "Ryan?"

"No," Lulu says.

"Hey, Lu!"

"Where are you?" Lulu turns in a circle in the hallway, like Cass is camouflaged in it somewhere.

"Walk to the end of the hall," Cass calls. Her voice is muffled by the space between them; she sounds like she's underwater. "Through the last door on your left."

In the room, Lulu is hit by a wall of sunlight, echoing white off the floors and the walls. She holds a hand up to her eyes instinctively, squinting.

This must be where whoever works on The Hotel when she's not around leaves their tools: The ground is littered with tarps and rollers and tool kits and cans of paint. Past them is a sliding glass door that opens onto a balcony. Cass is sitting out there in a folding chair with her back to Lulu. Her hair glimmers copper under the sun.

"Come hang," Cass says, raising a lazy arm in greeting.

"Hey," Lulu says. She makes her way across the room, careful not to step on stray nails in her thin-soled ballet flats.

"Did you see Ryan on the way in?"

"No."

"Huh."

"Should I have?"

Cass shrugs. "He wandered off a while ago. I thought he might be downstairs."

"Should we go looking for him?"

"Nah. I'm not worried." Cass stretches her legs out to rest them on the balcony's top railing. She's wearing a pair of jeans so worn that they might be actual vintage, not new-made-to-seem-old. Lulu wonders if the denim is as soft as it looks.

"I guess this is his place," Lulu says. "He can do whatever he wants."

"Exactly."

Lulu sets up so that she's facing Cass, sitting on the ground with her back against the balcony railings.

"Noooo," Cass says. "You can't sit that way! You're missing the best part."

"I wanted to keep the sun out of my face."

"Don't be a baby. Put your sunglasses on."

"What if I don't have sunglasses?" Lulu asks, just to be annoying.

Cass looks over the brim of her own pair, down at Lulu.

"Fine," Lulu says. She finds them in her bag and puts them on before turning around so she and Cass are facing the same way. "Now, what am I looking for?"

"The view."

The Hotel stretches out below them, a spread of white stone against the green and ochre of the winter hillside. Lulu feels like she's sitting inside of the curved cup of a bowl. The sun on her face is syrupy golden. She closes her eyes and lets it wrap around her limbs, slow and thick as honey.

"How are you doing?" Cass asks.

Lulu leans back against the door, letting the glass take her weight. "You know," she says. "I'm good."

"Cool."

Cass doesn't say anything else.

"My sister's home," Lulu says.

"From college?"

"Yeah."

Cass nods. "My brother too."

"Are you guys close?"

"We get along."

"Naomi and I don't, always."

Cass takes this in. "Do you fight?"

"No. We just—" Lulu lets the sentence drop.

"I thought about you the other night," Cass says.

Lulu concentrates on staying still and neutral when she says, "Oh?"

"Is that weird? I know we don't know each other that well."

"Depends on why you were thinking about me." It's hotter out here than Lulu would have guessed, once you sit for a while. Her thighs prickle with heat under her jeans. She wishes she'd worn a dress.

"Dylan—my brother—he was talking about his girlfriend. The way he described her reminded me of you."

Lulu goes for the easy thing, which is a joke. "Too cool for her own good?" she asks.

"No," Cass laughs. "That's not what he said."

"What did he say?"

"I don't know," Cass says. Lulu doesn't believe her. "Hey, you want anything? Water? Weed?"

Lulu almost says yes without thinking about it, the same way that, when Cass asked her how she was, she automatically said, *You know. I'm good.* The rules say: If Cass is stoned, she should be stoned. The rules say: Being fucked up is cooler than being sober, and gives you an excuse if you're a little weird too.

But she doesn't want to be high right now. She wants to sit in this quiet sunlight with Cass and talk to her slowly, their conversation going wherever it goes. She wants—she wants—nothing she's ready to name.

"I'm okay," Lulu says.

Cass smiles at her. "Glad to hear it."

And then, in that moment, Lulu wants something with sharp, specific clarity: for Cass to reach down and touch her hair. The desire goes through her so suddenly and violently that in order to keep herself from leaning into it, asking for the contact even just with her body, she leaps up to her feet. She walks to the far end of the balcony and peers around the edge of The Hotel.

"Hey," she asks, "what's over here?" There's something tall, a structure, glinting from among the trees just around the corner.

"Oh," Cass says. "The building, you mean? That's the greenhouse."

"Like, for growing stuff?"

"Yeah, like for growing stuff. Apparently it was one of the things The Hotel was famous for back in the day—it had this amazing collection of rare plants and things."

"What does it have now?"

"Dust, mostly. Ryan had the structure repaired and reinforced, but he hasn't put anything in it yet."

"Can we go there?"

"God, I should have known you were gonna make me get up."

"We don't have to—" Lulu starts, but Cass is already standing, and smiling. It doesn't look like she really minds.

The greenhouse is, in fact, dusty. The doors are propped open and it's sitting in the shade, but even still, it's hot inside. All that afternoon air, trapped and magnified by the glass. Lulu calls up to the rafters, a nonsense sound, but it doesn't echo. Tree branches brush the roof over their heads. For the first time since she's been at The Hotel, Lulu thinks the word *abandoned*.

"We don't come in here much," Cass says. She's lingering near the door, almost as if she's afraid to walk all the way inside.

"No greenhouse projects?"

"Ryan says he has a black thumb."

Lulu walks around the perimeter. There's nothing in here but space and air.

"You like it," Cass says. It's not a question.

"I do."

Cass smiles.

"What?" Lulu asks.

"I'm glad."

"Okay—okay."

Cass holds her arms out and twirls her wrists absently. Lulu likes the way the length of her takes up space.

"We have this little orchard that's my favorite place at my dad's house," Lulu says. "I like places where things can grow."

Cass's smile gets wider. "Lulu," she says. "Are you secretly kind of . . . a hippie?"

"Absolutely not." Lulu crosses her arms in front of her chest.

It doesn't stop Cass's grin. "I don't know about that," she says. "You play like you're some scary, too-cool party girl, but—"

"Hey," Lulu says. "You think I'm scary?"

Cass raises an eyebrow at her. "Not anymore."

But Lulu's not giving up that easily. "You *thought* I was scary?" She's fascinated. She can't imagine what it would be like to look at her and not already be tired of what you saw.

Cass frowns. "When we first met, you didn't look like you would be easy to talk to," she says eventually.

"I'm a very good conversationalist!" Lulu thinks of how often she got in trouble for whispering with her friends in class when she was in elementary school. Mr. Lindsey and Mrs. Garland and all the rest of them wish she had been hard to talk to.

"Not bad at talking, you absolute goose," Cass says. "Hard for *me* to talk to. I didn't know if we—if we could get along."

Lulu has been watching Cass walk around the space, but when she hears Cass say that, she has to look away. She can feel the way the afternoon is moving, the way Cass is peeling her apart in onionskin layers, so fine Lulu barely notices the process of being bared. *But we do, right?* Lulu could ask her, and Cass could read whatever she wanted into the question. *We do get along?*

Instead she goes back to the joke, the easy spar. "We *were* getting along," Lulu reminds her, "until you started making fun of me for having a feeling."

Maybe Cass senses their conversation is getting dangerous too, because her voice comes out high and a little strangled when she replies. "I was not making fun! I was—pointing something out. I was *observing*. Weren't you an indoor kid? Don't you know that's what we do? Observe?"

"I was busy being scary and going to parties," Lulu says.

Normally it makes her nervous to know that people are looking at her and seeing things she's not already aware of herself.

God, she likes the idea that Cass is noticing her, though.

"How did I ever entrap you in my secret garden?" Cass wonders.

Lulu hasn't taken any of the openings Cass was maybe-offering her. Now, helpless, she makes one of her own. "You didn't trap me," she says. "I wanted to come."

But now it's Cass's turn to avoid looking at Lulu. Or maybe she's just not looking anyway. Maybe she's not even thinking about what Lulu might mean by that, because why would she? Because they're just friends.

Cass changes the subject. "Did you ever read that book?" she asks. "*The Secret Garden?*"

"No."

"It was my mom's favorite when she was a kid, so she read it to me when I was little. I got obsessed with it."

"Huh."

"*Obsessed.* We watched all the movies together too. I made my brother play Secret Garden with me in the backyard so much he eventually stopped speaking to me for a while because he was so sick of it." Cass puts a palm up against the greenhouse wall. "So actually, this place should really be my favorite part of the property. It's got a very *Secret Garden* vibe."

Lulu takes this in. "That is," she declares, "pretty freakin' adorable. Also, see how I just acknowledged your feeling, and didn't make fun of it?"

"*God,*" Cass groans. She shakes her head. Then she says, quieter: "The funny part is, I didn't want to be Mary when we played it."

"She's the main character?"

Cass gives Lulu a withering look.

"We weren't all *Secret Garden* nerds!" Lulu says. "I don't know."

"Mary is the only girl in *The Secret Garden,*" Cass explains. "She starts out this sick, spoiled little princess, and then she plays in an English garden and gets hearty and healthy and in touch with nature and all of that. But I always wanted to be her friend Dickon."

"Why?"

Cass shrugs. "I think it made my parents wonder if I was gonna turn out to be trans or something," she says. "But it wasn't that. I didn't want to be a boy, exactly. Dickon just seemed cooler. He knew more stuff. And I didn't understand why everyone thought I should always want to be the girl, you know?"

Lulu has only ever wanted girl things. Pink ribbons and glitter lipstick. Long hair, high heels. Pretty dresses. A pretty face.

"That's exactly what I've always wanted," she says. "To be the girl."

"That's okay," Cass says.

Despite herself, Lulu believes her.

"What did you want to be instead?" Lulu asks.

Cass doesn't have an answer. "I don't know, just not that," she says. "You really never—you never just wanted to be something else for a minute?"

Lulu shakes her head. "I've always been a princess."

"Wild."

"I think you mean basic."

"Now who's making fun of you?"

"I'm not making fun. I'm stating a fact. Is there anything more basic than wanting to be a princess?"

"I don't know. I mean, if that's what you really want, there's nothing wrong with it."

As much as Lulu's been giving Cass shit about her hippie comment earlier, this contemplative, open conversation is worse, because it makes Lulu feel like she can say whatever she wants, and she isn't sure enough where things stand between them—what all of these little moments mean—to do that. Lulu feels her chin get stubborn. "Listen. I'm not dumb. I know what I look like," she says.

"What do you look like?"

"Like I'm dumb."

Cass barks out a laugh. She rubs a hand across her face. "Jesus, Lulu."

"Let's be honest. That first time you saw me, what did you think?" Lulu gestures to encompass the space she inhabits: the pale lavender of her sweater, the tangle of thin gold chains around her neck, and the stack of rings on her fingers. Her pink manicure and pink mouth. She's demanding something, and she's not entirely sure what it is. It just seems important to press Cass. To be sure of her. To *know*.

Lulu says, "It's okay. Scary party girl, right? You thought I was just some JAP bitch."

"No."

Lulu sighs and slumps down against the greenhouse wall. A puff of dust rises and then settles around her.

Cass comes to sit next to her. "We don't have to talk about this," she says. "I don't even know how we got into this conversation."

Lulu doesn't look at her, because if she looked, she would see how close Cass is to her. Instead, she leans her shoulder against Cass's, just the tiniest bit. Cass leans back.

"You were telling me about being into gardens when you were little," Lulu reminds her.

"I've always loved a hideout," Cass says. "That was really what I loved about it—not the garden but the secret. A place where no one was looking at me, and I could be whatever I wanted."

"You could be nothing," Lulu says.

"I could be anything," Cass corrects.

CHAPTER EIGHTEEN

• • • •

HER CONVERSATION WITH Cass shakes something loose in Lulu. All afternoon it buzzes against her bones, and that night, she can't fall asleep for its persistent, percussive force inside of her skull and against the backs of her teeth.

I could be anything, Cass had said.

Lulu has a lot of ideas about who she isn't and doesn't want to be: She doesn't want to be like her mother, whose life stalled out when her looks started to go, and has never been able to figure out what else about her might be interesting. She isn't like Naomi, who never cared about having looks in the first place. She isn't like Bea, who's smart and determined and knows, at least, that she wants to be someone, even if she isn't sure who she is yet.

Eventually, Lulu grabs her phone from where it's charging on her bedside table and jams her earbuds into her ears. She knows blue light isn't helpful when you're trying to sleep, but she's only looking at it for long enough to find the Connie Wilmott episode of the *Beauty, Power, Danger* podcast. Once it's playing, she turns her phone over so it can't glow at her, and stares up into the darkness, listening.

"Constance Wilmott was born right before the turn of the twentieth century in a tiny mining town somewhere in dusty Nevada; she moved to Los Angeles when she was eighteen, was cast as the wife in a silent film adaptation of the *Bluebeard* story that year, and married Avery Riggs before she turned twenty. She never made another film.

"So why do we know her name?" Christine L. Tompkins asks. "Most silent film actresses faded into obscurity as their talkie counterparts rose to prominence. In fact, most films of that era no longer exist, due to careless archivists and the film's extreme flammability."

Lulu finds it weirdly comforting to think that even the things people have *tried* to save have disappeared off the face of the earth. Like an accidental Flash, almost. Eventually, no one will ever be able to watch her kiss Sloane ever again. It might be a long while, but it will happen. Probably. Right?

"The answer to this question comes, as it so often does, in the form of her husband. Avery Riggs made sure that the film was preserved. He bought a then-unheard-of professional projection system so that he could screen it at his first hotel property, The Aster, every year on her birthday. The hotel, by the way, was named for Wilmott's favorite flower; the storied space ultimately couldn't hang on to its glamour, and was shuttered due to bankruptcy in the early 1990s."

So much for avoiding blue light. Lulu flips her phone over again and googles "the Aster hotel Los Angeles Riggs." The photos she turns up show a structure that's bigger and much more elaborate than the one she knows, but Lulu recognizes the landscape, and the thing Ryan's built to mimic it. So that's what The Hotel used to look like.

"Much has been made of Wilmott's decision not to act again after *Bluebeard*," Christine continues in Lulu's ears. "She insisted that it was a personal choice, rooted in her desire to be a mother first. But those who knew Riggs suggest that he was a jealous man and that, having seen the way the public loved his lovely wife in her debut, he refused to share her like that ever again.

"Why, though, would he then insist on screening the film repeatedly, creating and maintaining a legacy where he might simply have allowed her to be forgotten?

"Riggs's work as a developer was the building of monuments, and his tastes ran to structures that would dominate men, and outlast them. Whether or not he was behind his wife's decision to leave acting, he found a way to monumentalize her. He turned her into something lasting, attached to his name and under his control. Connie would age and fade; she would become a woman and a wife instead of a celluloid fantasy. But he would always own the vision of her body as eternally nubile and functionally mute.

"Riggs's real estate empire was, in some sense, built on the back of Connie Wilmott's beauty; the money she earned from that film funded his earliest forays in that world. Interest in *Bluebeard* has remained feverish in part because of her reluctance to appear in public to support or discuss it. Her silence has allowed a cult-like obsession with the film and with her to build up. Instead of remaining a woman, Connie became an icon onto which fantasy is eternally and seamlessly projected."

Lulu is more awake than ever. She picks up her phone again. Bea just messaged her a picture of herself in her hotel room with the texts:

> so switzerland is boring and cold everyone
>
> here really is a blond GIANT
>
> the skiing is good but that's all there is
>
> everything is just so . . . white

Lulu doesn't know what Bea means by that—if she's talking about the whiteness of the mountain, or the people. Bea talks about race so infrequently that Lulu forgets Bea isn't white sometimes, which she told Bea once, and Bea didn't like. So she doesn't know what to say to this. If she makes a joke about snow, will she be missing the point again? Or by *not* saying anything, is she chickening out, the way she did with Ryan at The Hotel when he was talking about Gypsies and she basically let him off the hook?

Considering this, Lulu scrolls up idly and sees something that makes her flinch: The last time she messaged Bea was the night of her party. It's been a full week and Lulu has been radio silent on her best friend. Shit.

Ughhhhhhhhhh I'm sorry, she writes back.

Bea responds right away. I guess LA must be pretty interesting

I'm sorry about that too, B

I promise

you haven't missed anything

You and Cass been hanging

out a lot?

Lulu stares at her phone screen. She doesn't know what Bea means by that.

Bea sends I haven't seen you in any of the usual suspects' flashes as if to explain herself.

Yeah I guess, Lulu sends, because she doesn't know what else to say.

When the Sloane Flash went up, Bea messaged, Heyyyy what's going on? everything okay, and Lulu sent back, I'm okay, I promise. She was lying, but she wasn't not-okay in any ways Bea could help with.

She didn't want help, because she didn't want it to be happening. Nothing about the Sloane Flash made sense in Lulu's life, which she had constructed so carefully. In a fraction of a second, she had undone all of her work to make herself a pretty girl, with pretty friends, and a nice, hot boyfriend—all of her efforts to only ever be seen in this one particular, legible way.

So what she wanted was to never have done it, or, barring that, to at least be able to pretend it away the way she'd pretended past every other inconvenient fact in her life.

Lulu thinks about Bea defending her at that party, being sharp and rude to Jason and then distracting and charming to Oliver. She would never have asked Bea to do those things for her—to take care of Lulu's messiness instead of leaving her to clean up after herself. But Bea did them anyway, and that's worth so much that it scares Lulu sometimes. To think that Bea loves her more than she loves her own social status, or her own rules. That Bea just loves her, just because.

I'm not up to anything cool, Lulu sends Bea. I miss your face.

> Well feel free to FaceTime me
> whenever then
> I got international data for
> daysssssssss

>> Don't answer your phone
>> while you're skiing please B

Lol never, Bea says. Def no.

CHAPTER NINETEEN

● ● ● ●

IT FEELS LIKE Cass is giving the days to Lulu like gifts: after-noons on the balcony, or down by the pool while Ryan practices skateboarding and takes pictures. Sometimes Lulu will wander off to the sunlit greenhouse and wait for Cass to come find her. Cass always does, and when she appears in the doorway, Lulu's heart kicks against her ribs. She's overcome with the sweetest, hottest ache: that Cass noticed she was missing, and wanted to know where she was.

Work on the property seems to have stalled out for the season. The Hotel looks finished, but there's nothing in it: no furniture except what Ryan's brought in for his own personal use. For days and days, nothing changes, and it's a relief. The days keep getting shorter, sliding into each other so fast sometimes Lulu feels like she can barely keep up, so it's nice that this one thing has arrested itself for her, just a temporary lacuna where she can sit still.

The tent has been relocated to The Hotel's lobby. It's too cold to sleep out of doors anymore. On the day they bring it in, Cass insists on stringing Christmas lights around the inside so they can get stoned and lie on their backs and watch the colors blink. Ryan takes a video of the scene, panning across their faces and then up to the lights.

He usually asks before he takes any pictures. "You guys good?" he'll say, and Lulu has never said no, but more and more she's been thinking about it.

She doesn't, though, because then he would ask why, and she wouldn't have a good answer. She's still filming herself basically every minute she's not at The Hotel—when she's getting dressed, or taking off her eye makeup, or little funny family things, like when she stops by her dad's to pick up a sweater she forgot and Olivia is putting on a fashion show in their living room—so she doesn't have that defense. She just doesn't *want* to, is all.

For just a little while, she just wants to be allowed to forget that anyone is looking, or that anyone cares what she looks like.

Plus, she's started listening to *Beauty, Power, Danger* from the beginning, and it's giving her all kinds of weird ideas about images and who owns them, and how and why it matters. She doesn't listen to it at The Hotel, but she's started reading the things Christine L. Tompkins mentions in the show notes— online articles, and sometimes even parts of actual books. Lulu can't believe she's reading, like, academic texts over vacation, but then, they're academic texts about interesting things: women and power and sex.

And she's a feminist, right? Or she's always thought she basically was, anyway. With Naomi for a sister you kind of had to be. But increasingly, Lulu realizes she didn't really have a sense of what that meant, other than for her own limited, personal purposes: that she wanted to be allowed to wear pants and own property and go to school and stuff.

Now when she goes to the mall with Naomi to try to get their mom a Hanukkah present and a man walking by says, "Pair of you, look at you, *nice*-looking girls," for no reason other than that he thought they might want to know what he thought of them, instead of ignoring him, brushing it off like she always does, Lulu thinks: *God, what a fucking pig.*

CHAPTER TWENTY

● ● ● ●

ON FRIDAY, RYAN has a project for the three of them. "What, you thought this would just be a free ride?" he says.

He's wearing paint-splattered khakis and a T-shirt with a rip at the collar. Even Lulu has to admit it's a good look on him: work-worn but not shabby. He's still so young-prince handsome. Those cheekbones. On his way to hug Cass he comes so close that Lulu scents the sweat of him: the funk of boy-skin, some kind of cologne. Sandalwood, maybe? Probably expensive. He smells good.

He doesn't touch Lulu. Instead, he says, "The painters fucked up the color in one of the rooms, and they can't get back in time to fix it, so I figured we'd take a crack at it."

"I'm an expert painter," Cass reports. "When I turned twelve my parents let me repaint my room, and I was going through a goth phase, so I went black, which was a mistake. Fixing it really sucked."

"Let me guess, Lulu, you're not as experienced." Ryan smirks at her dress and tights, her shearling-lined jacket, like she would have worn them if he'd just been a normal person and warned her about what they'd be doing.

Lulu's not going to be cowed. "What, Ryan, did you go to art school for this? Still photography and intermediate abstract wall painting?"

"I'm a regular Rothko," he says. "Nah, my dad made me do this stuff growing up sometimes. Builds character, whatever. Plus, that way you know if the guys you hire are lying to you, or being lazy. You know what a good job looks like and how long it takes."

The way he says it makes Lulu's skin crawl. She hates the idea of Riggs Senior teaching Ryan to dabble in manual labor, and how to keep an eye on his workers to make sure they don't slack or cut corners on his dime. It occurs to her that even as she's watched The Hotel transform in the last few weeks, she's been shielded from the sight of the men who've been making that happen. Like their work is shameful, or strange.

"I have clothes for you guys to wear if you don't want to get dirty," Ryan says. "Come upstairs so you can change."

Ryan's shirt hangs loose on Cass: It fits like proper boyfriend clothes. Lulu remembers the way he wrapped himself around her when they set up the tent that first night. It's hard not to feel like their bodies make sense of each other: his proportions and hers. One large, one small; one girl, one boy. On Lulu's curves, Ryan's clothes just look dumpy.

The job isn't hard, though. Dip a roller in paint; glide it up and down a wall. Stand close and check for evenness; wait for it to dry and check again. Layer after layer after layer. They turn the room from a pale yellow Easter color to a gemstone-y rose quartz pink.

"We get, like, sweat equity on this, right?" Cass says, midway through the afternoon. "This is the Shapiro and Velloro Memorial Suite. It's ours whenever we want it. The VellShap. The ShapVell."

"You guys looking to book a staycation together?" Ryan asks. There's acid on his tongue, and Lulu doesn't understand why. *She's wearing your T-shirt,* she wants to tell him. *She's asking you a question.*

"I've been thinking I want Lulu to teach me how to be a better girl," Cass says. "Manicures. Face masks. Loofahs? I don't know other kinds of girl accessories."

Lulu laughs. "That's a good start," she says.

Cass turns to Ryan. "We can do your makeup if you want," she says. "I bet Lulu could contour the shit out of you."

"I have highlighter in my bag," Lulu offers.

Instead, Ryan reaches down into the tray of paint and uses one finger to streak each cheek rosy. "How's this for contour?" he asks.

"Very good," Cass says approvingly. "I like a man who knows his angles."

Ryan smiles, but when Lulu turns back to the patch of wall she's been working on, he leaves, probably to go wash it off. She feels like she's won some obscure victory, though she couldn't say exactly what it was.

"I've been thinking about that conversation, actually," Cass says to Lulu. "About how you asked what I thought of you when we first met."

"You've come back around," Lulu deadpans. "It was JAP-y bitch. I knew it."

"Lulu!" Cass brandishes her roller at Lulu, but she isn't really trying, and it's easy to dance out of her way. "*No*," she continues. "What I was going to *ask* was why you wear that stuff if you think it makes you look so dumb."

Lulu paints a long stripe up the wall, pressing the roller from bottom to top. She looks at the pink streak she's left in her wake. She says, "I mean, I don't hate it or anything. But mostly it's just easy: I can do it without thinking about it. And when I do, no one thinks too much about me."

"It's, like, private school girl camouflage."

"Exactly."

"Okay but so then: What are you hiding?"

Lulu doesn't say anything. Cass uses her roller to go over Lulu's line of paint, turning it darker and more solid.

"The fact," Lulu says, "that I'm not very interesting."

"I think you are," Cass says. "Interesting." The sun is already starting to slide in the western sky, and the room is suffused with a rosy glow that makes Cass's cheeks look particularly pink.

Lulu shrugs.

"Okay," Cass says. "Fine, don't believe me. But I guess I should say—um—that you're only kind of right. The first night when I met you? Your camouflage worked. At first, I didn't notice you at all. But when I did, it was because of what you did. When I saw you sneaking upstairs—that's when I started wondering what your deal was."

Lulu forgets her self-pity instantly. She narrows her eyes. "Wait a minute! So when you found me, did you—"

Cass is definitely blushing now, the color coming on fierce and sudden. "I didn't know you were in the bathroom," she says. "I wasn't trying to follow you in *there*. I just wanted to know where you were going. I wanted to know what else there was to do at a party like that one."

"Not much."

"See," Cass says. "I had thought the options for that type of thing were to go, or not go. And then I saw you leaving without leaving, and it was like, I don't know. Like I hadn't imagined there could be this third thing."

"Well, I had never imagined I could really not go," Lulu says. "Not going is my specialty."

Cass leans over to dip her roller back into the paint; somehow, when she straightens, she and Lulu are standing closer than they were a moment ago.

It's weird to remember that night. Lulu was a different person then, in certain ways. She never would have imagined when she walked into Patrick's that a few weeks later she'd be so far from anywhere she's ever been before, wearing someone else's clothes, looking at a girl in this soft, gold, late afternoon light and feeling almost like she would be allowed to reach out and touch her.

She hasn't changed enough to do it, though.

Cass takes her roller and applies it to the next patch of wall. Ryan reappears in the doorway. "I Postmates'ed us some snacks, and it should be here in a few if you guys want to take a break," he says.

"Oh thank god." Cass puts her roller back down. "I think the fumes are starting to go to my head."

"I'm just gonna go over this once more so it can dry while we eat," Lulu says.

"That's the spirit," Ryan tells her.

And then Lulu is standing alone in an empty hotel room, surrounded by pink light and paint fumes. Feelings rush over her in waves: happiness and restlessness, and hope, and fear. It's too much and there's nothing she can do about it. She closes her eyes and holds her breath. It doesn't help. Her body is still buzzing, thrumming. When she opens her eyes again, she realizes she was standing alone in the room and smiling.

CHAPTER TWENTY-ONE

● ● ● ●

THE NEXT TIME Cass and Lulu come to The Hotel, there's a new car in the driveway: a little navy BMW 3 series parked neatly between two lines.

"Who's the company?" Lulu asks Cass.

Cass shrugs. "Ryan didn't tell me anything. Maybe he had a girl here last night or something. Gross." She mock-shivers. "I hate dealing with strangers."

"You brought *me* here," Lulu reminds her.

"You seemed like an okay stranger. You'd intrigued me, remember? And anyway, that was different."

"Different how?"

Instead of answering her question, Cass shoves something into Lulu's hands. "Don't you want to open your present?" she asks.

"I always want to open a present."

"I mean, it's not a big deal or anything. I was just at this bookstore the other day and they had a recommended shelf with a bunch of, like, feminist theorists and stuff on it, and I recognized one of the names you mentioned when we were talking the other day. I grabbed you something. I haven't read it. I don't know if it's good."

This is so cute Lulu wants to die. Instead she looks down at the book in her hands to give Cass a moment to recover. *The Argonauts*, it's called. A pull quote across the cover reads: *A meditation on the seductions, contradictions, limitations, and beauties of being normal.*

"I see," Lulu says. "You're trying to reading-list me out of being a JAP?"

"I want it on record that I have never called you that," Cass says. "That's all you, Lulu."

"I'm reclaiming my slurs," Lulu says. That's a phrase Naomi taught her, *reclaiming my slurs*, when she and Lulu got into a heated argument about whether or not Lulu could call someone a bitch.

Cass rolls her eyes. "C'mon," she says. "Speaking of slurs, let's go find Ryan and his random skank."

Only they don't find Ryan, or a skank. Instead, they run into Owen.

"Whoa," Lulu says. "I mean. Hi."

"Hi," Owen says. "Ryan texted me this morning to invite me over. Which was nice, I thought, since clearly you weren't going to."

Oh god. Lulu can't believe she forgot about her promise to Owen that she would bring him back here next time she came. In that moment, she assumed that he'd be on her mind, and that she'd want to hang out with him. It's a surprise to realize that, in fact, that hasn't been the case. And now she's mostly annoyed that he's here, interrupting her conversation with Cass.

"I'm sorry," Lulu says. "Um. Owen, you remember Cass?"

"Of course," Owen says. "And Cass, I don't know if you've met Kiley?"

Fuuuuuuuuuuuck.

"Hey guys," Kiley calls up from the bottom of the swimming pool. "Ryan's teaching me how to skateboard!"

"Fun for Ryan," Cass says. She sits down at the edge of the pool, feet and legs dangling into the emptiness below. Lulu joins her.

"This is quite a development," Cass says.

"Yeah," Lulu says. "There are five of us now."

"This is the first time Ryan's ever invited anyone over to hang out," Cass says. "Anyone but me, I mean. He'll bring girls back here sometimes, for the night, but they're usually gone in the morning."

Lulu takes this in. "Does that mean when you brought me—" she starts. She can't bring herself to say: *that was the first time you'd done that.* The night takes on a whole new cast. That Cass just brought her. And then let her bring Owen the next time.

"Like I said," Cass says. "You seemed like an okay stranger."

Owen settles himself next to them. Next to Cass, that is. Not Lulu.

"Are you going to learn to skate, Owen?" Cass asks.

"Nah."

"Owen broke his arm skateboarding when he was ten," Lulu reports. She still knows him so stupid well.

"Eleven," Owen corrects.

"Ten," she says. She wasn't there, but this is one of the first stories Owen's dad ever told her. "At your tenth birthday, when Gumball Eyeball came to play a backyard set and you fell in front of—"

"Ten," Owen agrees. "And don't make me relive it, god."

He puts a hand over his face, dramatic. Lulu laughs. She can't remember the last time they joked around this easily.

Cass can't handle this news. "You had *Gumball Eyeball* play your *birthday party*?" she says. "My god, I would have died. I was so obsessed with them in elementary school."

"I almost did die," Owen says. "Kind of literally. I was lucky that the arm was the only actual casualty. I was so excited when they showed I just straight-up forgot I was on a skateboard. Gravity did not."

"You must have some parents," Cass says. Lulu wonders if she doesn't remember Owen and Ryan meeting, talking about their dads. Or maybe she didn't know to notice that type of thing— what someone might be sensitive about. Every little nuance of every conversation.

"My dad knows people," Owen says.

"Hey!" Ryan calls from the pool's belly. "I almost forgot. New rule. No parents at The Hotel."

Cass looks around in mock confusion. "I don't see any parents, Ry," she says.

"You know what I mean. This place is going to be overrun with Riggses pretty soon, and until that happens, I want to be an orphan when I'm here. No parents. No family. None of that bullshit."

Kiley leaps off the skateboard and does a spin. She lands on the balls of her feet, silent, like a cat. She raises her arms above her head, an easy stretch, and Lulu's heart throbs and contracts at the idea of Owen and Cass watching her move right now. How beautiful she is; how easy she looks in the length of her body. Lulu has always wanted to be lanky like that, long and lean. It hurts to think about how much thinner she could be, if—if. She doesn't want to do any of the ugly stuff that would get her there, but that doesn't stop her from wanting the thinness itself.

"Like you're a Lost Boy," Kiley says. "Peter Pan, you know? I played Wendy once, in the musical. They tried to cast me as Tiger Lily, but I rebelled."

"Racism," Owen says wisely.

"Racism," Kiley agrees. Lulu recognizes the tone in her voice, a very slight warning, and it takes her a second to remember from where: When Mr. Winters screened a clip of *Birth of a Nation* and asked them to debate whether it was appropriate to interact with racist art, or if he should have left it off the syllabus entirely. Kiley sounded exactly as wary as she responded to his questions then as she does talking to Owen now.

"Whatever," she continues. "The joke was on them. It turned out that director had been doing all sorts of other, um, inappropriate stuff, and my complaint was just the thing that broke the camel's back, or whatever. He was a full-time creep. Children's theater is full of 'em."

"Is that why you quit acting?" Owen asks. "Because of the casting thing?"

Kiley does another spin. "I wasn't a very good actress," she says. "And at the time I was super serious about ballet, so it made sense to focus on that."

Ryan kicks the skateboard up to his hand like he thinks the conversation is done.

"Must have sucked," Owen says.

"The joke was also on me," Kiley says. "As it turned out, I hated playing Wendy. The whole play is fucked up, but Wendy's the worst part. Everybody else gets to be a Lost Boy, and in Neverland Wendy has to be everyone's *mother*?"

That's not really what Owen was asking, Lulu knows, but it's interesting to see how adept Kiley is at shifting a conversation without seeming to have taken offense. He wasn't going to change the subject, so she changed it for him.

Under other circumstances, Lulu might be trying to learn her secrets.

Owen hops down into the pool and goes to stand by Kiley's side. She takes her cue, and butts her head against his shoulder before sliding into his embrace.

"I think we're all Lost Boys here," Owen says.

"Lost boys and girls," Cass adds.

"Lost people," Lulu chimes in.

"Lost weekends," Ryan says. "Hey, Owen, when you showed up, you said you brought beer?"

In fact, Owen brought a six-pack, so Ryan and Lulu and Cass and him have a beer. When Ryan offers Kiley one, like they're his to offer, Kiley says, "I don't drink beer."

"Then why did you bring it?"

"It was Owen's call."

Owen says, "I'm the one with the ID."

Lulu is sort of annoyed that he's not more annoyed about Kiley hanging out with Ryan—does he really think he doesn't have anything to worry about with that? Lulu doesn't like Ryan, but he's cute, and he's rich, and he looks like if he saw a sliver of an opening with you, if that was something he wanted, he wouldn't hesitate to take it.

"I have whiskey in my room," Ryan offers. "Do you drink that?"

"I do."

"Okay," Ryan says.

Kiley grins. "Are you going to go get me some?" she asks.

She sits next to Owen, where he's spread out a blanket to lie on. He reaches up a lazy arm to pull her down next him. "You're a very rude guest," he tells her. "Extremely rude, Kileyrath."

"Go get it *please*?" Kiley beams up at Ryan.

"Very rude," Ryan agrees, but he's already turning toward The Hotel. "Should I bring cups for everyone?"

"I could level up," Cass says. She's been a little more than usually quiet all afternoon; Lulu hopes this means she's just being shy, that she doesn't want to, like, leave or anything. She hates the idea that she brought Owen and ruined The Hotel for Cass, even if it was Ryan who invited him this time.

"Me too," Lulu agrees.

"In that case, want to help me carry?"

It takes Lulu a second to realize that Ryan is talking to her.

"Sure," she says.

It isn't until they're inside the lobby, the heavy glass door swinging solidly closed behind them, that he says, "I'm sorry if this is weird for you."

"It's fine," Lulu says automatically.

"I guess you and Cass have kind of had your, like, girls' thing lately. I didn't think you would mind."

Do I look like I mind? Lulu wonders. Can Owen tell? Can Kiley?

"I don't."

"I mean, I invited him because I wanted another dude around, and then he brought Kiley. So actually it backfired on both of us, if that helps."

"I said it was fine." Lulu doesn't like Ryan's tone—the way he's insisting on talking about her unhappiness like it's something she wants to admit to, like it's something she's agreed to discuss.

"Sure it is." Ryan pauses at the top of the stairs and holds up both hands, like Lulu's got him at gunpoint or something. "It would be fine if it wasn't, though, also. You're only human. You guys broke up—what, a couple of months ago? If it helps, I'll admit it: I wasn't thrilled when Cass showed up with you that first night. I knew she was interested in girls, but I had sort of—"

"You knew *what*?"

The look on Ryan's face is awful. It's like the sheen of oil spreading across water, slick and shimmering. He says, "She hasn't told you? That's interesting. I just assumed— Anyway. Cass is gay. Or she says she is, anyway. She hasn't ever kissed a girl, so, you know, I hold out hope for my gender. Well. To be honest, I hold out hope for myself." He shrugs. "But the two of you experimenting together—I don't know. It makes sense."

Lulu is too stunned to say anything except "I hate that word. *Experimenting*."

"Oh?"

"It's not a fucking science project."

"I guess you would know."

Lulu hates Ryan completely. She doesn't know *anything*. Her whole life has been shadowed by this inconvenient desire, a thing she doesn't want to want and has never been able to help. Kissing Sloane wasn't anything like pipetting in a lab; there was no science, no method. It was dropping a lit match into a pool of gasoline, the way her body leaped helplessly toward the flames.

And now the idea that Cass really would—that they really, really could— Her brain overheats at the idea of it. The thought that she could stop messing around in the shallow end of her own desires and find out what happens when she swims all the way out is dizzying, disorienting.

Ryan is still talking, somehow. "She hasn't said anything about you either way, exactly," he continues. "But I thought it was obvious. I just assumed you had figured it out, Lulu. I'm sorry if I was wrong."

Not sorry for outing Cass, though, for spilling her secrets and acting like he's handing her off to Lulu, a temporary loan, till they can get their girl-kissing out of their systems and go back to the boys they probably really wanted all along.

They're in Ryan's room now, and he's handing Lulu a bottle of whiskey, a stack of cups.

She looks at the floor under their feet, the bottle in her hand, the view out the window, and thinks, *Ryan owns all of this*. It makes sense of him, she thinks: The possessive streak Cass mentioned on the beach is coming clear now, his selfishness matched, apparently, by a deeper vein of cruelty.

CHAPTER TWENTY-TWO

● ● ● ●

THE REST OF the day is haunted by questions. Lulu keeps looking at Cass and wondering: *Did you bring me here because you wanted me?*

Did you bring me here because you knew?

Maybe it's because Lulu is distracted, but it feels like night falls fast and sudden. Shadows slip across the concrete until they've swallowed the whole day.

Kiley looks it up on her phone; Ryan isn't paying attention, and by the time he notices, she's already putting it away. Lulu can't help being annoyed at watching her skirt the rules.

"It's the fucking solstice," she tells them. "Shortest day of the year. Poof! Gone. Whoops!" She gestures with the cup in her other hand and splashes whiskey and ginger ale onto the floor. They're sitting inside now, in the lobby, in the tent, wrapped in blankets. The Hotel's heat hasn't been turned on yet.

"That means it's the longest night," Cass observes. She's sitting next to Lulu. They're wrapped up separately and Cass is very drunk, leaning heavily against Lulu's side. The silk of her hair brushes Lulu's collarbone, tickles her cheek. Lulu thinks she must be imagining that she can feel some warmth radiating from Cass's body to hers through so many layers of fabric.

Ryan's voice keeps echoing in her head: the idea that Cass feels something the same way she feels something. Even if she's just an experiment, a convenience, the only girl in their private school web who's stupid enough to have basically sent a coming-out announcement to the whole damn internet. Even if it's nothing more than that. It's like someone's opened a door just a crack—not enough to walk through, but enough to spill light into a very dark room.

Cass likes girls.

Cass could like Lulu.

"What are we going to do with it?" Owen asks.

"You've been here, man, this is what we do," Ryan says. "This is pretty much—this is pretty much it."

"We should play a game or something," Kiley says. "You guys know kings?"

"Too complicated," Owen says. "And anyway, kings is just an excuse to play truth or dare. Why don't we just play truth or dare?"

"God, Owen, how old are you?" Kiley pokes him. "Do you think this is a middle school sleepover or something?"

"Fuck yes. And I say we play spin the bottle," Owen says. "Seven minutes in heaven."

"The ratio here isn't right for any of that," Kiley says. "Two boys, three girls. Although—I guess Lulu wouldn't mind."

Lulu blanches.

Cass says, "What?"

Kiley laughs. "Oh, sorry," she says. "But, like, do you not even know what Lulu's really famous for?"

Cass sounds very uncertain when she says "No?"

"Luckily for you, the internet never forgets." Kiley taps at her screen and then hands her phone to Cass. "Here," she says. "Look. You can see."

The volume must be all the way up. Lulu watches the screen's blue glow playing on Cass's face, that inhuman light, and hears the soft slur of her own giggle, the way it trips into a hitch in her breath. She looks down. She clenches her fists.

She doesn't even think of Owen until she realizes Kiley is tripping over herself as she hurries to stand up, saying, "Wait, shit, O—" and she understands that the clatter she's hearing isn't her own heartbeat in her ears. It's his feet on the stairs.

Ryan grabs Kiley's shoulder to stop her. "Give him a sec," he says. "He's fine, I'm sure he's fine. Just give him a minute."

"Fuck!" Lulu didn't realize how drunk Kiley was until she starts crying, all of a sudden, like a switch got flipped. Her tears are sooty with mascara and eyeliner. "Fuck!" she says again.

Lulu is glad she didn't see Owen's face before he left. She's always been spared that one small thing. She didn't have to see it when he realized that what he'd thought was a private message from her had actually been broadcast to her followers and, soon after that, halfway across the internet.

She's seen the aftermath, the wreckage, his body when it's near hers always crackling with the hurt of how badly she betrayed him, but she's never had to see the moment of it happening: the raw shock punching through him like a fist.

Because of course when he saw it for the first time, he didn't know she'd sent it out like that by accident. He assumed it was a selfish betrayal: that Lulu wanted attention so badly she'd share something private like that in order to get it. And once she knew he thought she was capable of that kind of thing—even though he wanted to forgive her—even though she wanted to forgive him—it opened up a chasm between them.

Lulu has looked at him across a gap for so many months now.

"I have to," Lulu starts. "I have to go talk to him." She waits for someone to stop her, the way Ryan did with Kiley, but no one does. Then there's nothing to do but walk up the stairs and face him.

CHAPTER TWENTY-THREE

● ● ● ●

OWEN IS SITTING on the floor in one of the empty rooms. His phone is out on the floor next to him, but he isn't touching it. He's just sitting there.

"Hey," Lulu says. "Is it okay if I'm here for a minute?"

Owen doesn't respond.

"I'm sorry," she says. "I'm sorry that you had to see that again, and I'm sorry that it happened, and I'm just—I'm still so sorry, O. I'm sorry I'm sorry I'm sorry I'm sorry. I feel like I could say it forever, and it still wouldn't change anything, or take back what I did, and I know that, so—"

"You shouldn't be sorry," Owen says. "I know it was an accident."

"That doesn't mean it didn't hurt you."

"I never liked it," Owen says. "I never wanted you to do that. I should have told you the first time you asked. I just—I don't know. It seemed like the kind of thing I was supposed to be into. And you seemed so sure that it was a good idea."

Lulu slides down the far wall so that she's sitting facing him. The room is surprisingly echoey, their voices tumbling around and coming back to them, little faint whispers of their conversation haunting the air.

"I didn't want to lose you," she says. "I was trying so hard to figure out how to make us keep working."

"Because you knew that we weren't."

"I didn't know."

"You thought."

Lulu takes a deep breath. "I did," she admits. "I thought. And I thought I could fix it too."

"I still don't understand how you thought that was gonna fix it. You kissing other people."

"They were just—" Lulu stops herself.

"What? They were just what?"

"Just girls."

Owen laughs. The sound is hollow and hurt. "C'mon, Lulu."

"I thought you would think that," she says. "That they were just girls." She thinks of the way Ryan talked about her and Cass experimenting together. She gave him shit, but isn't that exactly what she was telling herself? That it was all just silly, and fun, and it really didn't matter? "I guess I kind of wanted to think they were just girls too. I lied to both of us, if it helps."

"Watching you kiss her," Owen says. "Sloane. I thought, *It's been a while since Lulu kissed me like that*."

"I didn't want to lose you," Lulu repeats. "And I didn't want to hurt you."

"No," Owen says. "You definitely wanted to keep me. But

you also didn't want to be with me anymore, not really. You just already knew how we worked. I was the safe choice, and everything else was scary."

It makes a horrible kind of sense. Lulu never let herself wonder if she'd stopped wanting Owen—she was too busy wondering if he'd stopped wanting her. And so it was easy to not even think about whether she actually wanted to kiss girls, or if she just wanted to kiss other people, period.

In that moment, Sloane seemed like a way of having both at once. But, in fact, she was doing the thing people always accuse girls like her of doing: being greedy. It wasn't greedy to want boys sometimes, and girls sometimes. But to hang on to a person just to keep them, to try to have Owen and also someone else—anyone else—that was the thing she did wrong.

Lulu looks down at her body—her hands in her lap, the lines of her legs. She wonders if it will ever stop surprising or betraying her.

"I did love you," Lulu says. She sounds as helpless as she feels.

"I do love you," he says. This is the worst, best thing about Owen. He's so smart, and he's so brave, and he'll just *say* things. True things. Important things. "But it's a good thing for both of us that we're over."

Lulu feels something leave her. It's effortless, like a wave rushing away from the shoreline. She's been clutching at the edges of her old life like if she clung hard enough she might get to keep it. As if everything hadn't already changed. As if she really would have wanted it back if she could have it.

And now, just like that, she understands: It's gone. It's been gone.

And now she's nothing but scared. She has no idea what happens next.

"I love you," she says. "I still love you."

Owen comes to sit next to her. When he wraps an arm around her, she turns into his embrace and lets him hold her.

It's not until she's done crying, and raises her head to see the wet spot that she's made on his T-shirt, that it occurs to her that it was sort of a gross thing for her to do.

Owen is the first person she's ever been unself-consciously gross around. Sometimes it still feels like he'll be the last too. The only.

"I love you too, Lulu," Owen says. "Always, okay?"

It's the first time he's ever said it and not kissed her after. Lulu notes the absence. She allows herself to notice that it aches, but also that the pain is duller than it used to be. It's a little bit distant now. No longer a fresh wound. Instead she feels the particular dullness of the beginnings of a scar.

Downstairs, Kiley is asleep in the tent. Owen kneels at the entrance, about to crawl in and wake her. "I've got to get her home," he says. "She has curfew soon."

"You good to drive, man?" Ryan asks.

"I'm good," Owen says. "I quit drinking a few hours ago."

Ryan turns to Lulu. "What about you, Shapiro?" he asks. "Up for more?"

"You know," Lulu says. "I'm not."

She can't remember the last time she was this tired. She can't remember the last time she went home before she was sure the night was well and truly over. She never admits to her friends that she's tired. She never says out loud that sometimes, she'd really rather be alone. "I might call myself a Ryde or something." It'll be expensive, and even pricier to get back to pick her car up tomorrow. But she can't stay here anymore.

"Suit yourself," Ryan says. He turns away.

Cass draws up close to Lulu. "I was going to say I could drive you," she says, low. "But, you know. Actually I probably shouldn't."

"You definitely shouldn't," Lulu says. "And like—whatever. It's fine."

"Are you okay?"

"I'm fine," Lulu says.

"Are you—"

"I thought you didn't want to hear about this stuff," Lulu says, trying to sound light. "About *boys*."

"This is more than boys," Cass says. "And I just—I wanted you to know that you could stay. If you wanted. We'd want you to. I'd want you to."

"Are you trying to say that seeing that video didn't, like, *change* anything for you?" Lulu is demanding something, and she doesn't know what. She's so tired. There's nothing left in her but instinct.

"Ryan said he told you something, earlier. About me."

"He did."

"He shouldn't have."

All the hope Lulu has been nurturing contracts inside of her. "I can forget it if you want."

"No, you don't have to. I just meant—if anyone understands—I mean."

There are no words left. Lulu reaches out for Cass, and Cass comes. She curls against Lulu's body, and even though she's taller, she leans her head down to rest on Lulu's shoulder. She murmurs, "All I'm saying is, if you wanted to, you could stay."

Lulu FaceTimes Bea when she gets home. It's not even that late—the darkness, its early fall, just made it seem that way.

When Bea answers, she's still in bed in a pitch-black hotel room.

"Shit," Lulu says. "Sorry. Did I wake you up?"

"Yeah," Bea says. "Kinda. It's, like, seven in the morning." The screen shows Lulu more sheet than face.

"I can call back some other time," Lulu says. "I should go to sleep anyway. I just had a weird night."

Bea fumbles the phone as she puts on her glasses. "Weird how?"

"Owen and I talked for the first time since—you know. Like, really talked."

"Oh."

Bea doesn't say anything else. Lulu lets the silence linger. She really doesn't want to put anything heavy on Bea right now. She just wanted to hear a different voice in her head before she went to sleep—something that wasn't Owen saying goodbye to her, or Kiley laughing at her. Or Cass, saying she could stay.

"You've never really talked to me about that, you know," Bea says. "What happened. Why you guys broke up."

"What's there to say, B?"

"I don't *know*, Lulu." Bea's voice gets stiff. "Because you won't tell me."

"I just called you!"

"Yeah, because you're upset, but it wasn't because you actually wanted to tell me anything. Didn't you think, *Bea and I will have a gossip, and then I'll go to bed*?"

"Jesus. I just said I had a weird night."

"Yeah, no, I—whatever. I'm kind of out of it. I was out late with the cousins last night. Charles bought me some vodka shots. I shouldn't have said anything."

"Okay?"

"I should go. I'll be home for New Year's. Or you can call me tomorrow, if you want."

"I—okay. Sorry for waking you up."

Bea shrugs. She waves, blows Lulu a kiss, and presses END on the call.

Lulu stares at the black of her screen and feels like fucking shit.

CHAPTER TWENTY-FOUR

● ● ● ●

THE FIRST THING Lulu sees on her phone in the morning is a Flash message from Kiley that just says sorry.

She's feeling mean enough that she writes back for what. Then she drifts off to sleep again.

The next time she looks at her phone, Kiley has sent her a picture of herself with the text I am sorry, Lulu written underneath it.

Lulu's first instinct is to roll her eyes. Why does Kiley think a selfie, of all things, is the right thing to do right now?

But she presses her thumb to the screen to stay the image anyway. Kiley clearly isn't all the way up yet; she's not even wearing her usual no-makeup makeup. She's just . . . there. Looking at Lulu. Letting Lulu look back.

Another message comes in. you've been nothing but decent to me. you didn't deserve it.

Has she been decent? Lulu knows she hasn't been cruel to Kiley—not outwardly, anyway. But she hasn't liked her. Hasn't made space for her. Hasn't been nice to her either.

Now she has an excuse to be horrible if she feels like it. She could talk shit about Kiley forever and Kiley would probably just take it. She would keep saying *I'm sorry* over and over again.

Lulu probes at the edges of her own feelings, delicate. She's expecting to find anger, hot and fierce. Instead she finds blankness. She feels tender and tired. Lulu made the video. She posted it. Other people decided to make sure it would stay posted. It's not like Kiley told anyone a well-kept secret. She just pointed Cass toward something she was always going to end up seeing, one way or the other.

I don't know how I feel, Lulu sends.

Fair enough, Kiley says. I just wanted you to know.

Why did you do it? Lulu asks.

A long silence. Lulu gets up, brushes her teeth, washes her face, and gets back in bed with her laptop. Today seems like a Netflix-binge-type day.

Kiley messages her back just as Lulu is pressing SKIP on the title sequence of *Friends*. I hate seeing you and Owen together sometimes, she says. You look like you belong together. I was drunk. I shouldn't have.

She asks, do you ever just feel mean?

Lulu doesn't. She wants to be nice so badly it feels like it's eating her up sometimes.

But underneath that, inconvenient and irrepressible, she has felt things that were wild and impulsive and impossible to ignore, things that sang under her skin until she had to find a way to let them out.

I feel a lot of dumb things, Lulu says.

I wish I didn't, Kiley says.

Lulu says, Me too.

CHAPTER TWENTY-FIVE

• • • •

LULU IS FOUR episodes deep into Ross and Rachel's breakup when Cass messages her, Have you ever seen the Connie Wilmott Bluebeard?

No, Lulu sends back. I keep meaning to watch it.

My brother is doing a backyard screening thing here tonight, Cass says. If you want to come over for it.

Here? Lulu asks.

My house, she says.

Lulu has never been to Cass's house before. It's on the other side of town; there's been no reason to drive all the way east when they've got The Hotel to themselves.

Last night, Lulu found out Cass had never kissed a girl before, but that she thinks she wants to. Cass found out that Lulu has kissed a girl and told the entire internet about it.

Now she's inviting Lulu over.

Don't freak out, she commands herself. It may just as well be an elaborate no-homo-even-though-we're-both-kind-of-homos gesture. She should act like it is. That's the safest move, for her pride and her sanity.

                              Sounds dope

        Dope, really, Lulu?

                              Dope AFFFFF

        You're a dweeb

Lulu sends back a picture of herself sitting in bed. She showered last night after her conversation with Bea, trying to wash the discomfort off her body, and then fell asleep while her hair was still wet. Usually this would mean waking up to some kind of rat's nest nightmare, but instead for once it just looks tousled, like magazine bedhead and not the actual messy thing. She wrinkles her nose and sticks her tongue out at the camera.

Exactly, Cass says. She sends Lulu her address. Movie starts around 8, she says. But if you want to come over earlier we can get dinner or something.

Cool, Lulu says. I'm in.

Cass's older brother, Dylan, looks so much like Cass that Lulu sort of can't figure out whether it's weirder to be into him or not. They have the same angular faces and slightly suspicious gazes, the same slender, lanky limbs and flame-red hair. He lets Lulu in, and then balks when Cass appears wearing his plaid flannel, the same one she had on at the beach a few weeks ago.

"Oh come on," he says.

"What, this old thing?" Cass plucks at a sleeve.

"You could at least *pretend* to respect me."

"What would be the point of that?"

Dylan shakes his head and turns to Lulu. "I'm Dylan," he says. "By the way."

"Lulu," Lulu says.

"Do you have an older brother, Lulu?"

"Sister."

"Do you steal her clothes?"

"I would," Lulu says. "If they weren't so boring."

She deliberately dressed down tonight, trying to find something that felt bohemian-hipster enough for Silver Lake without making it too obvious to Cass that she was doing anything different. It seemed like an experiment, after their conversation a few days ago: What does she want to wear? Can she separate it from what she thinks she's supposed to wear? Lulu isn't sure she pulled it off on either count.

"Mmmm," Dylan says. "Attitude. Well, I see why you and Cass get along, I guess. You guys in for dinner?"

"What are you doing?"

"Ordering in from Pine and Crane," Dylan says. "Plus there's beer, if you're not scared of Mom coming down and seeing."

"What do you think, Lu? Chinese food with cinema bros? There's also a lot of great places around here—some really good Malaysian on Sunset, or there's poke, or, like, I don't know, what are you in the mood for?"

Lulu tries to imagine sitting across a restaurant table from Cass—interrupting their conversation to order and whenever a water glass gets refilled, trying to figure out what to eat and how much, making small talk in the car on the way there and back. It's so temptingly, terrifyingly date-like.

She chickens out.

"Chinese sounds good," she says. "If that's okay with you."

"I'm always happy to mooch off of Dyl."

"I'm stealing the shirt back while you sleep tonight," he tells her.

"You're welcome to try. But I'm not stupid. I'm not taking it off my body until you go back to school."

A couple of Dylan's friends drift in, carrying six-packs of beer with brand names Lulu doesn't recognize. Dinner arrives, and it's a mess of high-end Chinese food that smells so good Lulu almost forgets how bad she is at eating with chopsticks. She's thrilled when Cass grabs a fork and says, "C'mon, let's go eat on the front porch, away from these animals."

They settle into chairs there, plates balanced precariously on their knees. The sun has already sunk behind the hillside across from them, a last golden glow lingering above their jagged tops, turning their silhouettes flat black.

"This is nice," Lulu says. "The view."

"It's why my parents bought the place," Cass says. "My mom hates that we're so high up—makes walking anywhere a pain—but she couldn't say no to this."

"Where are they?" Lulu asks. "Your parents."

"Mom's in her office, upstairs," Cass says. "Dad's probably still at work? Don't worry, you won't have to do some awkward meet-the-parents thing. They stay out of our way, pretty much, which is nice."

A silence falls between them. Lulu breathes in the air, sweet with desert plants—sage, she thinks, and something else she doesn't recognize—and tries not to think about whether she's chewing too loudly.

"It's kind of random that Dylan wanted to watch this now," she says when she's swallowed. "Does he know Ryan?"

"Nah. We haven't been friends for that long. It's always weird to remember that."

"Yeah, I was wondering."

"About me and Ryan?"

"About, why—about how—you guys both seem like you're, I don't know—"

"We don't make friends easily," Cass says. "We're the same that way."

"How did it happen, then, I guess?"

"We were in English together freshman year. We were both new to Lowell—I mean, he knew people, kind of, because he'd grown up here, but we were both new. He was nice to me." She smiles. "I know. It's hard to imagine, right?"

"He's not that bad."

"He's not easy. Not for most people. I don't know. He's always been easy with me."

"Do you know why?"

Cass is gazing off into the distance. Her eyes are unfocused, and her voice is soft. "I think Ryan is scared of people," she says. "He grew up in this weird, isolated world, all private tutors and his parents terrorizing him about not getting kidnapped or used, or—I don't think he really understands how to make friends, or play the kinds of games people play at these schools."

These schools are the waters Lulu's been swimming in her whole life. She knows what Cass means, kind of, but then not really. Isn't this how everyone is?

"I don't either," Cass says. "It wasn't like that—high stakes like that—where I went to middle school, in Santa Cruz."

He likes you because you're innocent, Lulu thinks. But also, *He likes you because he thinks he can manipulate you.* Which is ungenerous. There's plenty about Cass to like. She knows that way, way too well.

"Anyway," Cass says. It's clear she's had enough of that subject. "I mentioned *Bluebeard* to Dylan at the end of this summer, and he got kind of obsessed. He's majoring in film, so now he's thinking he's going to write his thesis on it or something."

"I've actually been looking into it too," Lulu admits. "After Ryan mentioned it to me that first time, I got curious. You know. About the legacy. And"—she pauses, makes sure she sounds a little overdramatic—"*the curse.*"

Cass rolls her eyes. "It's not a curse," she says. "It's just a thing that happened."

"What's the difference?"

"A curse keeps happening. It stays alive in a place. You've been to The Hotel. Does it seem like it has ghosts to you?"

"Not angry ones."

"Exactly."

Dylan projects *Bluebeard* onto a sheet in the backyard. He's dragged a couch out from inside, which Cass and Lulu claim for themselves, a couple of sleeping bags wrapped around them to ward off the night's sharp chill.

It's very weird watching a silent movie: For one thing, Lulu can't look at her phone if she wants to keep up with the dialogue. And then the city becomes the film's soundtrack: helicopters buzzing by overhead and the distant wail of sirens, the rumble of traffic, music from a neighbor's party drifting by.

The plot of the film is fairly straightforward. Connie Wilmott plays Katherine, a small-town girl whose small town is bankrolled by a man with a presumably blue beard—in this version, everyone calls him Barbaro. He's been married three times, always to girls from outside the town; all three of those wives have disappeared under mysterious circumstances. The people in the town are suspicious, but they know better than to ask questions.

Barbaro owns the local factory, and the bank. When Katherine's father falls into debt, he invites Barbaro over for dinner in order to slyly introduce him to his beautiful daughters,

Katherine and her sister, Anna. Barbaro takes the bait; he forgives the debts in exchange for permission to marry Katherine.

Who is, understandably, not pleased.

She's taken to his house on a hill; she's given the run of the place, and keys to every room. There's one she can't enter, he tells her. There's a door she has the key to, but which she must never open.

For months, Katherine does as she's told. She comes to love the house, which is beautiful. She comes to a grudging respect for her husband, who does what he can to care for her. He seems like he might not be such an evil man.

Maybe that's why she looks, Lulu thinks. She can feel herself starting to trust him, and the animal part of her brain knows that she's wrong to do it. He's tame, maybe, but he is not safe.

Katherine opens the door she's never supposed to open. She sees the bodies of all the women he's loved before, bloodied, lifeless, hung on display.

She opens her mouth. There's silence where her scream should be.

She drops the key. Its gets stained with blood that won't scrub off. Barbaro comes home and sees it. He has his hands at her throat.

Katherine's sister is knocking on the door.

Barbaro lets her go. He's a patient man; he'll kill her after her sister visits. He'll let her dangle, helpless, and enjoy watching her squirm.

Anna is smart, though. She recognizes the terror on Katherine's face. She convinces Barbaro that she and Katherine need to be left alone, that they have some intimate sisterly business to attend to. They escape out a side door, and down the hill.

They go to the police—and find Barbaro at the station waiting for them. Of course the cops, partially funded by Barbaro's generosity, are all too happy to send his wife home with him again. She's being hysterical over nothing, he told them, and they had no reason not to believe him.

All seems lost, until the lovely Anna convinces the chief of police to go up to the house with her. They arrive to find Katherine tied to a chair in the secret room, and Barbaro sharpening his knife.

When the film ends, one of Dylan's friends lets out a long, low whistle. "Dude," he says, impressed, "that was fucked up."

"You didn't know the story?" another one asks. "It's, like, a famous fairy tale."

"Not really into *fairy tales*," the first one says. Everyone laughs.

"It's not really a fairy tale," Cass says quietly.

Dylan turns around in his seat. "It's from a collection called *The Complete Fairy Tales*," he says. "Charles Perrault. Look it up, little sister."

The attention of the boys shifts away from them.

"What is it, then?" Lulu asks Cass. "If it's not a fairy tale."

"A myth," Cass says. "It's like the thing at The Hotel that I was talking about—about what happens to beautiful women. All these stories are the same story. Violence and silence and fear. There are no fairies. There's not even any magic."

Lulu feels a small shiver go through her. "Guess I'm safe, then, at least," she says, trying to make a joke.

Cass's mouth curls up at one corner. She gives Lulu a look that Lulu can't quite read. "I'm cold. Do you want to go up to my room?" she asks.

Lulu does.

It's smaller than she would have expected, with a handful of vintage airline posters on the walls. The floor is littered with clothes, and the bed is covered by a colorful quilt. It looks so cozy. It's a very tempting place to get comfortable, Lulu thinks, and settles herself in the desk chair. Cass flops dramatically onto the bed.

"I hate watching movies with film majors," she says. "They always think they know everything about everything. Like just because they've sat in more classes than I have, they understand everything better than I can."

"I don't know," Lulu says. "At least it beats what would have happened if we'd watched it with my dude friends. Or, I mean, they never would have sat all the way through that, but if we'd tricked them into the first ten minutes. They would just have been pissed there weren't any explosions, or tits."

"So all men are exhausting," Cass says. "I don't know why you put up with them, honestly."

At least now Lulu is sure of what Cass means when she says stuff like this—even if she doesn't know what it means about things between the two of them. "I don't always," Lulu reminds her.

"Oh?"

"You saw the Flash."

"Plenty of girls kiss girls for a picture."

"It wasn't for a picture," Lulu says. "It's— That's why Owen and I broke up."

"Oh. Fuck."

"You really didn't know?"

"How would I have known? I joined Flash two days after I met you."

"Really?"

Cass flushes pink. "I'd been thinking about it anyway," she says. "But the truth is that Ryan mentioned to me that you were a big deal on it, and I got curious."

"You didn't follow me."

"Well, then I got shy."

Lulu feels bold enough to say, "That is, unfortunately, very cute."

Cass makes a face. Then she says, "Can I ask about why you posted it? The video?"

"It was an accident." Lulu has never said any of these words out loud before to anyone but Owen. She hasn't talked about it with anyone. "Posting it was. Owen and I were trying something out. Well, I had convinced him to try it. That video was only supposed to go to him."

"Whoa."

"Yeah." Lulu looks up at the ceiling. "It's fucked up, right?"

"No, I mean—I'm sure it sucked—to be publicly, like, to have people see. And were you— Did people—"

"I hadn't ever talked about it. What I am. I still haven't, really."

"You're talking now."

Lulu knows that if she looks at Cass the game will be up. She keeps her eyes trained on the ceiling. "Part of the thing is that I don't know what to call it. None of the words seems right. Like, technically, I'm bisexual. I'm, you know, as far as I know, I like both. But the word itself—I don't know. I don't like any of the words. Queer. Pan. They don't feel like me. Like they're mine."

"Yeah."

"Is that why you don't—um. I was wondering why you didn't tell me. When I asked about boys and stuff, you didn't just say— you know."

"*You* didn't tell *me*," Cass reminds Lulu.

"I wasn't sure what I'd even say."

"Well, yeah. Same."

Lulu risks looking down again. Cass is staring at her feet.

She says, "Bringing it up always feels *dramatic*. Like it's this announcement I have to make up front. So I put it off sometimes. I just don't . . . I don't. But then I hadn't told you, and we kept hanging out, and the longer it went on, the weirder it was to be like, *By the way, I forgot to mention, I'm pretty much a lesbian.*"

"Well," Lulu says. "Anyway. Now we both know."

"We do."

Lulu lets the silence settle for a minute before she says, "Can I ask you a question?"

"Okay."

"How can you be so sure?"

"Sure of what?"

"Yourself."

Cass throws her head back and laughs. "I am *not*," she says, "sure of anything." She runs a hand through her hair so that her curls rise and then fall again, a shower of sparks around her face.

"It's just that Ryan said something last night about, like, experimenting," Lulu continues. "And I—I hate that word. I hate that idea, but isn't that what I'm doing? Using other people to figure myself out?"

If Cass can hear the warning threaded, desperate, through Lulu's voice, she doesn't let on.

"That has nothing to do with being bisexual, I don't think," Cass says. "Or whatever word you choose. That's just . . . being a person. Right?"

Lulu feels like she's going to snap in half. She doesn't know how much of Cass's kindness she can bear. "Are you this nice to everyone?" she asks.

"No," Cass says. "No. I am pretty much only this nice to you."

Breath moves through Lulu's lungs: in, and then out again. "I'm glad—" she starts, but there's no end to the sentence she can possibly say out loud. "I'm glad," she says again. "I'm— Never mind."

"Are you glad we're friends?" Cass asks.

"Sure," Lulu says. "Of course."

"I—" Cass stops too.

Lulu would swear the air in this room is different from any air in any room she's ever been in before. It feels too thin, too shaky, like there's nothing at all that could possibly stop her from reaching out and touching Cass. There's nothing between them except her own hesitation.

And the possibility that Cass will say no.

But Lulu can't wait any longer. She's run out of questions and she's run out of answers. She's run out of everything but this desire, which doesn't seem to have an end.

Lulu comes and sits next to Cass on the bed.

Cass sits up.

Lulu isn't sure which of them leans in first, or faster. All she knows is that one minute she's not kissing Cass. And then, she is.

All she can think is: *It feels like I'm falling apart.* She's been holding herself together against this particular temptation so carefully for so long that letting go of it is like letting go of everything, every cell in her body suddenly floating weightless and free. She expected it to feel violent or terrifying, but instead it's like the world goes soft around her too.

Lulu stops thinking about what she looks like, what it feels like to Cass when Cass touches her stomach and it's folded slightly because she's sitting down. All she feels is the pressure of a hand where she wants it. All she knows is twisting her fingers in the tangles of Cass's bright, impossible hair and kissing her like she's been wanting to since the minute they met.

Cass's hands are nervous, birds' wings fluttering against Lulu's face, her arms, her stomach, her back. Lulu tries to lean into her touch, but as soon as she finds it, it's gone again. She wants to say something, but that would mean having to stop.

Instead, she starts to press Cass back against the sheets.

Cass's breath hitches. She stills. "Oh," she says. "Like this?"

"Like that," Lulu says. "If you want to."

"I do," Cass says. "I want you to."

CHAPTER TWENTY-SIX

● ● ● ●

NAOMI IS PUTTING away groceries when Lulu gets home, so she pokes her head into the kitchen and says, "Hey. I'm back."

"Cool," Naomi says. "Mom's still out." She shuts the fridge and turns around to look at Lulu properly. Then she smirks. "Also," she says. "Your shirt is on backward."

"Oh. Haha. Weird?" Lulu wills her hands to stay at her sides, not to betray her by reaching up to smooth her tangled hair or touch her swollen mouth. She can feel the ghost of Cass's touch all over her. When she was leaving the house, she liked the idea of someone seeing it on her right away: just how wild she feels right now.

She just didn't think through who that *someone* would specifically be.

"Please," Naomi says. "I know you think I'm a prude, but you don't actually think I'm a virgin, do you?"

Lulu blanches at her sister saying *virgin*. Yech.

"So who's the rebound dude?"

"It's not—" Lulu's mind does a series of calculations. Naomi saw the Sloane Flash. She asked to know things. It's good to start practice talking about this if—if. Most of all, right now, it feels too fresh to lie about. Like Cass would know somehow, like she would sense Lulu lying, and feel betrayed. "—a dude," Lulu finishes. "The um. The person, she isn't a dude. She's, you know, a girl."

"Oh." Naomi considers this. "Rebound chick, I guess?"

"I guess."

"That's fun. Who is she? Do you liiiiiike her?"

"Ugh. Naomi."

Naomi holds up her hands. "I'm just trying to engage with you," she says, the air quotes she wants to be making around "engage with you" almost audible. "Since Mom isn't around to do it. Oh, hey, does Mom know?"

"Know what?"

"Let's try, what *does* Mom know?"

"Not much."

Naomi makes a face at Lulu.

Lulu relents. "I told you," she says. "She and Dad didn't see the video."

"You could have come out, though. Separately from that."

"Well, I didn't. I'm not really into that whole"—Lulu waves her hands around helplessly—"extravaganza. Anyway, you didn't think I would tell her and not you, did you?"

Naomi shrugs.

"Also, you think she would have known and not called you? God, you know she would flip her shit."

"You think so?"

Now it's Lulu's turn to shrug. She hasn't ever thought too deeply about it, but when she does, she's never been able to figure out whether her mom would have a problem with her liking girls or not. Her mom's not a homophobe or anything, but having a gay-ish daughter is different from having, like, a gay friend. As far as Lulu can tell, mostly what her mother wants for her to is to marry rich, the way she did. Lock in those community property assets early. Make sure you always know where the money's coming from.

She tries to imagine joking with her mother that she can live off of some woman's divorce settlement as well as any man's, now that gay marriage is legal, and can't.

"She took me to get my abortion," Naomi says. "And didn't give me any shit about it. And I'm guessing, from the look on your face, she didn't tell you."

Of course she didn't. As far as Lulu knows, Naomi has never had a serious boyfriend. It's nearly impossible to imagine her, straightlaced sister accidentally getting pregnant, and then asking their mother for help—much less getting it.

Those must have been the bad nights Naomi was talking about.

There must be some kind of look on Lulu's face, because Naomi says, "I'm fine."

Lulu nods.

Naomi laughs. "No, really. It wasn't that big of a deal. It

doesn't have to be, you know. I didn't want to be pregnant. And then I wasn't."

"I know," Lulu tells her.

"It was a dumb mistake. Everyone makes them."

"I didn't know you did."

"I told you."

"I believe you now."

"Good."

Naomi gets this funny, firm, that's-enough-of-that look on her face, like she's buttoning up the conversation, and herself. Impulsive, Lulu launches herself at her big sister and wraps her in a hug.

After a moment, Naomi hugs Lulu back. "I will say that while she was driving me, Mom made an extremely upsetting remark about how I didn't want to ruin my lady parts by giving birth this young *anyway,* so, like, she's still very much Mom," she adds, because Naomi is incapable of just having a moment. That's fine. Lulu can live with that. "But she can be surprisingly all right about things when you need her to be. Way better than Dad is, anyway."

Lulu lets her sister go, dodging out of their embrace to snag a box of cereal Naomi was about to put in the cabinet. It's been an emotional day; she deserves a bedtime snack.

"I'll keep that in mind," she says before she goes.

● ● ● ●

Talking to Naomi takes some of the air out of Lulu; it punctures the cloud that carried her from Cass's house to her own, and she goes about the business of brushing her teeth and washing her face like any other night.

But then, in the morning, in her terrible tiny bed in her mother's dead-air apartment, there's a Flash from Cass on Lulu's phone. In the picture, Cass is lying in bed in a pool of white sunshine, the hollows of her throat cast in deep blue shadow. The imprint of Lulu's teeth is the faintest possible lilac, just above her collarbone. You're going to have to be a little more careful with me, the caption says.

The way Lulu's breath catches tells her everything she needs to know about how far gone she is already. She closes her eyes and presses her hands to her face, helpless and happy about it. *You're going to have to be much more careful with me, Cass, please,* she thinks, but doesn't send.

CHAPTER TWENTY-SEVEN

● ● ● ●

SO MUCH ABOUT this is unfamiliar, but certain things stay the same. When Cass texts Hotel today? the next morning, Lulu writes back:

> I think I'm gonna stay home today—
>
> got the apartment to myself
>
> You can come over if you want

Okay, Cass says.

They both know that Lulu means *Come over and kiss me*.

Cass does.

CHAPTER TWENTY-EIGHT

● ● ● ●

LULU WAKES UP on Christmas morning and sees that Bea has tagged Kiley in one of her Flash posts—some inside joke she doesn't even get. Her stomach clenches and her toes curl. So she's already in a bad mood when she sees she has a message from Cass that says, I'm worried about Ryan.

Lulu's immediate mental response is why, which makes her feel like an asshole. Maybe something really is wrong. So she writes back, What happened???

Nothing is wrong, though, because of course it isn't. Cass says:

Nothing, technically

I just haven't talked to him in a few days

Which I guess sounds psycho but we

always talk

And he hasn't answered my texts

Like I asked him a direct question and . . .

silence

Do you know his parents? Lulu asks. Could you call them?

I don't have their number

His dad and privacy, you know

Lulu does. She kicks her feet restlessly, irritated. A shopping bag that was sitting at the end of her bed tumbles to the floor. When she retrieves it, it has a card that reads *SURPRISE!* in her mother's familiar loopy handwriting tied to one of the handles. She pulls out the bag's contents and stifles a groan.

She and her mother and Naomi have spent every Christmas for years now at a spa in Koreatown, their own personal version of Chinese food and a movie. They sit and soak; they get wrapped; they get pedicures. They come home and eat vegan ice cream and watch *Love, Actually*.

It's corny, but it's fun too: It's a good reminder that as stressful as her family is, it could be worse. They could have to celebrate Christmas, with its gift-buying demands, and nightmare travel scenarios. This idea that twenty-four straight hours can be sugar-sweet and picture perfect. What they have is wildly imperfect, but at least it's theirs.

It's just that this year, her mother has given her a pair of sweatpants with *SHAPIRO* emblazoned across the ass, and Lulu is ninety-nine percent sure that she and Naomi are going to be expected to parade around the spa in matching outfits. With their mom.

Lulu returns to her phone. Cass hasn't said anything else. Lulu hates the idea of her having a shitty Christmas because Ryan's in a mood. So she asks, Can I do anything?

Cass replies:

That's why I texted, actually

> We have family Christmas stuff this morning
>
> & evening but I sort of want to go over to
>
> his house in between
>
> Just to check
>
> Again I know I'm being crazy

I'll come, Lulu texts, before she really considers whether this is possible or not. Her mom isn't usually a huge stickler about family traditions, but then they only have this one, and Lulu's never tried to get out of it before.

On the other hand, she actually has a present to give Cass, so if it works out, it's kind of perfect.

> Thank you so much, Lu.
>
> I'll pick you up around 1?

Lulu confirms with Cass and then goes to Naomi's room.

Naomi looks like a cat who's been stuffed into a dress: a haunted and miserable creature. Her hair is pulled back into a low, tight ponytail, and its no-nonsense severity is especially ridiculous—almost pathetically inadequate—against the force of the word *Shapiro* written in hot pink across her butt.

"This is a nightmare," Naomi says. "This is my personal, private nightmare."

"If I spill coffee on you in the kitchen this morning, will you do me a favor in return?"

"What kind of favor?"

"A friend is worried about her friend," Lulu says. "She wants me to go check on him with her this afternoon."

"A friend, huh?"

"Yes, Naomi, a friend. Will you help me convince Mom to let me out of the spa? I'll watch movies with you guys tonight, I promise. This is just—it's important to Cass."

"Cass, huh?"

"Yes. Cass."

"Is this Cass from—" Naomi makes a gesture. Lulu doesn't know what it's supposed to mean, but it's fastest if she puts both of them out of their misery.

"Yes," she says. "Okay, Naomi?"

"These sweatpants have to be unwearable. I cannot pull off this pink." The color their mom chose for the lettering is a little Malibu Barbie, even for Lulu's taste.

"I think they look adorable on you," Lulu says. "But on my honor, they will be fucking wrecked."

Cass picks her up at one p.m. sharp. There's just as much chaos and crap in her Volvo as there has been every time she's driven Lulu somewhere, and Lulu likes that she recognizes some of it now, that she knows to expect a couple of plastic army figurines tumbled over one another in the cup holder, so that an empty Starbucks cup has to be crammed into the side pocket next to her seat.

"I've only been to his house twice before," Cass says. "I don't even know if they have Christmas plans. They might not even be home."

"I'm sure it's fine," Lulu says. "You're being nice. Slightly crazy. But mostly nice."

Her gift—small, neatly wrapped, not particularly extravagant, even—feels like it's burning through her bag. She bought it before anything had happened between them, and it already felt crazy presumptuous. Now it's borderline unacceptable.

Whatever, she reminds herself. *I can always return it.* And it's not like it's unprecedented: Cass did buy Lulu a book for no reason at all.

"No but, like, Ryan's family has a whole *thing* about their house," Cass says, distracting Lulu from worrying. "He's barely allowed to have people over. His dad is super paranoid that someone will, like, leak details about the property or something. Compromise their security."

"Not to be the worst," Lulu says. "But we all know a lot of rich people. I feel like we know how to be cool about nice houses."

"I don't know a lot of rich people," Cass says. "Or I didn't, before Lowell."

Lulu tries to be delicate about her response. "Right, but you guys aren't—I mean, it's not like you're broke, right?"

Silver Lake isn't Beverly Hills, but she's pretty sure it's not a cheap neighborhood. She's pretty sure there are no cheap neighborhoods left in LA, or that's what Naomi says, anyway.

"You're right," Cass says. "We're not broke. Probably we're rich people now, actually. We weren't always, and I'm just not used to it yet, somehow."

One of the most important rules of all: Don't talk about money. It isn't nice. Lulu says, "I didn't mean to call you out or anything. We don't have to talk about it."

"No," Cass says. "I would like it, actually, if we could."

Lulu nods cautiously.

"Things just changed really fast," Cass explains. "Growing up, like, we were fine, we had a place to live, food, all that stuff—but then my dad got this new job and we moved to LA, and what had been just fine in Santa Cruz didn't feel like as much out here. But *then* the company he was working for got bought, and all of a sudden, you know. There was all of this money. I'm just—"

She shakes her head before repeating herself. "I'm still not used to it. The way people see me. I don't know how to look at myself anymore. Because also, when we had less, we hung out with people who had less too. And now we have more, but everyone I go to school with has so much more than *that*. It's almost like the more money we have, the more broke I feel, which is just . . . so dumb."

Lulu nods. "My first year at St. Amelia's, I complained to my mom that we didn't have anywhere to *go* for the summer, like a house or something. I think it was the angriest she's ever been with me. I didn't know. I thought maybe she just didn't know that's what we were supposed to do."

"She got mad about it?"

"Yeah. Well." Lulu watches the streets slip by as she tries to decide what to say. "I think in part she felt bad—like she was ashamed that we didn't have a summer house, and that I had finally figured that out."

She's never said these words out loud before. She's never put the thought all the way together—that maybe part of her mother's deal is that she's embarrassed that she can't give Lulu and Naomi everything their dad can give them, or that their friends' parents can give them. Maybe she wonders if they're embarrassed by her.

Lulu wishes she could figure out how to tell her that money is not why she's embarrassing.

"What a fucking world," Cass says. "You've always gone to private school, right?"

"Yep."

"You know, I remember the first time I was with Ryan and he valeted a car."

Lulu doesn't know where Cass is going with this, so she waits.

"We were going to dinner or something, and he didn't even look for parking. Just pulled up. Handed over the keys."

Cass drives quietly for a while.

"I just kept thinking about the guy who opened the door for me. What I looked like to him. What he imagined or even just, you know, assumed about me. If he could tell I wasn't rich like Ryan, or if he couldn't. If I was blending in, and if I even wanted to."

Lulu has had plenty of these thoughts herself. "He probably didn't think about you at all," she says.

"Probably not," Cass agrees. "But it was still—I—it was the first time I understood that other people were going to see me and assume things about what I had, what I was like, that weren't true. And there was nothing I could do about it. It's obviously not the worst thing in the world. But it is weird."

"People tell me all the time my life's not normal," Lulu says. "But no one has ever told me what normal actually *is*."

"Well, off the top of my head, normal definitely isn't knowing a half dozen people whose family names are on buildings," Cass says. "And normal isn't how everyone knows everyone, how you're all always talking about how *we met through JTD, The Center, Marlborough, Lowell, that summer program in Cambridge*, and like, I don't even know if you mean the Cambridge in Boston or the one in Europe. It's like your entire childhood was a very successful networking enterprise."

"I guess what I wonder is: Isn't it a type of normal? If it's what's normal for me?"

Cass doesn't answer. She pulls the car up to a curb. A lush stand of low palms and tall cacti form a hedge that hides the entrance to what must be Ryan's house.

Cass undoes her seat belt. She looks pale. "You don't have to come in," she says.

"Don't be dumb," Lulu says. "Of course I'm coming."

There's no bell on the gate to Ryan's house—not even a keypad. Over their heads, an orb regards them with dark, glassy silence.

Lulu looks up at it. "Hello?" she says.

"I think it alerts someone when there's movement," Cass

says. She fidgets. Lulu wants to put an arm around her, but she doesn't. Who knows who's watching.

An intercom buzzes to life. Lulu can't even see where the sound is coming from.

"Yes?" a woman's voice says.

Cass says, "Hi, I'm—we're—um—we're here to see Ryan?"

"What's your name, please?"

"Cass. Cassandra Velloro."

Cass nudges Lulu.

"Lulu Shapiro," Lulu says.

Silence.

There's another long pause, and then a faint clicking sound. Cass reaches out and pushes the gate, and it swings open. Involuntarily, Lulu takes a step back.

Then she makes herself step forward again. She can't wimp out on Cass now.

A tiny Central American woman opens the front door and stands aside to let Lulu and Cass pass.

"Hi," Cass says to her. "I'm here—"

"Arsema, I've got it," Ryan calls.

The woman slips away, dismissed.

Ryan stands in front of them in the hallway. He's wearing jeans and a button-down and a watch Lulu's never seen on him before. It looks heavy and expensive. His face is impassive.

"Cass, what?" he asks.

"Cass *what*," she repeats. "Are you kidding me?"

"Are you interrupting Christmas lunch?" Ryan gestures

behind him, and Lulu sees: the front foyer opens onto a palatial living room that, in turn, spills onto the back deck, the lawn glowing green and the pool shimmering aqua behind it.

The Riggs family is sitting at a long table on the deck. A Christmas tree is stationed at either end—Lulu would bet money they're honest-to-god firs—dripping in crystal ornaments that catch and refract light, dappling everyone in rainbows. There's wine in every cup and a delicate salad on their plates. It looks like a lifestyle shoot for someone's Instagram. Lulu doesn't think she's ever seen anything less cozy or intimate, or more icily, professionally beautiful.

"Ryan," Roman Sr. calls from the table. "Who's there?"

Lulu looks at Cass. Cass is still looking at Ryan.

"We can leave," Cass says, quiet, to Ryan. "I just wanted to make sure you were okay, and look. You're fine."

She turns, but Ryan reaches out and grabs her arm. "Don't go," he says. "We can talk. Upstairs."

Cass looks down at his hand on her wrist. "Okay," she says.

Ryan lets her go. He steps in close and wraps her in a hug.

It's Lulu's turn to look away.

Someone gets up from the table and makes his way to Lulu. As soon as he's close enough, she recognizes him: Flash makes good use of Roman Jr.'s looks in their ads. He has Ryan's handsome, striking features, but they're harder: He looks cut from stone instead of made of skin. "You want to sit for a minute?" he asks.

"I'm okay," Lulu says.

"Come on."

Lulu does as she's commanded: She goes to sit.

"I'm Roman," he says.

"Lulu."

"I figured. Ryan told me about you. I hear you're one of our premiere users on the Flash platform."

"Oh god, not premiere."

Lulu slips into Ryan's abandoned seat at the table. So this is what a Riggs-eye view of the world looks like.

It looks nice.

"He said one of your videos had gotten a lot of attention."

Lulu sucks in a breath.

"I haven't seen it," Roman continues. "But if you ever want to talk about opportunities with Flash—branded partnerships, that kind of thing—any friend of Ryan's is a friend of mine."

How many girls would die to be in Lulu's shoes right now? A young millionaire offering to help her get famous, to pay attention to her and help her promote herself. Six months ago she wouldn't have thought twice about saying *yes,* assuming that she could make him work for her even when it looked like she was working for him. Now, thinking that only makes her feel sick.

"Thanks," Lulu says. "That's generous."

"I trust Ryan," Roman says. "He has an eye for talent." He glances over his shoulder to the stairs Cass and Ryan walked up. "I never would have noticed Cass, but he's right. She photographs beautifully."

"I'm sure." Lulu has never seen prints of the pictures Ryan takes at The Hotel. She's never even seen digital thumbnails. He doesn't pass the camera around after, looking for commentary or praise. He seems so private about the images. Lulu is sort of shocked that Roman has seen them.

"He definitely knows how to pick 'em," Roman says. "Ryan has a real eye for girls."

"So what happened after you went upstairs?" Lulu asks Cass when they're safely in Cass's car.

Cass sighs. "He's pissed that I didn't come over the other day. You know, when I went over to your place instead."

"You couldn't hang out one day and he gives you the silent treatment?"

"It's a little more than that," Cass says. "He's been feeling jealous in general. Since you."

"Since me." Lulu catches Cass's eye and can't hold her gaze. She feels like there's a lit firework inside of her, something that could explode at any second.

"He's so sensitive," Cass says. "I should have given him space. He would have gotten over it. He said he was gonna call me tonight. He didn't think I'd worry so much."

Lulu frowns. She doesn't like that Cass has to make excuses for Ryan.

"I feel stupid," Cass says.

She's driving, and Lulu doesn't want to distract her, but she reaches out anyway to wrap her fingers around Cass's elbow. "I wish you wouldn't," Lulu says.

Lulu is almost out of the car at her house when she remembers that Cass's present is still sitting, ungiven, in her bag. She picked it up when she and Naomi were out shopping for their mom a few weeks ago, and it's not much. Naomi was the one who suggested it in the first place.

She hates the idea of it sitting around in her room, taunting her, so she leans her body back in the open door and thrusts the package at Cass so suddenly that Cass throws her hands up to defend herself before she realizes what it is, and takes it.

"For me?" she asks.

"Merry Christmas."

"I didn't get you anything."

"I don't celebrate Christmas," Lulu reminds her.

"Hm. True. Still."

"It's not—it's just sentimental," Lulu says. Great. Perfect. That's definitely gonna make this look casual.

"Can I open it?'

"Of course."

Lulu loves to watch Cass tear the paper off of something. She doesn't slide a thumbnail under the Scotch tape to preserve the wrapping. Instead, she rips it all to shreds.

"*The Bloody Chamber*," she says. "Angela Carter." The volume is a slim paperback with a beast's head drawn on the cover.

"It's a version of the *Bluebeard* story," Lulu says. "It's supposed to be beautiful."

"Thank you," Cass says. "I can't wait to read it."

She presses the book to her chest and looks up at Lulu, smiling.

Helpless against herself, Lulu smiles back, and leans in to kiss her.

Lulu keeps expecting Bea to message her, but it keeps not happening. They've never fought before, and she doesn't know how to handle it. Does Bea's silence mean she's still mad about their conversation the other night, and Lulu should leave her alone? Or is she taking Lulu's silence to mean Lulu is mad, and it's her job to make the first move?

She stews on it through Christmas dinner (delivery from Café Gratitude, so at least it's edible) and while she and her mom and Naomi watch *Love, Actually*. Finally she decides Christmas is as good an excuse as any, and sends Bea a picture of herself wearing her Shapiro sweats with the message:

Merry Christmas my goyishe princess!

Happy Jesus!!!!!

Can you believe what my mom

made us wear today

Haha, Bea sends back.

Classic.

And happy hanukkah to you

Hanukkah ended a few days ago, but of course Bea doesn't know that.

Lulu waits for her to say something else—something about how annoying her mom is, or what she's been up to with her family, but nothing comes. Lulu even puts her phone down, goes into the kitchen, and eats a paleo-brand yogurt (she doesn't think they had yogurt in the Paleolithic era, but whatever, it tastes fine), and still nothing.

She can't help herself. She writes, Not to be weird but since when are you and Kiley BFFs?

Bea responds, I thought you guys were cool?

She said you'd been hanging out

At that hotel place

Why are you even talking to her, Lulu types, and then deletes. Of course Bea wants to be friends with Kiley. Kiley's beautiful and cool and she's dating Bea's boyfriend's best friend. She's the kind of girl who messes up and then apologizes instead of freaking out and picking fights and making everything in her life elaborately weird.

We are. It's just still weird, Lulu sends instead.

Well she's not my BFF. You are!!!!! Bea says.

Lulu believes her. For now.

CHAPTER TWENTY-NINE

• • • •

WHEN RYAN TEXTS Lulu, Hotel has a reservation for you today, you gonna keep it, on the twenty-seventh, she feels like she has to go. If she doesn't, who knows what bullshit Ryan will try to pull on Cass. He's such a baby.

Cass does kind of let him get away with it, though.

Lulu finds Ryan, Owen, and Kiley sitting around in the lobby, which has been furnished with plush armchairs. She curls herself into one, grateful that its wide, high back keeps her from craning her head to see if Cass is walking in the door.

Instead she hears it when Cass enters: the whoosh of the door opening, and then the sound of her boots on the floor. Cass walks up to them and pauses next to Lulu, hovering for a bare moment. Lulu's eyes find the cup of coffee in Cass's hand.

"Can I?" she asks.

"Sure," Cass says.

Lulu lets their fingers brush in the handoff; she puts her mouth on the cup where Cass's mouth has been and pinks it with her lipstick. She licks a stray drop of coffee, pale with cream, from the plastic lid. She hands it back. The whole exchange takes maybe fifteen seconds, but Lulu feels like the rest of the room freezes, just briefly, to allow it to happen.

"I would have gotten you some if I'd known you wanted," Cass says.

"It's fine," Lulu tells her. "Next time."

Owen says, "Lulu always wants coffee."

Los Angeles is in the middle of a funny rush of desert weather, warm dry days and long, clear nights, and Cass is dressed uncharacteristically softly, in a loose white shift that stirs in the breeze that followed her through the door. It gives Lulu glimpses of the outline of her shoulders, her hip, the curve of one thigh. It's very distracting.

"What's up, Ry?" Cass asks. "Your message made it sound like there was something, like, happening."

Lulu's glad that she's not the only one who noticed the demand in his tone.

"Something is happening. It's by the pool," Ryan says. He laughs. "I mean, it *is* the pool, actually." He nods for them to follow him.

Lulu sees it before she understands what she's seeing. It's just so— She's gotten so used to—

The pool is a pool now. Full of water.

The concrete hollow where Lulu and Owen slept that first night, nearly a month ago now, and where Kiley taught herself to skateboard and Ryan photographed Cass draped in blankets in the tent—it's submerged now. Swallowed. Drowned.

"What are you waiting for?" Ryan asks. "Let's swim."

Owen tugs his shirt over his head without thinking twice. Lulu can't even imagine that kind of freedom in her skin.

She distracts herself by watching Cass as she slips off her shift. Lulu is so busy looking that she doesn't even have time to think about the fact that she's taking off her own clothes, skinning gracelessly out of her jeans. She's vaguely aware that she's glad she decided not to wear a thong today, that the chlorine probably won't do her bra any favors, that she's maybe three pounds heavier than the last time Owen saw her mostly naked, but she's still pretty tan, so—

Owen isn't looking. He's the first one in the water, cannonballing in with a splash.

"Go!" Ryan is yelling. "Go go go go!"

Cass dives in, smooth and easy, and Lulu watches her body disappear into the water. She follows her there.

She understands why Ryan wanted them to do it fast as soon as she's in. The pool is not heated.

The pool is *fucking freezing.*

"What the hell!" Owen heaves himself over the edge and onto dry land to tackle Ryan, who's laughing too hard to get away in time. "See, asshole, now you're all wet too!"

Owen is holding Ryan fast and flinging his hair around, trying to get him as damp as possible.

"Hey!" Kiley says, twisting from the spray. She didn't jump in either. In fact, she's still fully clothed. "O, come on, my hair!"

Owen lets up, and Ryan takes the opportunity to go after Kiley.

"You think you're exempt?" he says, wrapping his arms around her and butting his damp head against her neck. "You think you're too smart for me, Kiley?"

Kiley uses her elbows to keep him away from her head, but it just means he ends up with his face in her boobs.

Lulu looks at Owen, waiting for him to break it up, but that's not Owen's style. He doesn't get bent out of shape about what things look like. He's not gonna make a big deal out of some roughhousing.

Cass appears at the pool's lip, wrapped in a towel and carrying another. "Lu," she says. "Here."

Lulu swims to the edge and lifts herself up. Cass wraps the towel around her shoulders, her arm lingering as Lulu grabs the edges and pulls them tight. She can see the blue of the veins under Cass's skin.

"See," Ryan yelps from where he's allowed Kiley to maneuver him into a headlock. "There were other surprises! You animals!"

"Where did you find those?" Owen asks

Cass points to a pile in a lounge chair, and Owen proceeds to wrap himself in four towels: one for each leg, one around his torso, and another around his shoulders like a cape.

"Nice look," Ryan says. "But also, the pool's not the only thing that got an upgrade. The rooms are ready too."

● ● ● ●

The lobby is still mostly empty, but Ryan really has set up rooms for each of them: robes in the closets, chocolates on the pillows. There's no shampoo in the shower, though, let alone conditioner. Removed from the thrill of the moment, Lulu thoroughly regrets getting her hair wet. There's no way it's going to dry presentably. Her makeup is a lost cause.

At least the water pressure is strong, though, and the spray comes out hot. She stands under it and tries to adjust to this latest version of The Hotel. It's not like Cass didn't warn her that it was always changing. It's just that she wasn't entirely ready for this iteration, for it to stop being a safe, in-between space and start looking like everywhere else in the world.

She startles when someone knocks on the shower's glass door.

Cass is standing on the other side, looking uncertain. "There's a drought on," she says when Lulu opens it. "I didn't want to waste—"

"Come in," Lulu says. "Come in."

Afterward they can't stop laughing. Lulu doesn't know what's so funny, only that everything is: this improbable girl in this improbable place, the late afternoon light slanting through the window, Cass's stick legs and knobby wrists poking out from the ostentatiously fluffy robe she's wrapped in, the shape of the spot her damp hair leaves on the pillow.

Cass eats Lulu's chocolate and kisses her when Lulu

complains. *We could do this*, Lulu thinks. *We are doing this*. Something in her stomach zips tight, and she has no idea if it's excitement or fear.

Because she's done this before—with Owen, who's probably kissing Kiley right now, too serious to laugh about it. Because she did this with Owen and then he got tired of her and she got tired of him, and there's nothing there anymore. Or not nothing. But not enough.

She's never done this with a girl before, and it's different, and it's *so good*.

"Cass?" Ryan calls in the hall. "Cass, where did you go?"

Cass knows better than to keep Ryan waiting. She goes to the door and pokes her head out. "Here!" she calls.

Ryan brushes past her into Lulu's room. Lulu doesn't like the idea that Ryan can just insert himself into their moment like this. *We're on his property*, she reminds herself.

"We were just—" she starts to say, but she can't think of an excuse. What would she have here that Cass would need?

But then, why wouldn't Cass just come visit her? Like friends do?

And doesn't Ryan know anyway? What's the point in trying to hide it?

Still, she finishes her sentence, says, "Cass came to steal my chocolate," and tries not to hear how unconvincing she sounds.

"Good news for you, then," Ryan says. "We've got hot chocolate downstairs."

"And booze to spike it with?" Cass asks, coming around to hook her chin over his shoulder.

"And booze to spike it with," Ryan agrees, giving Lulu a smile that says, *Don't worry. Of course I know.*

This, at least, feels familiar and appropriate. Lulu texts her mom that she's spending the night at Bea's and lines the bottom of her cup in peppermint Schnapps, followed by enough hot chocolate to make it taste decent. Kiley and Ryan are still dressed, but the rest of them are in robes, hair damp and tangled, faces fresh and bare, and it feels like The Hotel is supposed to feel—off-kilter and unpredictable, a wild, lawless place.

It occurs to Lulu that Ryan must be sentimental about this goodbye too; he's gone to a lot of trouble to arrange the evening for them. There's the hot chocolate, and then the dinner he produces, an assortment of salads and sandwiches, cheeses and meats and crackers, more fancy little candies from a shop in Beverly Hills. It feels more like Christmas than anything that's ever happened to Lulu before, like a family celebration: the five of them sitting around on the floor and eating with their hands.

"No, but Lulu tried to learn to surf, kind of," Owen says at one point. Kiley has been telling them a story about her dad, one of his scars, Lulu wasn't really listening. Cass is sitting next to her, cross-legged, one bare knee touching Lulu's, and she can't stop thinking about it: whether anyone has noticed, if she cares if they do, or if she even sort of wants them to. "Last summer. She went out once."

"I went *three times*," Lulu says. "You just think it was once because you only *came* once."

"You only invited me once!"

"And you saw why!"

Owen shakes his head at her. Lulu thinks this might be the first time they've joked about something that happened during their relationship since it ended.

That day he wore a shirt Rich had made for him that said *Surf Groupie* on it. He sat in the sand, watching her wipe out over and over again.

It's true that the day he came was the last time she went. She didn't want to mention surfing to him again and know he was thinking about what she looked like flailing in the waves.

"I've always wanted to learn to surf," Cass says, "if you could be convinced to try again."

"Yeah," Lulu says. "I mean, I actually bought a wet suit and everything. So I probably should."

"We can find someone cool to take lessons from," Cass says. "It won't be warm enough until, like, July, but—" Lulu lets that *we* rattle around inside of her, trying to find a space to rest in her body.

"I'm really bad," she says.

"I'll be worse," Cass says. "I do not have the guns for it, let me tell you."

"You're saying I'm built for power?"

"Lu*lu*," Cass says. "No one is ever calling you fat. You know that, right?"

Ryan got up a few minutes ago to go to the bathroom; when Lulu turns she sees him standing just behind them, watching the little group they make without him, hovering as if uncertain.

Cass distracts Lulu by poking her in the hip. "Maybe I'll start calling you fat," she says. "Reverse psychology. Just tell you a thing that's obviously not true until you get so frustrated—"

"I love this," Owen says. "You hear that, Kiley? Next time you refuse to eat a croissant, I'm not gonna try to talk you out of it. And then you won't have any delicious pastry, and you'll be sad, but I'll have more, so I'll be very happy. I love this plan, Cass. Very smart."

Lulu doesn't know what to say. She knows she isn't—technically, she's not fat. That's just a numbers thing. But that's the word she knows to express that she's unhappy with her body, that she's always been unhappy with it, in a white-noise kind of way, a mantra that's been playing so long she almost never remembers to hear it properly anymore. She remembers Kiley asking her about what she ate at temple a few weeks ago. Who doesn't think about that stuff? What would it even be like to live in your body and not worry about its size?

"Girls thinking they're fat is so exhausting," Ryan says over her shoulder. Lulu turns and finds that at some point while she was distracted, he pulled out a camera. He's snapping a picture of them, all of them, together like this.

Lulu is helpless against imagining how it will look: her body, unposed. She straightens up, tries to make herself longer and more elegant. She realizes after she's done it that it might look to Cass like she's pulling away from her, like once she knew she was going to be photographed, she didn't want Cass in the same frame.

"*Girls*. Really, Ryan?" Cass asks. She turns away from Lulu and Lulu doesn't know if that means anything or not.

"Hashtag notallgirls," Kiley says, holding up her fingers to make the crosses of the hash.

"And anyway, there's nothing wrong with being fat," Cass says. "Which I have also—"

"Yes, yes, you've told me, you've told me." Ryan squats down to ruffle Cass's hair. She reaches up for him, and the two of them unbalance each other, tip to the side, and go sprawling to the floor. Ryan squawks, "My camera!" rolling away from Cass, hunched over the thing with panicked urgency.

"So-orry," Cass says. "You started it, though."

Ryan doesn't say anything.

"Hey," Cass tries again, softer this time. "Is the camera okay?"

"I think so."

"Good." Cass smiles and reaches out an arm for Ryan. He goes to curl up at her side, but before he does, he unloops the camera from his neck and puts it carefully out of everyone's way. Lulu gets up to go pour herself some water, and the least mature part of her wants to step on it—to see what he would do if something in his life ever actually went wrong.

CHAPTER THIRTY

• • • •

LULU SNEAKS INTO Cass's room this time. It hasn't been that long since everyone trooped off to bed, but Cass is already asleep, curled around her pillow. Her face is surrounded by waves of her hair, the gold and crimson of them turned pale by the moonlight. Lulu is about to leave again when Cass stirs. She blinks one eye open, sees Lulu, and then closes it again. She makes a noise that sounds like an invitation.

Still, Lulu is careful when she climbs into bed. Cass reaches one arm out across their bodies. She rests her hand on Lulu's belly.

"Do you like my body?" Lulu hates herself for asking the question. "You know. The way it is now." She knows that Cass will say *yes* no matter what she actually believes, and that even when she says it, it won't make Lulu feel any better. People have been telling her that she's thin her whole life and it's never made her feel like what she imagines a thin person feels like. Which is mostly: someone who doesn't have to ask this question.

"I was asleep," Cass responds. And then, a little less harshly, "I think you're so beautiful."

"Oh—" Lulu says. She feels guilty. *Stop being too much,* she commands herself, but she doesn't know how to do that. She never, ever has. "I—I'll leave before everyone wakes up."

"S'not what I said at all," Cass mumbles.

"I know. But still. I will."

Cass is half submerged in sleep again. She nudges her nose impatiently against Lulu's collarbone. "Don't—hiding," she says. "Silly. Unless you're ashamed of me. Are you, Lu?"

"Not you," Lulu says. She kisses the top of Cass's head. "Not—no."

"Very beautiful, asshole," Cass mumbles, and breathes out a long sigh that fades into the slow, even rhythm of her sleeping breath.

Lulu lies in the dark and stares at the ceiling.

She's out. Technically, she's been out. Cass is the only person she's ever said *bisexual* out loud to, but the Sloane thing happened, and she didn't, like, deny it, or do any damage control. She knew what people assumed and she let them assume it; she let those assumptions harden into things people repeated like a fact. Which it is. It's a true fact about her.

So she shouldn't mind now, the idea that she's just confirming what everyone already knows. And having a girlfriend is cool, right? Sexy, kind of. She knows that's what her friends at school would say if she asked them. *It's 2020, Lulu. You should date whoever you want, duh. Get it, girl.*

Instead she feels terrified. Liking Owen was so easy. There

was nothing to explain about her sweet, handsome boyfriend. What more normal thing could a teenage girl do with herself than have a crush on a boy?

Liking Cass asks Lulu to expose something about herself that people might not guess just by looking at her. It also exposes Cass, because if this is real, Lulu has to think about how to integrate Cass into Lulu's aestheticized, structured, constantly captured real life. And she's not sure she wants that—that she's ready for Cass to be public property any more than she's ready for The Hotel to open up and become a place anyone can visit.

Does that mean she's ashamed of her? That she's fetishizing her? That she's protecting her?

The questions swirl around Lulu so persistently that she can almost imagine them taking on weight in the air around her, thickening the darkness with their presence. Once again, something is happening that she doesn't have a strategy for. She doesn't know how to navigate it and keep herself and the person she cares about safe.

The difference is that this time she wants to let it happen anyway.

All she knows is that no matter how long she lies there driving herself crazy about what she wants, what Cass wants, what would be best for either or both of them, she stays anchored by the weight of Cass's hand on her belly.

And she doesn't set an alarm. She doesn't sneak off, she

doesn't take her questions with her and disappear, even though she wants to. She falls asleep eventually. When she wakes up her cheek is pillowed on the tangle of Cass's hair. Here they are, in bed together, she thinks. Here they are, in the light of morning.

CHAPTER THIRTY-ONE

• • • •

THE NEXT DAY Lulu gets an email from ryan@riggshotels.com. She opens it to find one of the fanciest email invites she's ever seen. Even the gold edging on the graphic looks luxe, somehow; gilt-flecked instead of cheap and cheesy. Ryan is throwing a New Year's Eve party at The Hotel.

She texts Cass a screenshot with the message, Does this mean it's open

I wish I knew, Cass responds.

He didn't tell you? that's shitty ☹

He didn't tell me about the party at all

Which

I'm sure seems like not a big deal

but again we used to tell each other

everything

Have you told him about us?

It's fine if you did I'm just wondering if

maybe like

He feels like you have secrets so now

he does too

I didn't

Tell him

I didn't know what to say tbh

Lulu doesn't know how to respond to that. She types and deletes, types and deletes. Then she FaceTimes Cass.

When she answers, Cass is sitting in her backyard, under a tree that dapples her face with leafy shadows and makes her expression hard to read. "Hey," she says. "What's up?"

"I didn't know what to say."

"You called . . . to say you didn't know what to say."

"Yes. No. I called— Usually when I don't know what to say, I don't say anything."

"That doesn't seem like such a crazy strategy."

"It isn't. But it can be. Sometimes I don't know what to say, but that doesn't mean I—" Lulu comes up short. For all the language she's learned in the last few months, she still doesn't know the words for this.

"It doesn't mean you don't—" Cass says.

"It doesn't mean I don't *want* to say something."

There's a long pause. "I think I get it," Cass says.

"Whatever you told him would be fine with me."

"You sure about that? What if I told him you were the curse incarnate, come to seduce me and kill me and make me The Hotel's most gruesome legacy?"

Lulu laughs. "Ryan doesn't really believe in curses," she reminds Cass.

CHAPTER THIRTY-TWO

• • • •

ON NEW YEAR'S Eve, Lulu tries on approximately a zillion outfits. It takes her two hours to get dressed, in part because she has to run back and forth between the half mirror in her bedroom and the full-length one in the bathroom down the hall. Then she has to do her makeup.

Naomi kicks her out of the bathroom twice to pee during this process. "This seems very exhausting," she says on her way out the second time.

Usually Lulu would take this for a veiled insult and make a rude, dismissive face at Naomi, but if Naomi wants to hear about what's going on in Lulu's life, she's going to have to get used to hearing about makeup.

"I actually enjoy it," Lulu says.

"You enjoy it."

Naomi stands in the bathroom door. She looks uncertain, actually, like she isn't sure of her welcome in Lulu's space.

"I like looking nice," Lulu says. "I like figuring out how to look nice."

"There isn't one way?"

"How to make myself *feel* nice, maybe. Or how I want to feel. Which changes."

Lulu's finally picked an outfit: a pale pink dress that she usually wouldn't pull out during the winter, but feels right, somehow, for tonight. She's accessorized it with a bunch of gold rings, and her plan is to dust her eyelids and cheekbones with loose shimmering gold powder, to make herself look as soft and glowing as she feels all over. This will probably be something like her and Cass's public debut. She wants Cass to be proud of her. She wants to be as beautiful as Cass, unaccountably, believes she is.

Lulu looks at the makeup bag on the counter, pens and brushes and pots spilling out of it, and at Naomi's face, reflected in the mirror in front of her.

"You don't just hang out with your friends like this? Do your makeup, get ready to go out?"

"I don't know if you've noticed, Lulu, but I do not wear makeup."

"I know you don't at home. But at school? When you're going to parties?" Lulu twists her head around to look at her sister. "Truly never?"

"I don't know how."

"Nao, it's not *hard*."

"You think that because you know how to do it."

"The dumbest girls in the world know how to do makeup. Don't you hardcore feminists think makeup was invented to keep women stupid and distracted or something?"

"Feminists think a lot of things about makeup," Naomi says. "I think it's okay to be interested in whatever you're interested in." She's such a goody-goody, it's truly incredible. "And," she adds, "I think yours usually looks really nice."

"Okay, well, if you want to see a master at work, watch and learn."

Lulu showered earlier, so her face is bare. She puts on primer and dusts herself with a mineral powder foundation, which she can get away with because her skin has been behaving itself, mostly, recently. She blushes the apples of her cheeks pink and streaks the lines of her face with highlighter.

"See?"

"It's like a magic trick," Naomi says. "Watching you do it doesn't mean I understand how it works."

"It's just angles," Lulu says. "Colors."

"Hmmmm."

Naomi comes into the bathroom and leans against the closed shower door. There's not a ton of room in here, but they both fit.

"Who's going to be at the party tonight?" she asks.

"It's at this hotel this guy Ryan is opening," Lulu explains. "He knows Owen, actually, so he'll be there."

"How's that gonna be?"

"Fine," Lulu declares optimistically. "And I—my—Cass will be there too."

"Nice."

"Yeah."

Lulu is working on her eyeliner now, always her least favorite part of this routine. Her hand isn't as steady as she wants it to be, and she never knows how dramatic to make her wings.

"Bea?"

"Oh," Lulu says. "No, not Bea."

B's back in town—she messaged Lulu yesterday, and Lulu didn't respond. She saw the notification and wanted to wait a few minutes so she didn't look like she'd been sitting around *waiting* for Bea to get in touch with her, and then she got distracted and forgot, like an idiot. She pauses what she's doing to send: Hey babe happy almost!!!! Have a good night see you soon? And then goes back to work.

"I was wondering," Naomi says. "I haven't heard much about her this break."

"We're fine." As soon as she says it, Lulu knows it's a lie.

"Okay."

Naomi doesn't say anything else, and Lulu is grateful for the silence, which gives her the concentration she needs to make her eyes look right. She finishes the liner, adds mascara. Now there's nothing left but gold.

"Where are you going tonight?" she asks Naomi.

"Over to Kevin's," she says. "Remember him?"

One of Naomi's high school friends.

"Just a house party?"

"Mmmhmmm."

"Want me to do your makeup?"

"Oh," Naomi says. "I don't, I mean—"

"Subtle," Lulu says. "Like, we could do just the eyes, or a bold lip. For fun. For something new."

"That would be really nice, actually," Naomi says. "If you don't mind. If you have time."

"I told you," Lulu says. "For me, this is the fun part."

She doesn't tell Naomi, but it's the first time she's felt completely like herself since the Sloane Flash. Just a girl getting prettied up, getting ready to meet her friends at a party, to kiss someone she's dying to kiss, to allow herself fizz and pleasure and beauty and fun.

Bea doesn't write Lulu back. Instead, Lulu watches Bea's Flashes of herself preparing for the night—she's spending it in, with Rich, while her parents are out at some party.

What are you wearing, Lulu asks Cass, and Cass responds with, No, no peeking.

Will I like it?

I hope so.

I think I will.

CHAPTER THIRTY-THREE

● ● ● ●

THE HOTEL IS dressed up for the occasion. There are lights in the trees that line the driveway and all of the cars are parked, neat and gleaming, in their spots. Uniformed valet attendants usher Lulu from her Ryde into the lobby. A waiter hands her a glass of champagne as soon as she walks in the door.

Lulu doesn't know what she was expecting, but this is a grown-up party. Roman Sr. is holding court in one corner, and she recognizes a handful of minor celebrities milling around too: a girl who makes a living doing sponsored content on her Flash; a guy who turned his YouTube channel's hyper-physical pranks into a career in action blockbusters.

There's something slippery in the air tonight. It's unnerving to watch a place that was a private hideaway become just another part of the adult world, a place you can transact your way into.

Lulu wishes she didn't feel so weird about it. Isn't she supposed to want to belong here? Shouldn't she feel special and sophisticated, to be drinking expensive champagne among all of these glittery, wealthy, well-known people?

She doesn't, though. She misses the raw quality that The

Hotel had before it was finished, when it was still a secret. When it was just her and her friends, and no one could see them, or find them, or make them behave.

This place used to be so uncivilized.

She wonders how Cass is handling the end of her secret garden. She can't find her right away. Instead, Lulu spots Ryan talking to the girl from Flash. He's wearing a black button-down and skinny black jeans. He looks remote, slightly, like he's one layer removed from everyone else in the room.

Cass is, predictably, trying to hide in a corner. She can't camouflage herself tonight, though, because she looks too beautiful: She's wearing a deep crimson dress cut low down the pale expanse of her back, revealing the line of her spine, the wings of her shoulder blades.

She looks like cream and blood, a breathing swirl of beauty and danger.

Lulu walks across the room to her. Cass has a champagne flute of her own. When Lulu kisses her, their mouths are made of sharpness and air. Cass smiles into the kiss. It only lasts a second. It sets Lulu's blood on fire.

"You excited for this?" Cass asks quietly.

"What, the new year? Of course I am. I like a fresh start."

"No," Cass says. "Didn't Ryan—he didn't tell you about the surprise?"

"There's another surprise? Is it going to be as cold as the pool was?"

Cass frowns. "He said he was gonna tell you," she repeats. "But I guess he's been busy. He probably forgot." She looks around for him. "I guess it's okay if I— So Ry printed a bunch of the pictures he took from the process, and he says the upstairs is all decorated in them. It's like an art show."

"Oh, cool!"

"Yeah."

"What?"

"I don't like looking at pictures of myself."

"No one does, Cass."

"Says the princess of Flash."

"Those aren't of me," Lulu says. "Well, not always. And I thought these weren't of you, mostly. Wasn't that his whole thing? That he didn't like taking pictures of hot girls?"

"Are you saying I'm hot?"

Lulu dips in and kisses Cass's neck, just because she can. Cass looks pink and pleased when Lulu pulls away.

"Yeah, no, I'm just being weird and paranoid," Cass continues. "When he took them, I sort of thought he'd let me look at them before he put them up. But I'm probably stressing over nothing. I'd bet he decided to scrap those, and it's just gonna be pictures of walls and wires and construction equipment."

"Dude stuff."

"Dude stuff."

Cass lifts her glass, and she and Lulu do a little toast.

"Heyyyyy!" Kiley slides over to them. The sequins on her

234

dress rub against one another, and give off a low, soft murmur when she moves.

"Hey," Lulu says.

"Happy New Year! You look great, Cass," Kiley reports. "You and Lulu both, duh. You guys want a picture together?"

"No phones at The Hotel," Lulu says automatically.

Cass shakes her head. "He changed the rule," she says. "Turns out the finishing touch on this place was Wi-Fi. The password is *aster*. I meant to Flash you when I got here, just to freak you out."

"*Whoa.*"

"I know. End of an era."

At the other end of the room, Roman Sr. is clinking a fork against his glass, trying to get everyone's attention.

"We have a little while till midnight, but I thought I'd get the introductions out of the way early," he says. "I'm Roman Riggs, and I'm thrilled to welcome all of you to the opening of Riggs Realty's newest project. This business has been in our family for generations, and I'm excited to introduce you to my son Ryan, who can tell you more about how this latest iteration came to be."

Roman turns and claps a hand onto Ryan's shoulder. Lulu wishes that Christine L. Tompkins, of *Beauty, Power, Danger,* were here to see this—the casual way men hand off power from one to the next.

"So as some of you know," Ryan starts, "it's a tradition in my family to take on a project when we turn eighteen. Each of us is given a chance to prove that we understand how money works, and that we know what to do with it. That we're ready to inherit our legacy.

"That's a big word to put on a kid: *legacy*. My great-great-grandfather made a name for himself, and every generation since has built on that foundation. I'm grateful to be a part of the Riggs family tradition, but it's also, you know, a little intimidating." Ryan pauses for a murmur of laughter to ripple through the crowd at how charmingly honest he's being.

"I was deeply inspired by my brother's creation of Flash, which you should feel free to use tonight, by the way, *hashtag TheFutureIsRigged*"—another chuckle—"because it showed real vision, I thought. Roman didn't just look at what our family's past was; he didn't do what we always do. He imagined, boldly, what our future *could* be. He radically re-thought what it meant to build something from the ground up."

Ryan gestures to the space around them. "I went a more traditional route, obviously. I used to come here with my grandfather when he was still alive; the Aster had been closed for years, but this property was the source of some of his favorite childhood memories. I wanted to restore it to its glory days, even if he wouldn't be here to enjoy it.

"But I also wanted something else." Ryan scans the crowd. He looks at Cass, and then looks away. Lulu feels something cold start to settle over her, so faint at first that she mistakes it for the air-conditioning being turned on, or a breeze blowing through an open door. As Ryan keeps talking, the cold takes on weight, settling around her shoulders like a cloak.

"Because I was thinking a lot about that question of legacy, of what it means to build something that lasts. What can stand up to history? Is it buildings? Is it art? Is it family? The answer, ultimately, is nothing. A thousand years from now, probably, no one will remember our names. This hotel won't still be standing."

"I wouldn't bet against the Riggses!" someone calls from the audience. More laughter; applause.

Ryan smiles and nods. "Thank you," he says, "but the idea was actually freeing. I stopped worrying about legacy and started thinking, instead, about desire. What do I want right now? What do I want most of all? That's the real genius of Flash. There's nothing to it, really—it's built on impermanence. It gets built and rebuilt every day, because people want to use it so badly.

"When my great-great-grandfather built this place, he wasn't thinking about the real estate empire he would go on to create. He wasn't imagining a great-great-grandson feeling the weight of the family's name heavy on his shoulders. His concerns were far more immediate: He had a beautiful new wife, and he wanted to build a beautiful place for her to live in.

"And I thought, isn't that what we're after, when we build buildings, and take pictures and post them on Flash? Aren't we just looking for ways to express and capture beauty?

"I thought, I don't know a better legacy for my family than that. Maybe it won't last forever, but it will make you *feel* something while you're here.

"Upstairs, you'll be able to see rooms as they'll be set when guests arrive. But you'll also be able to walk through the photographs I took in the process of changing this place from a derelict, abandoned site to the gorgeous space you're enjoying now. In that process, I excavated more than the land: I dug deep into my family's history and my own aesthetic preoccupations. I wanted to give you a sense of the history of beauty that the Riggs family represents, and hopefully, a peek at the future we're going to bring you."

Lulu is one of the first people up the stairs. She feels Cass behind her, but she's afraid to turn around and look at her. What did Ryan mean by all that?

The hallway is lined in the construction process shots Lulu was expecting: close-ups of rubble and walls tangled in vines. Trucks filled with debris that was emptied out of the pool, and trucks filled with tile for the bathrooms, piles of blue and gold. She starts to breathe easier.

Three, the room whose bathroom she used that first morning, after her night in the tent with Owen, is the one that's set up as a sample. It's in there that Lulu sees the first picture of an actual person: Kiley is hung up like art on the wall, captured sitting with her legs dangling into the empty pool, laughing up at the enormous blue sky stretched above her head. Next to her is a shot of Cass in the bathroom, wearing her pajamas, looking at herself in a mirror, caught in the act of brushing her hair. Ryan managed to keep himself out of the frame, so it's easy to forget that someone *took* the photograph. It looks like it was always meant to exist.

It makes Lulu's skin crawl a little bit. Cass was so anxious about her image earlier. She wishes Ryan would have checked with her before he put these up. It's a beautiful picture, but who knows if Cass will agree.

Lulu glances around for her, but they've lost each other in the jostle of the crowd.

Ryan, however, has found her. "You like them?" he asks.

"Sure," Lulu says. "Congratulations, by the way."

"Thank you."

He holds something out to her. It's small, gold, gleaming. A key.

"What?" Lulu asks.

"Look," Ryan says. "See for yourself." He gestures toward a door.

Three is part of a suite, it turns out: It opens right onto Four. Lulu fits the key into the lock and presses the door open. The walls in here are a pale seashell pink: the ones she and Cass and Ryan painted by hand. The only piece of this place she helped make real.

You can barely see the color, though, because of all of the bodies.

There's a moment before the rest of the crowd pushes in behind her when Lulu is alone with them: probably a hundred photographs framed and hung on the wall. All of them are pictures of women, women, women.

There are so many of them that at first she can't make out any details. She's rushed over by the repeating pattern of lips, teeth, eyes, hair, arms, legs, breasts, waists. The photographs are black and white or warm with color. The sheer number makes them impossible to parse. It's just a silent stack of slender limbs and disembodied smiles and deep, generous cleavage.

Then certain faces start to resolve themselves into something familiar. There's Constance Wilmott, captured on set and in stills from *Bluebeard*. Press photos of her, young and glamorous, are contrasted with later snapshots: Constance still alive in the '50s and '60s, no longer a star but still unmistakably, shockingly beautiful. Lulu recognizes Ryan's mother, who modeled before she met his father, posing in advertisements for cigarettes and cheap beer. Roman Jr. must have loaned out the use of some photos from Flash: There's the girl Lulu just saw downstairs, pictured taking a selfie in a mirrored hallway, her body multiplied endlessly out around her.

The movement of the crowd moves Lulu. She sees pictures of women she can't identify. There's so much. There's so many.

What is Ryan doing?

A flash of color on a far wall blinks at her. Lulu would know the flame of Cass's hair anywhere. She pushes through until she sees the picture.

The picture of Cass, and of herself.

All of the walls in the room are crowded, but mostly the images are diverse, scattered: like a collage clipped from fashion and art and social media and a few things Lulu suspects originated in soft-core porn. This wall is all Ryan's work, and the models are the same in every photograph: just Cass and Lulu, over and over and over again.

The first picture is the first one he took of the two of them sitting in bed together. Lulu is looking at Cass's mouth. It looks just as intimate as Lulu feared it would what seems like a hundred million years ago, the way she's leaning into Cass's body. What she can see now, which she was too nervous to notice then, is that Cass is leaning toward her too.

They march on from there: Lulu and her milkshake; Cass painting a wall; Lulu and Cass bent over a book, their heads together, talking. That one is in black and white.

Why? Lulu wonders. What's the point? Is it supposed to be artsier? Is it supposed to be—as she leans in closer to inspect it, she sees why. This photo is black and white and blurry because it was taken by a black-and-white camera. Not Ryan's fancy, expensive digital, and she knows that because you can see Ryan in the photograph: His body is a blur, midway through some skateboarding trick in the bottom of the pool.

Ryan didn't take this picture. The Hotel did.

Lulu doesn't know where they are, but she knows that they're here. They've always been here, the cameras. He mentioned them the first night, the security footage he was taking, how he needed light to do it by. That piece of printer paper taped up in the lobby: WARNING: THESE PREMISES ARE BEING MONITORED BY VIDEO. Of course Ryan needed to protect the construction site.

She hadn't counted on him using them to surveil her too.

Lulu races through the rest of the images: There's another black-and-white shot of her alone in her bathing suit, looking as docile and posed as a doll. She and Cass in their robes in color in the lobby, Owen and Kiley fuzzed out to vague background blurs. *Ryan took these*, Lulu thinks, and then, *He* took *these*.

The last images are three in a row of almost the same shot, all in black and white: Cass and Lulu asleep together in bed. They must have been taken over the course of the night they spent here. Their bodies shift around each other in the sheets, restless and random. It was dark when they were taken, and their limbs are grainy and indistinct. The images are perfectly innocent: abstract, almost. They look like shapes and shadows.

They mean that there was nothing Ryan was willing to let them keep for themselves.

The crowd around Lulu mills and swirls; it ebbs and eddies. Someone touches her shoulder, indicates the photograph on the wall, offers her a congratulations.

She sees Ryan talking to someone, some man in a suit. Ryan inclines his head to accept his praise. Lulu can almost see the crown that sits there, and how long he's been waiting to wear it.

And then he's under her hands. She shoves him hard. She drops the key she forgot she was holding. It clatters to the floor and the sound silences the room.

"You're a fucking piece of shit, you know that, right," Lulu says.

"Oh come on, Lulu," Ryan starts, and instantly she can see that she miscalculated. Because even though she's the one who's been fucked over here, he's mad. He looks contained and removed because he's clenching against a fury that's consuming him from the inside out. He doesn't care if he hurt her tonight. "You're really mad that people are looking at you?"

Maybe, actually, he wants to be allowed to hurt her worse.

The room is full of men in black suits and they're Ryan's friends. His dad's business partners. Lulu's pink dress feels so foolish, like she just had to go ahead and let everyone know that she's just a dumb, defenseless girl. There's no one here who's on her side, except Cass, but Cass—where is Cass? She can't find her in this sea of people.

Lulu is almost glad. She doesn't know if she could bear to look at Cass right now, to see Ryan taking all the privacy and intimacy he offered and turning it against her. He sold Cass on the idea that she could be anyone here, and now he's captured her, and pinned her in a frame.

The cruelty of it is staggering.

Lulu is sure that if she stays in this room her body will stop breathing.

She doesn't say anything to Ryan. Instead, she walks out of the room, into the hallway, down the stairs, through the lobby, and then out of its door at last, releasing herself into the cold, clear dark of the night.

CHAPTER THIRTY-FOUR

● ● ● ●

IT'S FIFTEEN MINUTES to midnight when Lulu shows up on Bea's doorstep. She thought about sending her a Flash on the way over, but then she figured Bea wouldn't be paying attention to her phone, and might especially not be in the mood to talk to Lulu if she didn't know it was urgent. It's not like her parents are home to be woken up, anyway.

It feels very strange and formal to ring the bell. Lulu listens to it echoing through the downstairs.

It takes five minutes and another ring before Bea comes to answer it. Lulu sees her dimly through the door's glass panes—the lights are mostly off down here, but Bea looks disheveled, and annoyed.

Her face changes when she realizes who's standing on her porch.

She opens the door.

"Can I come in?" Lulu asks.

"What the fuck?"

"Can I come in?"

Bea stands back. "Of course. Of course. Lulu, are you okay? Is that Owen? What's happening? What's going on?"

Owen is sitting in his car. He was the one who came out and found Lulu standing, shivering, mute, in The Hotel's driveway. He put his jacket around her shoulders and when she wouldn't go inside he coaxed her into his car. "Bea's," she told him. "If you want to do something, take me to Bea's," and he did.

Lulu sends a mental apology to Kiley for depriving her of her rightful midnight kiss. She waves at him, *Hi, I'm fine*, and he flashes his lights in response and starts backing out of the driveway.

"Are you okay?" Bea asks again.

"I'm fine," Lulu says. "Something bad happened. But I'm fine. Look at me. I'm fine."

"You always *look* fine, Lulu!"

Bea stands back to make room, so Lulu walks into the house, over the threshold, into the familiar space. There's mail on the side table and it smells like Bea's house always does, like her own almost-home.

"Where were you?" Bea asks.

Lulu follows Bea into the kitchen. "I don't want anything," she says.

"I might."

"Is Rich upstairs?"

"Mmmm."

"I was at a party," Lulu says. "At the—at the hotel property Ryan owns."

"Oh. Of course."

"Can we put that on hold for tonight?"

246

"Put what on hold?"

"Our argument," Lulu says. "Any argument."

"Oh, so now that you need me we're friends again?"

"Yes," Lulu agrees. "Now that I need you. I really need you, B."

Her voice must convey how desperate she is, because Bea just sighs. "Oh, girl," she says, and holds open her arms.

After a while, Bea goes upstairs to let Rich know what's going on. When she comes back down, she grabs a bottle of champagne out of the fridge and brings it and Lulu up to her bedroom.

"Where's Rich?" Lulu asks.

"Jerking off in the shower."

"Right," Lulu says. "I forgot. Happy New Year."

Somehow, that's what does it—breaks the seal of tension between them, so that they both dissolve into helpless, eye-watering laughter.

"Happy New Year!" Bea says, miming a jerk-off motion, her hands describing a dick so big they don't touch around it.

"Happy New Year!" Lulu cries, and pops the top off the champagne so that it fizzes and splashes onto her hands, and then the floor.

"My *rug*!" Bea yelps.

"MY LIFE," Lulu yelps back. She sucks the foam out of the bottle. It spills, wet and white, down her chin.

"Give me," Bea says. "Give it here," so Lulu does.

Out of habit, she checks her phone.

Ryan sent her a link to a website. When she opens it, he has the photographs for sale. He's calling the exhibition *LOOK AT THIS*. He's selling it like he owns it. Like he owns her.

"What?" Bea asks.

"Well," Lulu says. "You wanted to know what happened? This is what happened."

She hands her phone to Bea.

Bea clicks through the slideshow. Rich comes out at one point, hair damp, deeply pouty, and Bea waves him away. "Girl stuff," she says. "Urgent."

He goes downstairs to play video games.

Bea hands the phone back to Lulu when she's done.

Lulu can't keep herself from thumbing through the gallery some more. It's crazy to see herself as a model, a photograph, a thing that can be bought and sold. All of the magic of The Hotel sucked up and turned into a way to manipulate her into letting her guard down for long enough that he could capture the shape of her body for himself.

As if it even had to be that hard. Everyone knows Lulu is easy for a camera.

Bea takes the phone from Lulu's hands. Lulu doesn't resist. It feels so good to let someone else take care of her.

"I think we should talk about this," Bea says.

"What's left to say?" Lulu drains the last drops from the champagne bottle. "Is there more?" She likes the fuzzy faraway soft feeling the booze is lending her. She wants more of it.

"No," Bea says, "and, to start with, I need to know what

exactly happened here. Did Ryan not tell you he was taking the photographs? Or that he was going to sell them? Or post them online?"

"The black-and-white ones are security footage," Lulu says. "The pictures of us in bed? We definitely did not pose for those."

Bea sucks in a sharp breath.

Lulu says, "I just. I know it doesn't look that bad. But I didn't know he was watching. Much less that anyone else ever would be."

"Fuck."

"Pretty much."

"Wow. Wow. Wow. That's, like, that's got to be illegal, right?"

"I don't know. Probably. Kind of. There were signs up saying there were cameras at the hotel."

"Still, though. You should sue him."

"Sue the Riggs family?" Lulu's laugh is hollow. "Waste of time. Or money, I guess, mostly." Her family is rich, but there's a difference between second-generation immigrant lawyers and a hundred years of Riggs men getting away with whatever they fucking please in America. She thinks about that Supreme Court justice, the one who assaulted a girl when he was younger. No one believed the women who came forward against him. And the Riggses have way more money and history than he did.

"It would mess with his reputation, at least," Bea argues.

"I can't really think about this right now," Lulu says. "I'm sorry, B, I just—"

"No, no, that's fine, I'm sorry, I'm just—I don't know what to do about this."

"I don't either."

"You want to make Rich give up the PlayStation so we can watch a movie or something?"

"Yes," Lulu says. "Please. Thank you."

It doesn't seem possible, but Lulu falls asleep midway through the *Hannah Montana* movie. She wakes up to Bea shaking her gently, apologetically. "Rich just left," she says. "My parents are on their way home. They're gonna think it's weird if you're passed out here instead of upstairs."

"Right," Lulu says. "Of course."

Usually when she stays here she sleeps in Bea's room, but tonight Bea leads her to the guest room.

"You need anything?" Bea asks.

"Nah," Lulu says. "I'm fine."

"Okay."

Before she can talk herself out of it, Lulu says, "Hey."

Bea turns around.

"Thanks for letting me in."

"Of course."

"I know I haven't been an awesome friend lately."

Bea smiles gently. "We should probably have this conversation another time." Which isn't a *No! You've been great!* She doesn't move, though. Instead, she says, "But as long as we're talking about stuff. Can I ask you something?"

"Sure."

"Why do you keep doing it?"

Lulu frowns. "Keep doing what?"

"Flash," Bea says. "After—after Sloane. Did you ever think about stopping?"

Lulu closes her eyes and falls back on the bed.

Of course she thought about it. She wanted to do it. But she knew that if she did, she would be admitting something: that she'd screwed up; that everything had changed; that she wasn't who she'd said she was. Or who she wanted to be.

So she didn't.

"I'm not blaming you for what happened tonight," Bea adds hastily. "I've just been wondering."

"Well, I will now," Lulu says to the ceiling.

"I'm sorry," Bea says.

"Don't be."

"Don't tell me what to do!" Bea seems almost startled by the force of her own outburst.

Lulu has to laugh. "Okay," she says. "Be sorry. It's fine with me." She kicks her shoes onto the floor, and they land with a satisfying thump. "Why are you asking?"

"Um. In terms of you maybe not being the best friend in the

251

last few months. I guess it felt sometimes like you didn't want to talk to me about anything, but you were still always, like, performing. For this audience."

"I had a beautiful life," Lulu says. "Wasn't that what I was supposed to do with it? Make sure everyone knew just how beautiful it was?"

"Even when it was kind of fucked up?"

"Especially when it was fucked up."

Bea nods, and sighs. She says, "If you'd called and asked if you could come over, I don't know if I would have said yes."

"That's why I didn't call. I knew I shouldn't. But I also didn't want to go anywhere else."

"Well," Bea says, "for the record, I think I'm glad you did."

CHAPTER THIRTY-FIVE

● ● ● ●

IN THE MORNING, Cass has sent Lulu a text. Can we talk?

Sure, Lulu says. Should I come there?

Let's meet in the middle.

They pick a diner in the Farmers Market at Third and Fairfax, which is nearly empty at hangover o'clock on the first day of the year. It's been a long time since Lulu ate anywhere like this: a place that wasn't trying to be cute, or stylish—that just, like, *was*. They don't list a provenance for the coffee on the menu, or explain to her how it's been brewed. She sits in a booth drinking a cup, black, and worrying.

Lulu expects Cass to show up looking wrecked, but when she arrives she's just subdued. She doesn't look broken, but she doesn't look entirely like herself either. It takes Lulu a minute to work out why: She isn't wearing mascara. Her eyelashes are pale ginger, faint and delicate against the cream of her skin.

Lulu was ready to comfort Cass while she cried. She has no idea what to do with the stoic, steely-eyed Cass who's sitting across from her.

Cass breaks the silence. She says, "Hi."

"Hi," Lulu repeats.

The waitress tailed her in, so she takes Cass's coffee order and they're spared the pressure of making conversation for a minute more.

Then she bustles away, and it's just the two of them.

"I—" Lulu says, but she can't get the rest of the sentence out of her throat.

Cass asks, "So where did you go last night?"

"To Bea's."

"Oh."

Talking to Cass has always been almost too easy. Now Lulu feels like she's sitting with a stranger. "How did you— Did you end up staying long? At the party?" she asks.

"No, Lulu."

"Did I miss something?" Lulu asks. "Something else?"

"No, Lulu."

"Okay." Lulu wishes she had done something right—with Bea, with Cass—so that people wouldn't keep being so mad at her, but it's too late for that now. "I'm sorry I left without you. I wasn't thinking straight. I wasn't thinking at all. I just had to leave. I felt like I was gonna die if I didn't."

Cass's coffee arrives. She takes a long swallow and looks out the window. She doesn't say anything. Then, after a while, conversationally: "He broke my heart, Lulu."

"He what?"

"My heart, Lulu. He broke it."

"I thought you guys weren't—"

"He was my best friend. For a while—before you—he was one of my only friends. I trusted him, and I loved him, and he got pissed that I wasn't paying attention to him and he betrayed me. He took something that he knew was important to me and made sure everyone could see it. He exposed me, even though he knew it was the last thing I'd be able to stand. He broke my *heart* last night, Lulu." Cass can't keep the emotion out of her voice anymore. "And you just left. You went to hang out with Bea. You didn't text. You didn't call. You didn't ask if I was okay—"

"I *know*." There's nothing Lulu can do to change it. "I know," she says again. "I couldn't bear to look at you, Cass. It felt like it was going to make it too real. It was selfish. That's the truth about me: I'm a very selfish person."

"Don't ask me to feel sorry for you."

"I'm *not*," Lulu snarls. God, she's angry. All of the rage she's been suppressing comes roaring to life, and before she knows it she's saying, "He did this to me too, you know."

"Not like he did it to me."

"Oh, because of your special friendship?" Lulu couldn't let herself be angry with Ryan, not the way she wanted to be. She couldn't let herself scream or curse, get ugly and wild. But there's nothing and no one stopping her from dumping the fury that's been simmering in her blood—at Ryan, but also at her stupid, stupid self—onto Cass.

"Or," Lulu continues. "Do you mean, because I've already

exposed myself on the internet? That it just shouldn't bother me as much? I was always going to be damaged goods, I guess."

"That's not what I said. That's not even remotely what I said."

"What are you saying, then?"

"I'm saying that I get the sense you disappeared on Bea when you met me, but when I stopped being easy, you went back to Bea. I'm saying that I thought there was *one person* I could completely, totally trust, and he fucked me over, and I'm scared. I'm scared of him, and I'm scared of you too. I'm scared that I'm gonna keep falling for you, and you're gonna abandon me when I stop being convenient."

"I didn't do anything!"

"Exactly. You don't do things. You let things happen to you. You waited for that Flash to break you and Owen up; you were never gonna tell me you were into girls, were you, until Kiley forced the issue—"

"I'm here, aren't I?"

"Yeah, and who texted first?"

Lulu puts her head on the table. Its surface is hard and cold. She likes that. She likes that it's exactly and only what it is.

"Okay," Lulu says. "I already told you: I'm bad. I'm the worst one. What do you want from me, Cass?"

Cass doesn't say anything for a while. She drinks her coffee. Lulu thinks this is the longest she's sat with someone in—she can't remember how long, where neither of them is saying anything, or looking at her phone.

"I read the book you got me," Cass says, finally. "For Christmas. Have you read it?"

"No," Lulu says, and thinks, *Another strike against me.*

"It's beautiful," Cass says. "But mostly it got me thinking. Do you know how many adaptations of the *Bluebeard* story there are?"

"No." *And another.*

"A lot. There are . . . a lot. Just like, all of these retellings of this story about a man who compulsively kills women. Who murders them. That's what we watch for fun. That's the story we've been telling each other as entertainment for hundreds and hundreds of years."

"She gets away in the end," Lulu says. "Slays the monster. Lives happily ever after in the castle."

"First, though, she has to escape."

"I don't know what you *want* from me, Cass."

"I don't want anything," Cass says. "From anyone. Or I just— god. I just want it to stop."

She puts a ten down on the table and leaves.

Back in her car, Lulu does what she always does when she feels like she's dissolving. She flips the camera in her phone on and takes a selfie. It looks like all her other selfies: She knows exactly how to angle her chin to catch light on her cheekbones, to make her mouth look full and her eyes look wide. Usually it helps make her feel solid again: taking a photo, and posting it, and knowing exactly how everyone else is seeing her. Being able to look at herself the way everyone else in the world does.

But today the image on the screen doesn't make her feel any better. Lulu recognizes the girl in the picture, but not the one sliced into pieces by the rear- and side-view mirrors, reflecting off the windshield's glass. She doesn't understand what she's feeling, sitting here, coming and coming apart. The girl in the pictures has nothing to do with her today. She's untouchable, and Lulu—everyone's had their hands all over Lulu, haven't they.

Lulu puts the car in gear and starts driving.

CHAPTER THIRTY-SIX

● ● ● ●

THE HOTEL BEARS all the signs of a long, late party. The catering company took the glassware and the linens, but the lobby is still forested with bare tables, and the walls are lined with empty bottles and abandoned jackets and wraps. The front steps are covered in cigarette butts.

The lobby door is open and even though it's sunny outside, inside it's all blue chill. After Lulu left, someone plugged in a projector down here, and the images from upstairs blinked onto one of the lobby's bare walls while guests danced. Lulu watched Flashes of it this morning. Thanks for nothing, #TheFutureIsRigged.

Ryan is exactly where he was the first time Lulu showed up here: in room Four. This time, though, he's in bed, asleep. He doesn't stir when Lulu opens the door. She stands there, looking at him.

He's sweet in his sleep just like everyone is, slack and young looking, pale and vulnerable. The thought comes to Lulu: *I could do anything I want to you.* Anything at all. Is that what he felt every time he saw her and Cass wander away from him, thinking they were alone, and knowing better? This surge of sick, seductive power?

She kicks his bed to wake him up.

Ryan spasms, startled, but he recovers quickly. He's shirtless, passed out in last night's jeans. As soon as he's fully conscious he looks dangerous again, rich and handsome, rumpled but unfazed. "Shapiro," he says. "What's up."

"Yeah, I don't know, Ryan. What is up?"

Lulu's mind is spinning. What does Ryan value? What does Ryan need? She has no answers for these questions. God, what an idiot she's been. She showed him exactly where she was vulnerable—with Owen, with Cass—and all he ever showed her was this place where she could act out her fantasies, and let him watch them unfold. She can't believe that she let herself forget, even for a second, that she was playing a game.

The only thing she can cling to is: Lulu Shapiro is very, very good at this particular game.

"You're pissed," he says.

That's not too much to give away. "Of course I am."

"I'm sorry it was such a big surprise," Ryan says. "I wanted to show you two the pictures first. I really think they're great. But I also didn't want to risk you trying to stop me."

"Is that supposed to make me feel better? At all?"

"I do have a conscience," Ryan says. He grins at her, infuriatingly pleased with himself. "I listen to it. I just try not to let it affect my behavior, or my work. The images are beautiful, right?"

"Self-indulgent. Just pretty girls being pretty girls. I thought you were better than that."

"Pretty girls are enticing, though," Ryan says. "If there's one thing I learned from Roman, it's the kind of business you can build if you make pretty girls your first customers. And really, I just couldn't pass up the opportunity to photograph someone with such a big reputation."

He thinks he's already thought of everything. Lulu wants to see if she can rattle him. "Aren't you worried that I'll sue?"

"Not really," Ryan says. "Sure, you didn't sign anything, but there were signs up about the cameras. I told you they were there. I took pictures of you guys all the time, and I always asked, so you knew that was happening. And I'm only eighteen. How could I have known that I needed anything other than verbal consent?"

"This is how your dad raised you, huh. He must be proud."

"You know what," Ryan says. "He is."

"That's because he doesn't know how pathetic you are. Building a whole hotel to keep a girl interested in you. And she *wasn't*, Ryan. She wasn't ever going to be, so you decorated it with stolen photos and called it art. This is all self-indulgent bullshit and you know it. That doesn't surprise me—you've been a self-indulgent bullshit artist since I met you—but even I can't believe you'd do that to Cass."

"I didn't do half of what I could have," he spits back. Finally, finally, she's got Ryan unguarded, Ryan too furious to hold back.

This is who he really is—a wounded animal, and once Lulu would have felt bad, seeing him hurt. Now all she sees is how intent he is on hurting her, and everyone else who gets too close. "You want to see what I could have done to you and Cass?"

"No," Lulu says. But when has Ryan ever listened to *no*?

She already knows what this will be. If the cameras were on that night, they were on in the morning. The light would have been better. They would have gotten a clear view of Cass and Lulu waking up, and what happened after.

She doesn't know what's crueler: Ryan letting her know that he saw it, or Ryan making sure she knows he kept it to himself. It's the most violent tenderness she's ever experienced, the way he assures her that he was careful when he was carving them up. He exposed them, but not the way he could have.

Lulu understands that she's supposed to be grateful.

"This is what's disgusting," Ryan says. "You two sneaking around my property, getting each other off, pretending you were *just friends,* like nothing had changed. Like I couldn't tell! I'm not stupid, Lulu!"

He unplugs the hard drive from the computer and tosses it in her direction. Lulu is so surprised that she catches it.

"You're the one who releases revenge porn," he says. "Poor Owen. You're the one who's always making herself the goddamn center of attention. Well, if you need some more footage to release, go right ahead. That should make you the center of attention for the next six months at least."

"Fuck you. *Fuck you*, Ryan."

"I'm done now. Get out of here. I want you to leave."

Lulu tosses the drive back at Ryan. "Keep it."

"I wouldn't do that if I were you."

"I don't give a fuck about what you'd do."

"Still. That's the only copy. You really want to let me have it? You trust me with that power?"

"I don't believe you."

Ryan shrugs. "Good news for me: I don't have to care."

He might be lying, but why take the chance? If there are more copies, it doesn't matter what she does. If there aren't—she should do this. She should just take the stupid thing.

Mutely, Lulu reaches out a hand. The weight of giving in settles on her shoulders. She's done lots of things that people told her were dirty, but she's never felt stained by anything until right now. Making any kind of deal with Ryan feels like a bargain with the devil himself.

"Cass will forgive me eventually," Ryan says.

"I don't think she will."

"Oh please." Ryan says. "You think you love her or something? That she loves you? You barely know her. You give yourself away for *nothing,* Lulu. I went ahead and made something, at least. God, it's so sad. I know so many girls like you."

"Girls like me."

"Empty," Ryan says.

Lulu stands still and feels her beating heart, the pressure of air in her lungs and blood in her veins. She's purple-bruised and incandescent with rage.

He doesn't deserve a response, so Lulu doesn't give him one. "Thanks for this," she says, and then she leaves.

When she gets home, she texts Cass. I'm sorry about everything.

Cass doesn't write back.

Lulu remembers this. She remembers how to be this person, scared and blank and numb. She knows how to hold still until it's safe to feel something again. It's like slipping into a second skin to crawl into bed, and sleep, and sleep, and sleep.

CHAPTER THIRTY-SEVEN

● ● ● ●

NAOMI WOULD HAVE questions about Lulu's disappearing act, but luckily for Lulu, Naomi has to leave on the second. Once she's gone, their mom leaves Lulu alone, letting her drowse away the days with Netflix on autoplay in the background.

On Saturday night, Lulu sees her mother standing tentatively in the doorway of her bedroom. "I was going to make some dinner. I was wondering if you wanted some," she says.

Lulu's been surviving on Postmates and misery for like thirty-six hours, which is the only reason she says yes. Probably she should eat a vegetable before she has to go back to school with sodium bloat testifying to just how badly she's been handling this.

Her mother's not one to let that kind of thing go either. When Lulu appears in the kitchen to help set the table, her mom pauses her and takes Lulu's face in her hands. "You don't look good," she says. "All this staying inside. You got pale."

"I am pale, Mom. We're white, remember?"

Her mother shakes her head. "You should have gone away for break. At least for a week, to get some sun. You're like me—you look better with a tan."

"Sorry about that," Lulu mutters.

Her mother has the audacity to look hurt by Lulu's tone.

Dinner is awkward. Lulu listens to her fork tines scrape across the plate and the sound of water in her mouth, gulped down her throat. Her mother asks desultory questions: *What time will you head back to your dad's tomorrow? Are you excited about the new semester? Any news about college?*

When Lulu's exhausted her answers (*The afternoon, at some point; Sure, yeah; No, Mom*), the quiet stretches out, thick and heavy between them.

"Did you—" her mom starts. "It seems like maybe you and Owen broke up again."

"No. Just once."

"Okay."

When Lulu looks up, her mother is looking at her plate. She's taken off the day's makeup, and her long, dark hair is pulled back from her face, and just for a moment, Lulu can see her sister in her mother's features—not a vision, but an echo or a ripple, knowable only in motion. If Lulu spent years thinking Naomi was a stranger, she's never even bothered to wonder about her mom.

"I got dumped by someone else," Lulu says.

"Who was he?"

Lulu says, "She."

"She," her mother agrees.

Lulu takes a deep breath. So that's it, huh.

She's glad her mother isn't going to make a big deal out of it or anything.

She allows herself a moment to wish it hadn't felt like a big deal to her to say it.

She tries to imagine what it would be like to live somewhere—to know someone—she wouldn't *have* to tell. Who would expect it. Who would have seen it coming, because they'd been there themselves.

"It doesn't matter," Lulu says.

"Okay," her mother says again.

Lulu takes a last bite of her dinner. She chews and swallows it. "Have you ever thought about doing anything other than acting?" she asks.

"What, sweetheart?"

"I was just wondering." Lulu shrugs.

"Not really." Her mother touches her napkin to the corners of her lips, even though she's not wearing any lipstick. "Even if it's not what you'd call *fulfilling* these days, it certainly pays the bills."

"Yeah. No. It just seems like it could get exhausting, being looked at that much."

Her mother gives her a mock-demure smile. "Who doesn't love attention?" she purrs. She tosses her ponytail over her shoulder. She looks past Lulu, into space. "Some days it can be a little much," she says. "Some days—but then, it used to bother me more when I was younger. Now if I'm not on set, no one looks at me at all. I'm too old for that." Her gaze shifts back to Lulu, frank and certain. "So no. I don't think about stopping. At least not for that reason. I could do without the hours. And some of these directors—well, you know how it is. This *town*."

Lulu relaxes into the familiarity of her mother's monologue on how disgusting the men are in Hollywood. She's heard it all her life, and she's always thought of it as a brag: her mom's way of reminding everyone that she's still hot enough to get hit on every time she goes to work.

Tonight, though, for the first time, she can hear the nerves in her mother's voice as she delivers it. This apartment, this dinner, all the things she can give Lulu, which she worries aren't enough—they all depend on money, which depends on those men still wanting to look at her.

FLASH POST BY CLAIRE SAWYER, JANUARY 4, 11:00 A.M.

"So like . . . can we talk about Lulu Shapiro, you guys? Is she trying to make some kind of move to be an actual model or something? I didn't think the lesbian thing in the fall was a stunt—I have friends who go to school with her and they said she didn't, like, talk about it, so it seemed like maybe it really was a mistake. But now Ryan Riggs is posting all of these pictures of her on his Flash, and there's rumors that there's another picture of her kissing a girl in his show, and it's juuuuust a little sketchy if you ask me."

FLASH PHOTO POST BY FIONA VERACRUZ, JANUARY 4, 12:27 P.M.

[Photograph of Lulu in her bathing suit from Ryan's show]

Fuuuuck why is @lulululu always so #goals

FLASH VIDEO POST BY JULIET HILLIER, JANUARY 4, 2:13 A.M.

"I guess I had to be drunk to talk about this, but I just wanted to say fuck the way Lulu Shapiro uses her sexuality for attention. Okay great. Bye!!!!!"

FLASH PHOTO POST BY BRENDAN POWELL, JANUARY 4, 4:44 P.M.

[Photograph of a shirtless teenage boy, flexing in the mirror]

@Lulululu listen if you still like dudes you know where to slide

THREE IDENTICAL POSTS FROM TAE YOUNG KIM, ASHLEY GUINESS, AND MOLLY KETCHUM

[A selfie of each girl, standing against a neutral background, with the text #DEFENDLULU posted over their eyes and mouths.]

**DIRECT MESSAGE FROM SIERRA
CARPENTER TO LULU SHAPIRO,
JANUARY 4, 10:49 P.M.**

*Heyyyyyy sorry if this is weird because we don't
know each other but I just wanted to say I've
always thought you were hot and if you're not
dating that girl from the pictures maybe, like, let
me know?*

**DIRECT MESSAGE FROM JAMES
BRONSON TO LULU SHAPIRO,
JANUARY 4, 10:44 A.M.**

Keep posting those pix 😸 😸 😸

**DIRECT MESSAGE FROM FRANK
WALKER TO LULU SHAPIRO,
JANUARY 4, 11:03 P.M.**

[Explicit photograph]

CHAPTER THIRTY-EIGHT

●　●　●　●

LULU DRAGS HER corpse out of bed on the last day of break in order to go to Sephora. She doesn't need anything—she doesn't even want anything. But after days of lying around, she's actually starting to feel kind of antsy, and the mall seems like a place she can just, like, *go,* without needing a companion, or more of a reason than *I want to try on lipstick.*

Century City is nightmarishly busy, and it takes her so long to park that she thinks about just leaving, but then a spot opens up, and the inertia of already being there—of not wanting to have to go home again, or anywhere, really—tugs her into it.

The only nice thing about the crowds is that the salespeople in the store are too busy to bother her while Lulu swipes a thick fingerful of La Mer from one of the sample jars she normally doesn't touch—all those germs. She taps on Tom Ford bronzer to give her the glow her mom was looking for, and makes her eyelashes thick and full with Dior mascara. Lulu builds her face into something pretty and expensive in a series of tiny, hot-lit mirrors.

She expected some sort of hunger to come over her once she

was here—usually she loves to shop—but there's no magic in the bottles and brushes today: just her sad face and its bright mask. Lulu rubs it all off again before she leaves the store.

She heads upstairs to the food court to get a snack before she goes, in the hope that she'll honestly be able to tell her mom that she isn't hungry for dinner later.

"Lulu!"

Lulu hears her own name and whirls around, too surprised to pretend she's not startled. Before she even really understands what's happening, Molly Ketchum is flying at her, a blur of blond hair and enthusiasm, yelping, "Oh my god I was just *talking* about you! How *are* you? It's been so much *drama*!"

"Hey," Lulu says. "Yeah, huh. Drama."

Molly lets Lulu go, but she stays close and tilts their heads together conspiratorially. "Kiley won't say anything," she reports. "I have questions, and she's being all secretive, and I'm like, *Ki*ley, Lulu and I have been friends forever, I think I can know what's up." She rolls her eyes.

Molly and Lulu have known each other forever—their moms met in some parent-and-me singalong group when they were babies. And they are friends, technically, though sometimes Lulu feels like that's mostly so Molly can keep pumping Lulu for gossip.

"What do you want to know?" Lulu asks.

"Everything! You've been so mysterious. Are you and Ryan planning another show? Is that why you took your Flash down?

Are you and that girl dating now? Or are you dating Ryan? Because I've heard it both ways."

"I'm not dating anyone," Lulu says.

"Oh my god, this is why you can't listen to gossip. KILEY!" Molly calls to a group of girls who are sitting on a bench eating froyo. Kiley separates herself from the pack and comes over to them. Has she possibly gotten taller since the last time Lulu saw her? She looks lankier than ever, just, like, miles and miles of limbs.

"Lulu says she isn't dating anyone. Which doesn't seem like that big of a secret to me. So can you please tell Kiley there's no need to be Fort Knox?" Molly asks.

"Actually," Kiley says. "Can I talk to Lulu for a second?"

"Soooooo mysterious," Molly sighs. "Whatever. Go ahead." She skips back to the bench where her friends are waiting.

Lulu looks at Kiley expectantly.

"I don't even know the answers to most of her questions," Kiley says. "I don't know why she keeps asking."

Lulu shrugs. "Tell her whatever you want," she says.

"Look, Lulu, I apologized—"

"I'm not mad at you anymore." At least Kiley did what she did on impulse. She didn't spend weeks plotting and planning to fuck Lulu over as thoroughly as possible. And anyway, that video was already out there. Lulu put it out there herself.

Lulu glances over and sees that Molly is still watching them. "Can we walk?" she asks.

"Sure." Kiley falls into step with her as they turn away from the girls and the food court and head off in a random direction.

"What did you want to say?" Lulu asks.

"Oh, nothing," Kiley says. "I just figured you didn't want to talk to Molly."

"How did you guess?" Lulu catches Kiley's eye, and they both laugh, and then look away. "I didn't know you two were friends," she says after a minute.

"Same ballet studio," Kiley says. "When we did ballet. She quit before I did."

"Right. When did you stop?"

"Last spring."

Lulu had forgotten what it meant to be out in the world. She had imagined having to talk to people, but instead, she can ask Kiley to talk to her, and that means not having to listen to the inside of her own head.

"Why?" she asks.

"Do you really care?"

"I don't want to talk to myself any more than I want to talk to Molly."

"In that case. Um, I guess the short version of the story is that I had basically never not done it, and I wanted to know what it would be like to stop."

"Can you start again if you want to?"

"In theory. I've already lost a lot of time."

"Did that scare you? Giving it up?"

They pause in front of a store that appears to sell an array of shapeless, colorless garments. Lulu doesn't even know what they are: dresses? Tops? The salesgirl inside is almost inhumanly beautiful. Kiley examines her reflection in the plate glass window.

"Of course it did," she says.

They move on, walking in silence. Then Lulu says, "You said, before. You said that sometimes, you just felt like being mean."

Kiley sighs. "Yeah. Especially if—when I get tired of being the different one. The youngest at these parties, the only black girl, the one who has to explain—see. Just like this. I try to be nice. Sometimes I'm not."

"I feel horrible," Lulu says. She thought she could get away with saying it out loud and sounding—something, okay, maybe, but her voice betrays her and comes out harsh, broken and raw. "I feel fucking horrible all the time."

"Why are you telling me?" Kiley asks. There's no malice in her question.

"I don't know." Lulu scrubs a hand across her cheeks to make sure her eyes aren't leaking traitor tears.

"We're never gonna be friends, are we," Kiley says.

"No," Lulu agrees. "Probably not." They've wandered themselves near the parking garage entrance; she has to leave soon if she doesn't want to have to pay for her spot. "I should go," she says. "Thank you for talking to me." And, after a pause, "Thanks for listening. Thanks for saving me from Molly. I owe you one."

Kiley nods. "Sure," she says. "I'll remember that." She pulls her phone out of her pocket and glances at it. "Oh," she says. "Bea just got out of a movie, if you want to say hi to her before you go."

CHAPTER THIRTY-NINE

● ● ● ●

BEA GREETS LULU like nothing is wrong, like the last time they saw each other it wasn't midnight on New Year's Eve and Lulu wasn't in the middle of a minor mental breakdown. "Hey," she says, slinging an arm around Lulu's shoulders before resuming the story she was telling Molly. "—Anyway, it was like, the *nastiest* on-screen kiss I've ever seen," she says with a shuddering flourish.

"Ugh." Molly shudders. "I'm so glad we decided not to go. Wanna see what we got at Madewell while you were suffering?"

"I would, but I'm, like, starving," Bea says. "Lulu, you hungry?"

"I was thinking about eating," Lulu says, and it isn't even a lie.

"Wear it all on Monday!" Bea advises Molly. She blows kisses at Kiley and the rest of the group, and hustles herself and Lulu out of there so neatly that even Lulu, who's watched Bea work for years now, is impressed.

"God," Bea says when they're clear. "That was already too much. I'm so not ready for school tomorrow."

"That makes two of us," Lulu says.

"What should we eat?"

"I really don't care."

"Hmmmm." Bea contemplates their options. "Maybe let's go to Eataly, and get a lot of snacks?"

"You know I love a snack tray." This is a tradition they developed when Lulu first started sleeping over at Bea's house: going to the grocery store and plundering the aisles for Doritos and Ruffles and Sour Patch Kids to eat while they streamed movies onto Bea's parents' flat-screen.

Eataly is way fancier than the Gelson's they used to go to, though: Lulu accidentally picks out a twenty-five-dollar hunk of cheese before Bea notices, and makes her trade it out for something less outrageous. "Unless you want to put it on your credit card, princess," she says.

Cass flashes in front of Lulu—Cass arguing with her about whether she was a JAP. Cass saying, *I could be anything.* "I don't," Lulu says.

"C'mon," Bea says. "If we're gonna get mozzarella, we need bread or crackers or something."

"Sure."

"Hey, Molly said you said you weren't dating anyone. That girl is a gossip black hole, I swear. She sucks in information like it's her job." Bea pauses, but Lulu doesn't say anything, so she continues. "Was she wrong? Or did you and Cass break up?"

"I don't know if we were ever really dating."

"That sounds like semantics."

Eataly is the fanciest grocery store Lulu's ever been in, but it's still just a grocery store: fluorescent lit, with aisles of small, brightly colored things. When she and Bea used to do this, Lulu felt like such a grown-up.

"We're not talking," she says.

"I'm sorry."

"It's okay."

Bea pauses them so that she can examine a display of preserved fish. "You aren't an anchovy person, right?"

Lulu shakes her head.

"I was excited about you and Cass," Bea says.

"Yeah, well, me too."

"It seemed like she was good for you."

Lulu balks. "What's *that* supposed to mean?"

"It wasn't an insult."

"No, I know, but it makes her sound like . . . vitamins, or something."

Bea selects a tin of anchovies anyway, and tosses it in their basket before moving down the aisle. "Well, maybe that's what you needed," she says, and Lulu's still catching up to her, so she almost misses it. "At least you wanted to talk to somebody."

"What do you mean?"

Bea's standing in front of the olives now, which Lulu knows she doesn't like. Still, she scrutinizes the labels like they're important documents. "I don't know if you know what the last few months have been like for me, Lulu."

"For you?"

"Yes, for me! For me, trying to take care of you, and having you just insist on pretending everything was okay. Which it clearly wasn't! It, Lulu, it *clearly* was not." Bea pulls a jar of black olives off the shelf and then replaces it again. "So when you started hanging out with Cass I was pissed, selfishly, because I missed you, but mostly I was glad, at least, that you were excited about *something*. I figured, at least she's talking to someone. Since you wouldn't talk to me."

"I talked to you!"

"Not about anything that mattered. Not about what was really going on." Bea has had enough of the olives. She spins to face Lulu now, and that's when Lulu realizes, *Oh, we're really doing this*. In front of a display of imported olives in a fancy food store in a fancy mall. Why not? Where would be better?

So she says, "You wanted to hear, what? A big gay sob story? A tender coming out?"

"Jesus, Lulu. I wanted to hear whatever you wanted to tell me."

"Well, I just wanted to stop embarrassing myself. Stop embarrassing you. You understand that, Bea, don't you?"

"You think you were *embarrassing* me?"

"I wouldn't blame you. I've been behaving pretty badly."

"God, honestly, that's the meanest thing you've ever said to me." Bea looks like she's on the verge of tears. "I *love you*, Lulu, you fucking asshole. I don't care if anyone else thinks you're cool."

Lulu doesn't know what to say.

"Is that what you think we are to each other? That I'm gonna ditch you for Kiley because she's dating Owen now?" Bea puts the basket she's carrying down and cups her hands around her mouth like a megaphone. "Attention!" she shouts. The other people in the aisle look at her, startled. Some just keep walking. "This is Lulu, and she is my best friend," Bea continues. "My best! Friend!"

"High five for friendship!" Some dude offers Bea his palm, and she slaps it.

Bea turns to Lulu coolly. "What I just did," she says, "was embarrassing. You're not embarrassing. You're just a mess, like everyone else."

Lulu has never wanted to laugh and cry so hard, at the same time, in her whole life. Who even is Bea? Who is she?

"Okay," Bea says. "Your turn."

"My turn?"

"Even if you were embarrassing me," Bea says. "I wouldn't mind. So what is it, Lulu? Do you feel the same way about me?"

In the last six months Lulu has accidentally uploaded a video of herself mid-make-out to the internet. She's made the first move on a girl she wasn't sure liked her. She's stripped off her clothes and leaped into freezing water. She has changed her whole life. Somehow, it's still hard to curl a hand around her mouth and yell out, "ATTENTION SHOPPERS.

"BEATRIZ OCAMPO IS MY BEST FRIEND.

"SHE IS A BETTER FRIEND THAN I DESERVE.

"JUST THOUGHT YOU SHOULD KNOW."

Then she collapses into a ball on the floor.

"I was gonna say, 'That wasn't so bad, was it,'" Bea says, somewhere above her. "But, um. Did I kill you?"

Lulu realizes that lying on the floor of Eataly is not much less dramatic than yelling in the aisles of one. She gets up and dusts herself off. "Incredibly," she says, "I survived."

A security guard approaches them cautiously. She looks like she isn't much older than they are, and she isn't at all sure what the protocol for a situation like this one is.

"Um," she says. "I think? I think I have to ask you to leave."

Lulu has never been kicked out of anywhere before in her life. She doesn't know what to say to Bea once they're standing outside. They weren't even allowed to buy the snacks they'd picked out, so they're empty-handed.

The big declarations are over. Lulu feels better, and also like that doesn't mean that everything is better yet.

"I'm sad about that mozzarella," Bea says, after a minute. "It looked really good."

"It did," Lulu agrees.

They both laugh, and then stop laughing.

Lulu asks, "What happens next?"

Bea says, "I don't know."

"Do you have anything else you want to say to me? Before we stop acting like we're on a CW show or something?"

Bea smiles, and then sighs. "I do," she says. "I feel like—like you have this idea that you need to take up less space. That it's easier for me, and for other people, if you're just this, like, boilerplate teen dream thing. But if you're unhappy, and you're hiding, it doesn't make it easier. It makes it harder. I know you thought—I know that a lot of people thought your life looked good lately. But for me, up close, it was hard to watch."

"I'm sorry," Lulu says. This time she doesn't explain for what. She's sorry for whatever's making Bea look at her like that—like she's afraid of Lulu, or for her. "And thanks for sticking around anyway," she adds. "It means a lot to me."

"Thanks for letting me."

It occurs to Lulu that maybe Bea has been just as scared to be there for Lulu—no questions asked, no rules, just *there*—as Lulu is to let herself be loved when she doesn't understand why anyone would want to.

Bea nudges Lulu with the point of her elbow. "I mean, someone's got to keep an eye on you," she says. "And usually I'm good at it, so I figure, you know. Might as well be me."

CHAPTER FORTY

● ● ● ●

BEA DRIVES THEM both to school in the morning. Lulu is wearing a short black dress her mother gave her for Hanukkah with a quilted black bomber jacket, black tights, and black boots. The sun is so bright when she walks down the driveway that she has to put her sunglasses on.

"Jesus, Lu, that's a statement," Bea says when she gets into the car.

"It's just black."

"You look like you're going to a high-class funeral."

"Yeah well," Lulu agrees. "My own."

The first two periods pass uneventfully; Lulu gets her midterms back and can barely remember taking them. Her grades are fine. Of course they are. *You always look fine*, Bea had said, and it's true.

She's ready to spend her third period free hiding out in the library, but just as history ends someone knocks on the door with a note for her. It's from Mr. Winters; he wants her to come by his office for a chat. Lulu considers not going, but she has Cinema Studies later today, so she's going to have to see him soon anyway. Better to just get it over with.

"I haven't listened to it yet," Lulu lies. *"Beauty, Power, Danger—*I haven't had time." She's hoping against hope that that's all this meeting is about—that he wants to follow up with her and tell her more about how he knows the Riggs family, and Christine L. Thompson, and whoever else.

Mr. Winters dashes her hopes, waving them away with a hand. "Whenever you're ready," he says. "Though I would especially recommend checking it out now, given what you were up to over the break. Sit down."

"What I was up to?"

"Ryan's parents told me about the opening," Mr. Winters says. "To clarify. I'm not the kind of teacher who goes looking my students up online or anything. I mean, I'd hope you know that, but can't be too careful, I guess."

"Have you seen the pictures?"

"I think a lot of people have," Mr. Winters says. He squints at Lulu. "Is that a problem?"

"No."

"Are you—"

"I said *no.*"

"Okay!" Mr. Winters holds up his hands, like he didn't mean to start anything. As if he weren't the one who brought this up.

"Because I just wanted to say that I think they're beautiful. Ryan's so talented, but in particular, the pictures of you I thought were just fantastic. Really raw and brave, Lulu. Roman—Ryan's father—suggested I take a look at some of your previous work, to give some context to—"

"What previous—"

"Your Flash posts," Mr. Winters says. "He sent me a link to an archive, and I only glanced through a few, but I really thought that the images represented a huge step forward for you, in terms of achieving naturalism, and more effectively blurring the lines between life and art. The Flashes were so composed, largely. Whereas there's—I already said *raw*, didn't I? But there is. There's just something so real about what happens when you put down the camera and let someone else capture you. Are you interested in modeling at all? Because I think you have some real talent, and I'd be happy to introduce you to my contacts. Such as they are, of course."

Lulu is totally, utterly stunned. She finds herself at a complete loss for words.

"I don't want to model," she says eventually.

"I don't mean to suggest you don't have a future in photography, being on the creative side," Mr. Winters says, too fast, like he's worried he's offended her. "I just know Ryan was the driving creative force behind this project, behind the camera, so I assumed, but I certainly don't think that's all you can—all you're capable of—"

"I'm not sure what I want to do yet," Lulu says.

"Well, that's fine too, of course. And truly, if you ever want to talk—you know I'm happy to—"

"I know," Lulu says.

Mr. Winters isn't done with her for the day, though. He starts class with an announcement. "Usually Cinema Studies is a general survey," he says. "But a general survey, as many of you know, tends to be a general survey of the history of white men."

"Mr. W, so *woke*!" Isaac Levine pipes up from the back of the class.

"Woke Winters," Doug Anderson agrees. "Winters woke."

Mr. Winters laughs. "I'm not trying to earn any brownie points," he says. "Or—what is it on the internet now—cookies? I just feel like, as one of the few teachers at this school not bound to get you to pass any kind of standardized test, maybe it's my responsibility to broaden your curriculum a little bit. And I've been thinking a lot lately about how women are depicted on screen."

The hand that's been lingering, loose, at Lulu's throat tightens its grip. It's hard not to imagine his smile is directed at her.

"We'll still be watching plenty of the classics—don't worry, no one is taking *A Clockwork Orange* or *The Usual Suspects* off the syllabus," he says. "But I wanted to start the semester with a little clinic on feminist filmmaking. So that when we watch the men, you have something to compare them to."

Lulu's hand is in the air before she can stop herself. Has she ever volunteered a comment in class before? Much less an *opinion*? But that was Lulu before, she thinks. This is Lulu *after*. This is scorched-earth Lulu; Lulu scorned. Lulu who isn't going to get to say what she thinks about so much stuff, so she may as well say what she can, where she can.

Mr. Winters doesn't exactly call on her, but Lulu starts talking anyway. "So the women are just, like, context," she says. "For the work that the men have done?"

"I wouldn't say that, exactly," Mr. Winters says. "I think they're both context for each other. You've been watching cinema made by men—"

"My whole life, I know that," Lulu says. "I think we all know that. So, like, I'm just wondering: Why give it so much space, still, here? If you want to teach a feminist film class, why not do it right, and do a whole semester on it, instead of just cramming it into your syllabus at the last minute? Oh, wait, sorry, I know the answer."

"Lulu," Mr. Winters says warningly. *You didn't tell off Doug and Isaac,* Lulu thinks. She's about to get an earful when Kiley interrupts him.

"Can I ask why you decided to think about diversity just in terms of men and women?" she asks. "What about race? I've noticed that, other than our detour into Confederate propaganda early in the semester, we haven't focused much on filmmakers of color. If we're making this class inclusive, I'd love to see some racial diversity as well. Especially since most of the women we're watching this week"—she indicates the syllabus Mr. Winters has written onto the whiteboard—"are white."

This earns her an appreciative hoot from Rob Sullivan, the other black kid in the class, and Charlie Andrews, who probably thinks he has a chance with Kiley just because she's a sophomore and he's a senior.

Everyone else is silent.

"Exactly, Kiley," Lulu says. "You can't just shove a handful of films onto your existing syllabus and say you're making a real change. There's more than a week's worth—more than a semester's worth—there's so much, um—"

This is why she doesn't talk in class: no time to strategize how best to express herself. *Woke Winters,* she thinks, already imagining what Doug is texting Isaac under his desk. *Loony Lulu.* She's being shrill. She can't stop herself. Her voice keeps squeezing itself out the narrowing channel of her throat.

"But that's true of cinema in general," Mr. Winters says, looking at Lulu, then turning to nod at Kiley. His tone is infuriatingly placid, as if to highlight how emotional Lulu is. "There's no way we can cover everything—even if we picked an incredibly niche topic, let's say feminist filmmakers just 1960 to present, or black filmmakers in the 1970s, we couldn't really do it justice in two semesters, probably. The class has always been a survey. I'm just trying to start broadening the survey a bit.

"I'd love to hear your suggestions for what else should be

included. Lulu, Kiley, anyone else. And it might be interesting for you to petition the school for courses specifically on black history, or feminism. They always respond more strongly when they know there's student interest and enthusiasm for a proposed course."

He's right. He's reasonable and he's right. Lulu knows this. She's the one yelling at him in his classroom. It's just—it's so—it's so frustrating! It's so frustrating. To have to be thankful that she is being included, that she is being listened to, that she's being encouraged. To be grateful that someone cares enough to give women a week. To have to be the one who speaks up, who takes time, who goes to a dean's office and lobbies about her *feelings*. Boys never have to do that.

But then, boys don't have to do so many things.

Lulu steals a glance at Kiley, but Kiley isn't looking at her. Probably she's thinking: *White girls don't have to do so many things.*

She's not wrong.

"Lulu's taken a renewed interest in women's issues," Doug says, and his voice is just loud enough that everyone can certainly hear him, but not so loud that it sounds like he's making a point of it or anything.

"And I applaud that," Mr. Winters says.

Lulu knows he didn't have to take that at face value, to pretend that Doug wasn't implying *Lulu's a lesbo now.* He saw the pictures. He gets the joke.

But he decided to pretend he didn't, because he's woke, sure, Mr. Winters, and he's patient, and probably he's trying, but he's still a man. Deep down inside, he's still a boy, and his instinct is always to belong with them, to think their jokes are funny. To think their jokes are just jokes.

Lulu catches up with Kiley after class. "Thanks," she says. "For having my back in there. Made me feel less crazy for speaking up."

"You're welcome. But it wasn't about you," Kiley says. "Sometimes things aren't, you know."

CHAPTER FORTY-ONE

● ● ● ○

IF SHE'S GOING to be a full-time feminist crusader now, there's someone she should be talking to, so that night Lulu calls Naomi. She can't remember the last time she called anyone—much less her sister. For advice.

The world really has been turned upside down.

She doesn't know how to start telling the story, though. Instead, she says, "Naomi, you've read the book I got Cass for Christmas, right?"

"Yeah, a couple of years ago," Naomi says. "When I thought I might be a lit major freshman year, I took a course on fairy tales. Did she not like it or something?"

"No," Lulu says. "She liked it."

"What about it, then? Just curious?"

"Cass said something about it. About how many stories we tell about women getting murdered."

"Oh, yeah, the SVU thing."

"*Law & Order?*"

"A whole television show about violence against women. And you know, those serial killer podcasts and stuff? People are obsessed with hearing about ways women die."

"Yeah."

"You okay, Lulu?"

"Something happened. No one died. I don't want to talk about it."

"Okay." There's a pause. Then Naomi asks, "You want me to talk to you instead?"

"Sure."

So Naomi does. She tells Lulu about her classes, and how she thinks maybe a grad student in one of her upper-level seminars is flirting with her. She tells Lulu about how the other night she and her friends went out to a bar and played pool. She tells Lulu a bunch of sort of funny, sort of boring stories, until Lulu's lulled her brain into quiet, until, when there's a pause in the conversation, Lulu says, "The thing is that it turned out that Ryan was spying on us."

"I'm sorry," Naomi says. "But what? And who? And what the fuck?"

Lulu tells her the whole story.

After she's explained, Naomi says, "I'm so sorry, Lu."

"What are you sorry for? You didn't do it."

"Of course I didn't do it. I just didn't want anything like this to happen to you."

"Well, yeah. But it did."

"Have you talked to someone? A guidance counselor or anyone?"

"No."

"Oh Lu. I wish you would."

"Well, I don't want to."

Naomi sighs. There's a long silence. "I don't want to tell you what to do," she says. "I know that usually doesn't work. But I just—I don't want this to be your secret either. I don't want you to live with this alone."

"I don't, though," Lulu says. "You know. That's why I called you. Bea knows. Cass—"

Cass knows. Even if they never speak again, they'll have this between them. They're the only people who know this specific betrayal, inside and out.

"Still," Naomi says. "It's different. But it's up to you. As long as you know it's an option." And then, "God, no wonder Cass has been thinking about *Bluebeard*."

"We didn't *die*," Lulu says. She doesn't understand why she has to keep explaining this.

"No, of course not. But it's—the things men do to women. The ways they think they get to be in charge of you. The way it never seems to stop."

Those retellings too, which is what Cass was talking about: The way that, even when the physical violence stops, their stories get repeated, and reimagined. Again, and again, and again.

Naomi continues, "I will say, in that class, one of the things we talked about was how people read that story like it's a warning to women—to trust your intuition and not marry creeps, or, if you do marry a creep, not to be curious about him. To leave things be. Which weirded me out, because he's the villain. Whatever else happens in the story, he dies at the end."

"That's what I said! That's what I'm saying."

"It can be about both things, though, is what I thought was interesting. This idea that it's a story about how women die, but it's also a story about how women survive."

Lulu's dad's favorite joke is to short-circuit their Passover seders. A seder is supposed to be a long ritual dinner, hours and hours devoted to telling a story everyone already knows. His parents, observant immigrants, used to make him sit through all of it. Lulu's whole life, he's sat everyone down at the table and said, "You know how this one goes, right? They tried to kill us; they couldn't; let's eat!" and tucked right into his matzoh ball soup.

Bea's parents left the Philippines decades ago, but their siblings are still there; they don't work in politics, but her grandparents used to. She doesn't talk about it much, but she mentions, every now and again, how violent things are over there, under the new president. How glad she is that part of her family is here, and how impossible it is not to worry about the rest of them, who are still there.

If you're telling the story, it means you're still alive. If you're telling the story, it means you're still haunted by it too.

"Survival is a privilege," Naomi says. "And it is also kind of a burden."

"I don't want it. Either of it. Any of it."

"What do you want instead?"

Lulu doesn't have an answer for that.

After a while, Naomi says, "Thank you for telling me."

"You're . . . welcome?"

"I know you want to handle it on your own. So I appreciate that you chose to let me help. Or try to."

Lulu doesn't know what to say to that. She doesn't think of herself as being particularly tough, or self-sufficient. She doesn't think of herself as being someone who doesn't want help. Only someone who's trying desperately not to.

"I love you, little sister," Naomi says.

Lulu's thought so many times that being hard would break her, that she would crack in half under the pressure. But somehow it's Naomi's tenderness that does it, that finally makes her feel like she's suddenly, totally come undone.

Lulu goes and sits on one of the stone benches in the grove of fruit trees in the backyard. It's dark out and it has been basically since she got home from school. The dark here isn't romantic the way it was at The Hotel; she can see the neighbors' lights, and the ones from her house up the hill. She can hear city noises and see the buzzy ambient hum of urban fluorescence brightening the world around her, making all of it seem mundane and comprehensible. She closes her eyes and it presses harder against her, demanding her attention, insisting on being let in.

"No," Lulu whispers. Her eyes were squeezed shut but at the sound of her own voice against the night they fly open. "No," she says again. "No!" she yells. "No no no no no no no no!" By now she's howling. "NO!" She screams. "NO! I WON'T! YOU CAN'T MAKE ME!"

She doesn't know what she's talking about, or even who she thinks she's yelling at. Definitely not Naomi or Ryan. God, maybe. Whoever, whatever made a universe like this one.

She's yelling at herself, for not being able to keep Ryan from hurting her, and the women who raised him, who raised him like this. The men who raised him, who raised him like this. His great-great-grandfather and all of his money. His great-great-grandfather and his money and his property and the woman he saw on the screen and then plucked off of it to keep for himself. Avery wanted what Ryan wanted: to own a woman's body. To control her any way he could.

"No," she says again, and this time it comes out in a raw, hurt whisper. "No. No. No."

But the world doesn't care what Lulu has to say about it—whether she hates it. If it seems like it's trying to kill her. *Good,* it's probably thinking. *You weren't tough enough anyway, then.*

Lulu knows what she wants, now: to look the indifferent universe in the eye, defiant, and triumphant and recklessly, impossibly, alive.

Despite it. Despite everything.

Lulu looks around at the orange grove, her little tiny oasis of quiet in the big busy noisy city night. She remembers standing here with Owen, plucking fruit from the trees, letting their heaviness tug them off the branch and into her open palms. That was when she first started to understand that she was really, really going to lose him. That was the day after she met Cass for the first time. That was a different life, she thinks, and yet here she is again, her bare feet in the same earth.

The world is indifferent to her, and that means she can do whatever she wants as long as she's in it.

"Fuck *you*," Lulu says to the night. She wipes her eyes on the sleeve of her sweater. She turns and goes inside.

CHAPTER FORTY-TWO

• • • •

BEA DRESSES LULU up for the party. That's the condition: Lulu will go with her, but only if Bea is responsible for her outfit, and for driving, and for making Lulu feel like less of an ass for being there.

"Act like everything's normal, right?" Bea said when she proposed it. "And, like, fuck anyone who wants to mess with you."

"Didn't you say I shouldn't do things I didn't want to do?" Lulu replied.

"Ugh," Bea said. "Technically, I did."

But Lulu doesn't want to be home alone, so she lets Bea put her in one of her dresses—something loose and flowy, which turns perilously tight and short on Lulu's curves—and get her in the car. She's actually almost looking forward to it by the time they arrive. Whatever it is when she gets there, at least she'll know. It can't be as bad as she's imagining. Right?

Even thinking that was asking for trouble, she realizes, when she walks into Jules's house and the first person she sees is Sloane.

"Um," Bea says.

Jules introduced them. Jules introduced them at that party in August. He's how Sloane came into her life in the first place, so Lulu should have known. She shouldn't have been surprised, but Lulu's been so distracted that she forgot to worry about this single particular thing, so of course this is the thing that's happening. Sloane Mori is sitting on a couch next to Patrick, drinking what looks like a rum and Coke.

She sees Lulu and she smiles and then she looks away, and Lulu has no idea how to respond. She knows what she wants to do, though, which is what she does: walks into the den where they're hanging out, sits down in one of the chairs, and pours herself a drink. She swallows it in two gulps and makes herself another.

"Hey-o, Shapiro," Patrick says. "What is *up*."

"Feel you, girl," Sloane says. "That's exactly the mood. Also. Um. Hey."

They haven't seen each other since That Whole Thing happened. They haven't spoken since they came downstairs at the party where they met, and one of the boys said, "Rude of you to let the internet watch, but not the people who are actually here."

For an infinite, split-second moment, Lulu didn't know what he meant; then he held up his phone, and she did. She fumbled her phone out of her pocket and deleted the video, and even then, fingers shaking, nausea roiling through her, she knew, instinctively, that she was already way too fucking late.

"Hey," Lulu says to Sloane now.

Bea comes and balances herself on the arm of Lulu's chair. She nudges Lulu with an elbow. "Bartender," she says. "Make me one?"

"Sure," Lulu says.

She busies herself pouring while Bea introduces herself to Sloane, as if she doesn't know who she is. Rich shows up and distracts Bea; Jules and Cristina Vega and Faye Samson arrive with him, and then there's more people to say hi to and drinks to pour and sip and distractions, and somehow Lulu is at a party, a party with *Sloane*, and it's—fine, she thinks. Somehow it seems like everything is actually kind of almost fine.

Bea disappears with Rich, which was the actual point of them coming to the party. Lulu stays in the den, mostly. She feels like a prey animal or a spy, keeping her eyes on the door so that no more surprises sneak up on her tonight.

There's only one bathroom down there, though, and someone has been in it for a *while*. Lulu really has to pee. The second-floor bathroom is just at the top of the stairs—safe enough, she figures, and it is. She pees, washes her hands, redoes her topknot, wishes she could touch up her eye makeup, which has gotten a little too smudgy for her taste.

Sloane is standing outside the door when she opens it.

"Sorry," Sloane says. Her facade of calm has fallen slightly with the wash of drunkenness. She's twisting her hands together, biting the inside of her lip. Lulu feels a swell of the thing she felt over the summer, the ease of desire, of sheer, sharp *want*.

And then she immediately feels disloyal to Cass, which is— No. She pushes the thought away. Cass still hasn't texted her back. Lulu assumes this means they're over.

Sloane continues. "I didn't mean to ambush you. I just wanted to talk, and I didn't want to do it in front of everyone."

Lulu looks around. The second floor is open plan, mostly—a living room that unfolds into the kitchen; the bedrooms are all on the third floor. There's no one around to hear them, but still she feels terribly exposed.

"Do we need to?" she asks, trying to keep it light.

"I just—I saw the thing," Sloane says. "That Ryan made. And I heard a rumor that you weren't, like, totally down with it."

"I guess," Lulu says.

"I mostly wanted to say: That fucking sucks," Sloane says. "I knew him growing up, you know. And he—"

Lulu's had enough of watching girls take responsibility for Ryan. "He's not your fault," she says.

"Thank god." Sloane laughs, and then turns to go.

"I'm sorry," Lulu says.

"What?"

"About the summer. About the Flash," Lulu says. "I'm sorry."

Sloane shrugs. "Nothing people didn't already know about me," she says. "And I know you didn't do it on purpose."

"Do you?"

Sloane smiles. "I was there. I know what happened. Plus, you had a boyfriend."

"I did."

"He's not here tonight."

"Yeah."

"I heard you guys broke up." Sloane waits for Lulu to respond, and when she doesn't, she continues. "I sort of figured it would be temporary. I don't know why. I just thought it might blow over, after."

"If you heard about the pictures, you must have heard the rumors about me and Cass." Lulu hasn't said her name much lately. It makes her seem more real, somehow, not just the memory of her, indistinct, but her name like currency, something anyone can use to conjure her.

"I guess I did," Sloane says.

"And Owen has a new girlfriend," Lulu adds. Now that she's got a knife in her own side, may as well twist it a little.

"And you and Cass?"

Lulu shakes her head.

Sloane steps in closer to her. "Do you want me to kiss you?" she asks.

Lulu feels the same sting of disloyalty, the idea that this is wrong, that it will hurt Cass. But Cass is the one who stopped speaking to her. *May as well*, she thinks. And Sloane is still so beautiful. "I do."

Sloane kisses her in the hallway. She puts her hands on Lulu's waist, under her shirt, and now that Lulu isn't so overwhelmed by the fact that it's happening, that she's kissing a girl for real, it's easier to notice details: that Sloane's hands are bigger than Cass's were, but smaller than Owen's, and softer, that instead of being slick with summer like last time, she's cool and dry. Sloane touches Lulu easily, certainly, like she's trying to tell Lulu something, to convince her that she knows what she's doing.

Sloane is the one who pulls away after a while, takes Lulu's hand, and leads her silently up to one of the guest bedrooms. Lulu thinks about last time this happened, and all the things she didn't know, didn't know how to do. Now she could be in charge, if she wanted to. She could ask for the things she wants.

It feels good, though, to give in. To follow Sloane, to lie down on the bed, to kiss until her mouth is numb. Lulu takes Sloane's shirt off; she surrounds herself with the distraction of someone else's skin. She loses herself to the moment and lets it go further than it should. Usually she tries to be careful about things—ask questions about where someone's been, what they're doing, should we get a condom or whatever. But tonight Lulu can't find a way to care, and before she knows it, she's grinding mindlessly into the pressure of Sloane's palm. She's just a body now, something seeking satisfaction and release. No thoughts. No ideas. Just the distance she has to cross between where she is, and where she wants to be.

The thing is, she can't get there tonight.

Lulu's body has always been easy for her, this one way: She

doesn't usually need to be in any particular headspace to come. It's not an emotional experience for her, the way it seems like it might be for some girls. It's just a matter of friction and rhythm, someone who's willing to be a little bit patient. She's been patient for enough boys to know that she doesn't actually take all that long.

Tonight, though, she seems to have climbed to the top of some plateau. Everything Sloane does feels good but she stays restless, in her own skin, unable to find a build to anything, a way to open the door to true mindless abandon.

"You don't have to," she says at some point.

"Are you not going to?" Sloane says. "Because if you aren't, I'll stop, but I don't mind. I know sometimes—"

"I don't think," Lulu says, and shyness flashes through her, which is so ridiculous, when Sloane has two fingers hooked inside of her. "Um. I don't think I can right now. I'm sorry. Can we—I might need a sec to—"

"Don't be sorry," Sloane says. She kisses Lulu once, quick, and rolls off of her. Another thing Lulu is still trying to get used to, with girls. Owen would have been nudging his dick against her, saying "Can I still?" and she would have said yes. It's not like she would have minded. She liked having sex with him, whether or not it was, like, going anywhere for her.

It's just weird to have sex where someone getting her off is a much bigger part of the point.

"This isn't about feelings," Lulu says. "I'm just drunk."

"Okay."

"I'm not—" Lulu says, and then stops, because she's being defensive, and that's never a good look.

"Even if you were," Sloane says, "it would be okay, you know. Breakups aren't rational. Feelings aren't rational. It takes a while for your body to get over someone, sometimes. Even when your mind is like, *I'm ready to be ready,* you know?"

"That's not what's going on."

"What is?"

Lulu doesn't say anything.

"I won't tell."

Lulu is teetering on the edge between the spin of being drunk and the toxic, pinching flush of her hangover. She wants a glass of water. She sits up and pulls her dress on, realizes her bra is still on the floor somewhere. She puts her head between her knees.

Sloane puts a hand on her back.

That's what does it. Lulu says the words into the curl of her body, but Sloane seems to hear them. Lulu tells her the story. She tells her what Ryan did. All of it. The pictures. And the tape.

"Yeah," Sloane says when she's finished. "That's—Jesus. He's a nightmare. But I can't say I'm surprised."

"What, because I deserved it?"

"No. Fuck. Has anyone said that to you? That this was your fault?"

No one but Lulu herself. She shakes her head.

"You know this isn't the first time he's done something like this, right?"

"What?"

"Do you know Emma Kushner?"

"No."

"She's our year at Sanderson. I think she went to the Center. I know her because—never mind. It doesn't matter. It's just that they dated for a little while when we were freshmen, and, you know, she sent him some pictures. He said he deleted them after they broke up, but it turned out he didn't. Instead he was selling them to dudes he knew. Twenty dollars per image, fifty for the set. Emma's dad went to Ryan's dad and Ryan's dad said Emma was a slut, and Ryan had good entrepreneurial instincts."

Lulu remembers sitting next to Cass on the couch in her backyard, huddled next to her, pretending it was for warmth. Watching Connie Wilmott on screen as she opened a door and saw all of the bodies that had come before hers. How she knew, in that moment, that she was going to be next.

Lulu can't save herself or Cass, but what if she could spare whoever Ryan falls in love with next.

"Now I'm sorry," Sloane says. "If I'd known you were hanging out with him, I would have warned you. Emma bought the pictures back from all the guys who had them and got one of them kicked out of school for other stuff—he was selling amphetamines to freshmen on campus like some kind of criminal idiot—so people don't talk about it, and I don't like to spread the story. But I wish more people knew about Ryan."

"Me too," Lulu says. "Me fucking too."

CHAPTER FORTY-THREE

• • • •

JUST TYPING CASS'S name into the *to* field of a text makes Lulu feel like she needs to lie down and take a nap. They almost always messaged each other on Flash, so at least she doesn't have to have the app reminding her how long it's been since they spoke. Still, though, her pulse picks up with each letter she types. C-A-S-S. Lulu has never made a fool of herself for anyone before, not on purpose, anyway. She's always figured out how to do the flattering thing.

Fuck flattering, she thinks, and writes:

> You can ignore this or tell me to shut up,
> but I just wanted you to know that I saw
> Ryan after we talked, and he gave me a
> hard drive with some, um, "extra footage"
> on it. It's been sitting on my desk and I
> haven't known what to do with it, but I'm
> going to destroy it. I thought you might
> want to do that with me?

She adds four hammer emojis for effect.

Lulu has no idea if hammers will actually be involved. She

just wants to be clear she isn't trying to get Cass to, like, forget everything and start over. She's just trying to facilitate a little bit of healing revenge and stuff-smashing. She wants to erase as much of Ryan from their lives as she can.

That sounds kind of ideal, actually, Cass writes back. Bonfire at mine?

You don't think that's a recipe for like . . .

an explosion?

You were being literal about
the hammers?

Could be cathartic

Hang on, I'm googling.

Lulu is sitting in front of her laptop, but she figures she'll let Cass run the search.

Instead, while she waits, she does something she hasn't done in a long time: She googles herself. Owen's dad's fan sites come up first, the ones that were archiving her Flash. She wonders if they've figured out that she and Owen broke up, and if so, if they've stopped following her. She wonders if they're on Kiley now instead, imagining her life as voraciously and inaccurately as they pictured Lulu's.

She's surprised to find, though, that a little bit farther down in the results, there are a couple of blog posts people have written about her. Maybe one of them is Naomi's friend.

She can't tell about that, but Lulu is mentioned in some feminist website's essay about the Selfie Generation and, like, what does it *mean* that kids these days are documenting their lives? The essay mentions the Sloane video, of course, a "radical, virtual, viral coming out that announced her sexuality not with language or labels but by enacting it on a very public stage." It praises her for her courage.

Then there are people's responses to the essay, which argue Lulu's actions and intentions, what other people think she meant and did with her Flash in general and that Flash in particular. They were all written before Ryan's pictures came out; Lulu wonders what they would have thought of her if they had had that evidence at their disposal. They'd probably all still be wrong.

No one knows what it's like inside of her. It's not their fault, and it's not hers either.

It's strange to think of herself as the subject of feminist critique and debate, the same way the women she's been hearing and reading about for months now are—to think of herself as a woman, much less a woman artist. Lulu imagines responding to all of these essays: "Thank you so much for your consideration, but I was just drunk and dumb and horny, tbh." How hilariously disappointed they'd all be.

You know, you might be right about the hammers, Cass texts her. Weirdly, I think analog is our best bet in this case.

Let me know when you're ready, Lulu says.

Can't tomorrow, Cass says. What about Wednesday night?

CHAPTER FORTY-FOUR

• • • •

WHEN CASS OPENS her door, Lulu holds the hard drive out between them like an offering, or a shield. "I brought it," she says.

Cass smiles briefly. "Good."

"Are your parents or anyone home?" Lulu asks as they make their way through the house. It's 4:30 p.m. and starting to get dark already. She's ready for spring, but it's still a few months off.

"No."

"That's nice."

"Mmmm."

Cass's backyard looks bigger without all of the stuff that was in it last time she was here, the couches and projector and screen, and all of those boys. She leads Lulu to a corner where apparently at some point someone tried to build a fire pit; now there's just grass-free dirt and a circle of rocks. Cass has already laid down a tarp; she has a toolbox off to one side.

"So do we just go at it?"

"Hang on a sec."

Cass sits on the tarp and opens the toolbox, pulls out a screwdriver. After a moment, Lulu comes to sit with her.

There's a cover on top of the drive that she's trying to pry off, working on unscrewing the screws. She does the first three before Lulu stops her.

"Can I do one?"

"If you want to."

"I do," Lulu says. "I just. I want to feel it come apart."

Cass nods. She hands Lulu the screwdriver and the drive. "It's sort of more prying than unscrewing."

"Cool," Lulu says. She tries to do what Cass did. It takes her a while too, but the screw pops loose, and there it is: the vulnerable inside of the thing. An object she can attack and destroy.

"Hah!" she says.

"Very nice."

Cass is smiling indulgently and Lulu looks up at her and thinks, *I want to kiss you*. It reminds her of thinking it and trying to swallow it all those times before; it makes her realize how silly she was to imagine that this was something she could ignore, or deny. She's never not going to want to kiss Cass when Cass is around. There's no *just friends* about this.

But she did not come over here to make that point.

"There are discs inside," Cass is saying. "See? Those are the things we want to ruin. That's where the data is stored."

They're so small and ordinary looking. For a second, something in Lulu wavers. What did those little pieces of metal ever do to her? What does she really think she'll accomplish by putting them in pieces? The world will still be fucked and Cass will still be mostly not speaking to her. Ryan will still be able to do this whole thing to someone else again.

But then she looks at Cass and remembers that there are other things in the world than pure justice, or vengeance. There's her, and there's Cass. There's this one small thing they can do to make themselves feel safe.

The first fall of the hammer is tricky: the aim and balance, making sure the blow lands exactly where she intends to place it. Soon, though, the tool is light in her hands. Her body knows how to do this, when she lets it: to smash up ugliness, to erase the evidence of how much she gave away, and how that still wasn't enough, so that even more had to be taken from her. It's another way of saying *no*, and Lulu says it until she aches all through her palms and fingers, in the muscle of her shoulders and her bones.

When they're done, Cass gathers the corners of the tarp and ties them together; she puts the whole bundle in a trash bag, and the bag in the can, out on the street, to be collected in the morning. "Well," she says. "So."

"Yeah," Lulu says. "Okay."

"Thanks for coming over," Cass says. "I'm glad we got to do that."

"Me too."

"What are you going to do now?"

Lulu shrugs. "Go home," she says. "My homework, I guess."

"Oh, no, I meant . . ." Cass gestures at the evening around them with one hand, and laughs. "In general."

"I don't know."

"Me neither."

For a bare moment, they smile at each other.

"I did delete my Flash account," Lulu admits

"I did too."

"Yeah. I, um, I realized I was tired of contributing content to the Riggs family."

Cass grimaces. "Roman Junior! Jesus. He is, believe it or not, way worse than Ryan."

"No, I believe that."

"Or I guess actually he's more obviously a creep? Maybe that's better. Because I always knew to stay away."

"Here's some important work for the young women of the world to be doing—deciding which kind of asshole is the less-terrible kind."

"You are a feminist now, Lu."

"Books got to my head, I guess."

"All that reading." Cass reaches out thoughtlessly to ruffle Lulu's hair.

Lulu holds perfectly still, hoping. Cass pulls her hand back.

"Anyway," Cass says. "It sucks that Ryan got to ruin Flash for you. I mean, not that it's like a super-tragic loss or anything, but you were so—I don't know. You were good at it. Is that a weird thing to say? I felt like you cared about it. Like it was so part of who you were."

"That's who I was? That's sad."

Cass rolls her eyes. "You know that's not what I meant."

Lulu tilts her head up to the sky. It's pale, undifferentiated blue above her, going dingy and dim with gray at one edge as the sun fades behind the hills. "I don't know that," she says, at last. "I don't know how you think about me. Especially since we—whatever. Broke up."

"Did we?"

"The last time we talked felt pretty final."

Cass sighs. "I didn't mean for it to be that way. Necessarily."

"What did you mean for it to be like?"

Cass twists her mouth into a complicated shape. "I mean, it wasn't even personal. I didn't break up with you; I broke up with everyone, basically. I was just so angry and sad. I just didn't have the energy for anything. I couldn't make any decisions. I couldn't handle anyone else's feelings. I could barely fucking handle my own."

Lulu tries to imagine what it's like to have such a certain sense of yourself that you can walk away from other people's feelings: to not always be thinking about them, or imagining them, or trying to shape yourself around the fact of them. That's what she meant to say to Bea, when B asked her about staying on Flash. It's Lulu's way of asking someone else to answer a question she can't seem to stop asking: *Am I doing it right? Am I doing it right? Am I still doing okay?*

"Talk about selfish," Cass is saying. "I was mad at you, but I was also—it was easier to be mad at you than at Ryan. To make sure to be mad at you so I didn't have to feel anything else. After, it was like I wasn't even there. Like my skin was a shell, and I was a ghost floating inside of it. Like I was nothing."

She swipes the back of one hand against her cheek where a tear was starting to fall. "Which, like, I didn't want to—nothing really changed, you know? They're just pictures. He didn't really take anything important, even. Not in the way that, you know, he could have. This video. Or something else." Cass might be crying, but Lulu doesn't know, because her face is tilted to the ground.

Lulu doesn't touch her. "Do you want," she starts. "We could go inside and talk a little bit more."

Cass keeps looking down, but she reaches out a hand to Lulu. Lulu takes it, and lets Cass guide her inside.

CHAPTER FORTY-FIVE

• • • •

THE LAST TIME Lulu goes to The Hotel, it's the middle of January. She wears the same boots she had on that first night, but everything else is different. It's day, for one thing, an ordinary blue-and-white Saturday, and it rained yesterday, so the hillside she and Cass drive up is lush with new green and small, open flowers. Even the thick, pale skins of desert plants and cacti are washed clean and dustless. The gate stands open and ready for them.

The first time Lulu came to The Hotel, the only person who'd ever betrayed her was herself. And so she trusted everyone else.

Cass parks out in front, straight on in one of the spots, like she's always been civilized here. Ryan comes out of the lobby to meet them. He looks bristly and wary and uncertain in a way that makes Lulu want to make sure she doesn't look at him too long, in case she starts to hallucinate tenderness underneath it. She's not here to imagine anything about Ryan. She's just here to make sure Cass survives the reality of him.

There's a moment just before they open the car doors. "You ready?" Lulu asks Cass.

Cass looks at her softly. "Yeah," she says.

"You sure you don't want me to come—"

"I've got this."

Cass gets out of the car.

Lulu stays where she is. She looks down at the last moment, so she doesn't have to see Cass and Ryan navigate greeting each other. So what if he took the option from her—she's still decent enough to feel the instinct that he deserves privacy. She stares at her hands for long quiet minutes. The habit of not taking out her phone at The Hotel is so deeply ingrained.

When she looks up again, Cass and Ryan have their backs to her. They're walking over to the pool. Lulu waits for them to disappear from view before she eases her door open and steps out of the car.

The front door of The Hotel is still unlocked. Of course it is. Ryan is so used to believing that he's invulnerable.

The lobby is set up like an actual lobby now: a small lounge with couches and plush chairs, a coffee table, a bunch of art magazines; a front desk with flowers on it, though the space isn't supposed to open for another handful of weeks. The elevator is probably working by now, but Lulu takes the stairs out of habit.

She's glad it looks so normal. The Hotel she wants to revisit doesn't exist anymore, for anyone. In Ryan's room, a laptop is sitting on the desk, its screen black with sleep. It's hard not to look at it and see the evidence of how Ryan thought he was master of this space: that he could know everything that happened in it. But that's not what happened—that's not what's happening now.

He saw things, but he couldn't control them. He couldn't stop her and Cass from finding each other, or from falling into each other. And he can't stop them now from saying this last goodbye and leaving, and never, ever coming back.

Lulu goes downstairs, out the front door. She's trying to be quiet, but as soon as she walks outside and hears Ryan's voice she knows he's not listening for anything. He and Cass are over by the pool, but in the silence of the afternoon his words echo off the concrete, bouncing right to her.

"What was I supposed to do, Cass?" he's saying. "I was just trying to show you what it was like on the outside. What it looked like looking in on you, like some *stranger*. I didn't want to hurt you. I really didn't."

"Well, you did." Cass's voice is fluorescent with pain.

Ryan says something indistinct.

Lulu walks closer.

". . . I wanted you to see that you were hurting *me*," Ryan is saying, when she can hear him clearly again. "I didn't know how else to make you see that, Cass. You just brought her here. You didn't even ask! And then it was like I didn't matter anymore. Like *we*, what we *were*—"

"Nothing changed!" Cass says. "You were still my best friend. I told you that, Ryan."

"We weren't just friends. You know we weren't."

"Maybe that's how you felt about it," she says. "But for me, we were. I'm sorry if that wasn't enough for you. I'm sorry if I couldn't be what you thought I'd be for you, or what you wanted, but—Ryan. It wasn't ever going to happen between us like that."

"You don't know that."

"I don't know what I want?"

"You don't know the future," Ryan says. He sounds petulant, childish. "You don't *know*."

"I'm gay, Ry," Cass says. "That doesn't have anything to do with you or Lulu. It's not gonna change. It's just a fact."

"You were gay when I met you," Ryan says. "That didn't used to stop you from loving me."

"Nothing stopped me from loving you except you," Cass says. "What did you think? That I would see it and feel sorry for you? That I would suddenly realize your dick was the magic one for me? And that if I did, I would forgive you for exposing me like that?"

"I don't know what I was thinking." Ryan is talking softly now, low and coaxing, but Lulu can still hear him, which means she's gotten too close. She knows this. She should go back to the car. This is private. This isn't hers to hear.

But she can't make herself move. Lulu almost—*almost*—feels bad for him. He sounds so totally, helplessly lost. She's felt that kind of lost. She knows what it is to wonder if you know how to love anyone, and if anyone else wants to love you.

That doesn't mean it gives him license to hurt her, though. Or to hurt Cass.

She pulls out her phone, pulls up the voice notes app, and hits RECORD.

"I can't explain it," Ryan is saying. "It just felt like—like you'd forced me into a corner. It was the only thing I could do. I was losing you. I was desperate. I was desperate to keep you, Cass."

"To trap me, you mean. To keep a record of me, whether I wanted to be recorded or not."

"It was our project," Ryan says. "We made it up together. We talked and talked. We had so many ideas. And then *she* came along and it was *let's just chill, Ry, we can do other stuff every now and again, are these photos really going to be that great anyway.* So yeah, I figured out a way to get content. Because I don't abandon shit that matters to me."

"Don't say 'get content' like that. You didn't *get* content. You took it. You took me and turned me into content."

This is it. This is it this is it this is it. Lulu's hands are shaking. This is the clearest admission of guilt she'll ever get from him.

This is how she reminds him that other people can see him too.

"Sure," Ryan says. "It wasn't, like, ethical. I should have told you about the cameras, especially in the rooms. I should have told you about the pictures before I showed them. But really, Cass, look at who you're dating. You think she's not gonna do something like this to you, someday? You think Lulu Shapiro is going to keep your secrets?"

"Don't talk about her. This isn't about her."

"You're fucking stupid to trust her. She's not even interesting, Cass. She's not who you think she is."

"I don't forgive you," Cass says. "I never will."

Lulu's thumb presses down once, hard, on the END RECORD button.

They look up when she comes through the pool gate. They're both crying, Cass quietly and Ryan miserably, determinedly, like even still he needs them both to *see*, to *know*, to witness him. Like they've done something to him. Like any of this is either of their faults.

"Go *away*," he says.

"Cass," Lulu says quietly. "Are you ready?"

"Yeah," Cass says. "I'm ready."

Ryan's temper flares. "Do you want to make me your enemy?" he asks. "Do you really think that's smart?"

"I don't care if it's smart or not," Cass says. "*Fuck* you, Ryan."

"You were always our enemy," Lulu says. "I guess I should say thank you for making sure we'd never forget it."

CHAPTER FORTY-SIX

• • • •

LULU DRIVES THEM home. She doesn't put on her GPS or ask Cass for directions. She just drives: down the hill, into the hum of the city, through sleepy weekend traffic. Cass stares blankly out the passenger-side window.

Lulu feels like a kid again, like she's in her dad's car on her way to the airport on the first day of vacation. Like the rest of the world is still cogging its way along, and she alone has been cut free—suspended, dangling. Suddenly loose and light.

She has power now. Not much—not enough—not anything that will make any big, real difference in the world. She can't make Ryan take back what he did. But she can make it harder for him to do it to another girl.

She knows what she wants to do. For herself. For everyone else.

Lulu drives them to her house, where Cass picked her up just a few hours ago. It feels like it's been days. She turns the car off but can't make herself get out.

"You can come in, if you want to," she says.

Silence.

"Not like—I'm not trying to start anything," she clarifies. "Like, if you want to drink a glass of water before you head back. Take a nap. I won't even walk you up to my room."

Cass says, "I should probably go. I'm kind of exhausted."

Lulu remembers the last time Cass came over to see her, at her mom's apartment, the first day after they'd kissed. What happened; what it meant to her. To both of them. That first night at Cass's they'd opened a door together; at Lulu's the next day it was like they stepped through it and into the same room. *Oh*, Lulu remembers thinking, *this is* happening.

She can't imagine how terrifying it must be to have something like Ryan happen to you: to know that no matter what you do or say, someone is going to take the presence of your body in the world as an invitation to do what he wants with it, and then blame you if you tell him you don't like it. At least when he did it to Lulu, he didn't pretend it was because he loved her.

"Okay," Lulu says.

Cass yawns then, a huge, face-cracking thing that moves through her whole body. "Okay," she says. "Maybe actually I could come lie down for a minute. Will I be able to find your room without you?"

Lulu laughs. "This isn't Patrick's batshit maze mansion," she says. "Through the front door, up the stairs, second door on your left. You can put whatever's on the bed on the floor."

"I don't even know if I can sleep," Cass says. "I just need to be alone for a minute. Or a lot of minutes."

"As many minutes as you need."

"What are you gonna do?"

"I don't know. Watch TV?"

"You don't want your room?"

I want you to have it, Lulu thinks, and doesn't say. *Just for right now.*

"I'm okay, I promise," she tells Cass.

It's early evening by the time Cass comes downstairs. She sits down next to Lulu on the couch, where Lulu is knee-deep in a *Benton and the Billions* marathon. Lulu mutes the television.

"So I did fall asleep," Cass says. "Whoops."

"You probably needed it."

Cass gives Lulu a side eye. "You sound like my mom."

"You *did*!"

"Speaking of which, she's home tonight, and I promised her I would be too."

"Yeah, yeah. But before you go—I have to show you something."

"I thought you said you weren't trying to start anything."

Lulu has to laugh at that. "Not like that, perv." Then she sobers up. "I just wanted you to know I had it. I won't do anything with it if you don't want me to. And you don't have to make a decision right now, but—"

"Jesus, Lulu, you're making me nervous. Just show me already."

"Whip it out?" Lulu suggests.

"Something like that."

Lulu takes a deep breath as she hands her phone to Cass. "I recorded this at The Hotel earlier," she says. "It's probably not enough to go on, legally or anything. But if we wanted to put it out there, it might hurt Ryan's reputation. Might keep him from thinking he could get away with something like this again."

Cass hits PLAY on the recording. Lulu watches the television screen and listens to Ryan's tiny voice saying "I was desperate to keep you, Cass" and "It wasn't, like, ethical."

Cass hands her back the phone.

"You can delete it," Lulu says. "It's. I mean. You're in it."

"Yeah. I am." Cass sighs. She pulls her feet up onto the couch and rests her cheek against the tops of her knees. "Did you know you were going to do that?" she asks. "Is that why you wanted to come?"

Lulu shakes her head.

"You want to put it online?" Cass asks.

Lulu nods.

"Why?"

"Like I said. I don't want him to try what he did to us with anyone else. Because he has, before."

Cass lets out a shaky breath. "Emma," she says.

"You knew?"

"He told me. He cried, Lulu. He cried when we talked about it, and he told me he would never do anything like it ever again."

"That fucking—"

"You think that's the worst part." Cass's hands are on her knees, and she's staring at them intently. "The real worst part is, I *still* feel bad for him."

Her voice is so soft Lulu can barely hear her.

"I know it's fucked up, and I don't want to forgive him or give him another chance, or—but I still feel bad for him, Lu."

"I don't."

Cass looks away from her. Lulu feels bad for her fierceness. "I never loved him, though," she says. "So it's less complicated for me. I always thought he was kind of a monster. Turns out I was right."

"He's not a monster, though," Cass points out. "It would be different if he were, because monsters can't help being like that. There's nothing they can do about it. Ryan is just a guy. I knew him—this person. He knew me. And he chose to hurt me. Us." Cass closes her eyes. "I don't want revenge, but I want him to *stop*."

Lulu knows she's holding her breath, and can't make her lungs relax.

"You should," Cass says. "You should post it."

"Really?"

"This isn't just about me," Cass says. "You're right that this is about Emma. And other girls, maybe. Whose names we don't know. And then, maybe, whoever's next."

Lulu nods.

Cass nods back.

"Are you sure?" Lulu asks. "I don't want to—"

"I'm giving you permission," Cass says. "But then you have to actually do it, Lulu. I can't do it for you. And you can't just do it because you think it'll be good for me."

"Fuck," Lulu says.

"Fuck," Cass agrees.

Then she leans in and kisses Lulu so swiftly that Lulu finds herself chasing the ghost of Cass's mouth, leaning forward as Cass stands up and straightens the hem of her shirt self-consciously.

"I really have to go," she says.

"Okay," Lulu says.

"Bye, Lulu."

"Bye, Cass."

CHAPTER FORTY-SEVEN

● ● ● ●

LULU TAKES SOME time putting the whole thing together.
She's not going to post it to Flash—who knows what a Riggs-
owned platform will do with this information.

Instead she stitches together a video of her own. She starts
with a series of portraits of women, pictures she takes from
the little thumbnails in her art history textbook. *SUBJECT/
OBJECT* she writes over each of their faces, across their eyes.
Five of them in a row, picked at random: women staring into
their era's versions of the camera. Then five of her own selfies,
same treatment: *SUBJECT/OBJECT.*

Then, black screen, just text:

> HAVE YOU CONSIDERED THAT WHEN I DO
> THIS WHAT I AM LETTING YOU DO IS LOOK
> THROUGH ME

then

> NOT AT ME

then

> MOSTLY.

Lulu blocks the camera and films the sounds of herself getting under the covers, making herself comfortable in bed.

She keeps the camera blocked and makes a video that's just the sound of her own voice saying, "I'm not trying to tell anyone how to live, but I would stay away from Ryan Riggs if I were you." And then, almost as an afterthought, "And any of his hotel properties too. They seem to have a way of seeing you even when it doesn't seem like they're looking."

Then comes the audio from the afternoon.

It ends with one of Ryan's stolen shots: a still from the security footage of Lulu and Cass lying on their backs near the pool, looking up at the sun, talking. Lulu doesn't remember what afternoon that was. Even she has no idea what they're saying.

When it's ready, she registers *RyanRiggsIsaCreep.com* and posts the video there. She reactivates her account and Flashes the link out to her five thousand followers.

Then she sends it to Mr. Winters. The body of the email says:

> *I know it's non-traditional, but please consider this my midterm project.*

When Lulu wakes up in the morning, people are sharing it so ferociously that the hashtag #CreepShotsArentHot is trending on every social media platform she knows about. By mid-afternoon, Curbed has a write-up with the Riggs family's real estate dynasty as the peg; the feminist film blog *Celluloid & Cellulite* does something on Connie Wilmott and the *Bluebeard* legacy around dinnertime. Local news outlets do segments that get picked up by national ones. Everyone loves a juicy story about fucked-up private school kids.

None of it means anything until Lulu gets a text that says:

> hey it's Sloane
>
> Got your number from Jules ran into a
>
> certain someone at a function w my parents
>
> last night and he was in a frothingggg rage

Lulu replies: Ahhhhhhhhhhhhhhhhhh

Sloane says, They're replacing him on the hotel project. They're keeping his name off of anything real estate related going forward. And they're cutting off his trust fund until he's 21.

That's just another few years, Lulu knows. The family is certainly already at work on a redemption narrative for him. They'll do what it takes to clear their name—never mind that they're just teaching Ryan that his bad behavior is tolerable, encouraging him to do it again. She hasn't changed anything, really.

But now Ryan Riggs has felt afraid the way she has. He knows that he's vulnerable. He knows that he's not the only person in the world with feelings, or power, or rage.

This probably won't teach him to be kind. But that's not Lulu's fault. She gave him the opportunity to understand something. She can't be responsible for making sure that he takes it too.

Thanks for telling me about Emma that night, Lulu sends Sloane. And thanks for being so cool about all of this.

What can I say, Sloane responds. I am cool.

Lulu looks at her phone, trying to decide what to say next. When she got back to school after the Sloane Flash came out, Angie Dallow immediately tried to talk her into joining St. Amelia's Out & Proud club, which meets Thursdays after school and organizes a couple of assemblies every year where queer speakers come talk about how it's, like, *so* fine to be gay or whatever.

Lulu brushed Angie off; she didn't understand why being openly bisexual meant she had to start hanging out with a bunch of people she'd never wanted to be friends with before. But lately, the idea of having friends who understood certain things about her without her having to explain them, friends among whom she'd be standard, instead of a deviation—that's started to sound appealing. Lulu will never love anyone more than Bea, but Bea can't be everything to Lulu, the same way Lulu can't be everything to Bea.

I was thinking, Lulu says, what if we started being, like, friends

WILD, Sloane sends back. And then, but also, yeah, I'd be super into that

CHAPTER FORTY-EIGHT

● ● ● ●

OWEN FINDS HER between periods on Monday morning. "Lu," he says.

"Hey." She tries to weave by him, but Owen isn't having it. He texted her three times on Sunday, and called her that night. She had hoped that ignoring him would be enough, but clearly he isn't getting the hint.

"What's up?"

"I need to talk to you."

"Well, I have class right now."

"After school, then. We can go up to the overlook or something. Please, Lu."

She's never been good at saying no to him. "Sure," Lulu says. "After school."

"Okay," Owen says. "Okay good. I'll see you then."

The overlook is at the end of a little dead-end street a few blocks from St. Amelia's, tucked up in the hills: ten feet of flat dirt and scrub before the land drops out from under you. From the cliff's edge you can look out over the campus and have a little secret smoke or drink or whatever.

They used to come up here sometimes when they were together—not to smoke, even, just to kiss and talk. To be alone. It's weird to think now how precious it was to Lulu then, getting any time alone with Owen: how he would try to say hi, ask about her day, and she would already be kissing him, tucking a hand into the waistband of his jeans, reminding herself of all of the parts of him that were hers, just hers.

When she arrives, O is leaning against the trunk of his car, legs crossed at the ankles, staring placidly into the middle distance. Lulu looks at him, and the distance between them feels uncrossable. Not dangerous, exactly, but definitely, like, *there*.

"Hey," she says.

"Hey."

"You wanted to talk?"

"I saw, um. I watched the video you posted. I wanted to check in with you."

"Well, great news: I'm fine."

"Don't be like this, Lulu. I'm asking how you are."

"So ask, then."

"I just did." He looks genuinely confused.

"No you didn't. You said you wanted to check in."

"What's the difference?"

Lulu is tired. "I don't know," she says. "I guess maybe the difference is, I don't want to check in."

"So why did you even come here?"

"You said you needed to talk to me!"

"What were you expecting?"

"What do I ever expect anymore?" Lulu spreads her arms, exasperated. "I don't know. I really don't. My life has been nothing but nightmare circus crazy *things* for weeks now. Maybe you want to tell me you're getting in on the revenge porn game too. I don't know, O."

"Jesus, Lulu, you really think I'd do that? That's honestly—I know Ryan turned out to be a dick, but that's, like, very deeply twisted. To think that about a person who . . ."

"Who what?" But Lulu knows why he can't finish the sentence. It's because he genuinely doesn't know what to call himself—whether to say *who loves you*, or *who loved you*.

She doesn't know which one she wants him to say.

"I wanted to know how you were doing," Owen says. "I'm sorry if that's, like, an imposition now."

Lulu shrugs.

"I wanted to know if I could do something to help."

Lulu shrugs again.

"I wanted—"

Lulu looks at the sky. She says, "I want you to consider: I might not know if I'm okay right now. And this might not be about what you want."

Owen goes quiet again.

Then he asks: "What are you saying? That I'm not a part of your life anymore?"

"I'm saying that you're asking me to make room for you right now. To give you some of my feelings. I didn't ask for that, O. For you to do that."

"You *never* ask," he says. "You have never in your life asked me for help when you wanted it, Lulu. How am I supposed to know the difference?"

Bea said kind of the same thing. Lulu looks down at her shoes. "You're not supposed to be a person I ask for help from anymore," she says.

Owen sighs. "I know that," he says. "I do. But this is an extreme circumstance. This is—god, Lulu, I hate this. I hate Ryan. I hate that someone so small, so *nothing*, could do this to you. He doesn't deserve to get to hurt you. You know?"

"I very much do."

"I wish I could change that."

"I wish you could too."

Lulu wishes she could give Owen more, but she can't. There's nothing there to offer. Her feelings are still too tender, and tangled, and private. He used to be the one person she would turn herself inside out for, but she can't do that anymore. Even though he's sweet to be asking. That doesn't mean she's wrong to refuse.

"Listen," Lulu says. "I don't like anything I'm feeling right now, for the record. The last thing I want is to give Ryan Riggs any power over me or my life. But like, the whole point is, this is not about what I want or deserve. Sometimes people just take things from you. They just take them! Whether you like it or not! Whether you asked for it or not!"

She pauses. Takes a deep breath. "I could pretend I didn't hate it, but that would be a lie. And I think it would be a worse lie, honestly. I think it would be way more fucked up to sit here and pretend that I was fine so that you felt fine, and I felt fine, and tough, and brave, or whatever. There's nothing either of us can do about it right now. I'm fucked up about it. I just am."

Lulu turns away from him, faces out over the canyon, the houses and the roads, the cars, the school, the brush and the trees and lawns below. "I'm! Really! Fucked! Up! About! This!" she yells. She half expects her voice to echo, but it doesn't. There's just the sound of it in the moment, and then the quiet that comes after.

She hears Owen moving behind her, but then he stops. Probably coming to hug her, and then thinking better of it. It feels nice, much nicer than his offer to talk: his holding himself back, and letting her have this series of moments to herself.

She looks at the city underneath her, the sprawl of Los Angeles, the spread of the Valley, already turning burnished gold as the sun starts to fall behind the hills. She looks at all the places she could be, and isn't.

She feels an echo of the thing she felt in the car with Cass, coming down from The Hotel on Saturday—that sense of displacement and of hiddenness. Like even if someone was looking for her, they wouldn't know where to find her. Like at last, she's somewhere private, and secret, and hidden, almost all the way alone.

Lulu watches the sunlight drift across the city. Owen is standing right next to her, but she's still the only person who sees it from exactly that angle. She's the only person who knows exactly how this moment feels inside of her skin.

CHAPTER FORTY-NINE

● ● ● ●

THAT NIGHT, LULU takes a video she doesn't post anywhere. It's simple, kind of dumb, even—just the steam in the air after she's taken a shower, the swirl of shed hair she made on one wall so that it wouldn't clog the drain. In the morning she takes another one: the rumple of her sheets and the impression her head made on the pillow.

At school she takes footage of her desk at the end of Spanish, and her plate after she's finished with lunch. She doesn't know what she's doing with any of it yet, exactly, only that she likes recording what she sees, reminding herself that only she's seeing it. She likes making a picture that's specifically about herself, but doesn't include her body in the frame.

CHAPTER FIFTY

● ● ● ●

IT TAKES A few days, but eventually Lulu starts sending the videos she's taking to Cass: her clothes laid on the floor in the morning before school; a stack of her books with their pages marked for studying; a shot of an open book that's near-neon with her highlighters and her notes.

All day long Cass doesn't say anything. In the evening, just: So this is what you're doing now, huh.

I think it's a project, Lulu says. A proper Art Project. Mine, this time. Not trying to show the world what she thinks it wants to see from her, but showing it what she sees, instead.

Cass doesn't ask her to stop, so she keeps sending them, day after day after day.

A week later, she asks, Do you know why you're doing it yet?

I have some ideas, Lulu says. Then, daring: Want to get coffee and hear about them?

I can do that, Cass says. This weekend?

"We don't actually have to talk about them," Lulu says as soon as Cass sits down.

"I haven't even said anything yet."

"Sorry." Lulu ducks her head. "I'm just. I think I'm really nervous?"

"What, am I suddenly going to decide I don't like you?"

"I don't know!"

Cass gives Lulu an assessing look.

"Don't do that!"

"I mean. It's not why I came."

"I'm glad to hear it."

Someone at the counter calls Lulu's name, so she busies herself picking up their drinks, making a show of tipping a splash of almond milk into Cass's coffee, the way she knows she likes it. She delivers them to the table with a flourish.

"I am kind of curious about them, though," Cass says. "The videos. If you don't mind talking about them."

"Did I tell you about Mr. Winters?"

"No. I don't think so?"

"My Cinema Studies teacher."

"I can honestly say I don't think you ever told me you were taking Cinema Studies."

"Oh. Well. I am."

"Makes sense."

"Yeah. Anyway, our midterm project can be a creative submission. And he knows Ryan—his family. He'd said something about liking me as Ryan's model. So I sent him the thing I made, the first one, for a grade."

"Daaaaang."

"I know, right? I'm a whole new Lulu."

"What did he say about it?'

"He's not that stupid. He gave me an A and moved on." Lulu shrugs. "But then it started to seem kind of cheap to me, because, like, that was not actually a movie, or a thing about movies. And so it got me thinking: What would it mean to do my own work? Really do it? In a way that was deliberate, and intentional. Not, like, fooling around on Flash and being dumb."

"Those weren't—"

"I wasn't serious about them," Lulu says. "I'm, um. I think I'm being serious about this."

"You seem serious. Or at least productive."

"They're boring, right?"

"I don't know what they are," Cass says. "Honestly. It's hard for me to imagine what it would be like to watch them if I didn't know you. If I couldn't picture you just outside of the frame."

"That's sort of the point, I think," Lulu says. "To look at how many places in the world my body has made an impression. Just an ordinary one. How many places it was, and isn't anymore. It's like—sorry, this is *so* pretentious—but it's like, how can I construct a self-portrait that I'm not in, if that makes sense."

Cass mulls this over. "It almost sounds like you're trying to pull some disappearing trick," she says. "To be in a place, and also not be, at the same time."

"I'm just trying to figure out where I am first," Lulu says. "It's like, process of elimination, almost? Like, here's not-me. Here's not-me. Here's not-me. But also: Here's what I see. Here's me from the inside. Not out."

"You're the—like when you look at a Magic Eye thing," Cass says. "You stare at that center dot and the design comes into focus around it. These pictures are the dot. Your life is the design."

"That's a way of thinking about it."

"You're the one in Cinema Studies. You're the one who should have the theories."

"I'm just trying to figure out how to live in the world," Lulu says.

Cass quirks her mouth, wry, and takes a long sip of coffee. "Tell me about it," she says.

That night Cass sends Lulu a picture of her empty sneakers, tongue loose, laces tangled. In the morning, a close-up of the damp fibers of a towel.

Am I getting the idea, she asks.

If you're doing it it's your project, Lulu writes back. But I mean, I think so, yeah.

CHAPTER FIFTY-ONE

● ● ● ●

FOR WEEKS AFTER, that's how they talk—by sending images back and forth of spaces their bodies used to occupy, and don't anymore. The funny little pockets of emptiness that they find during the course of their days. Lulu learns more about Cass than she actually knew when they were hooking up: that she sits in the back of every classroom, and what the insides of Lowell's classrooms look like. How long she sits in traffic on the drive home from school, some days. How often she eats dinner alone.

It's a peculiar kind of intimacy, but it's theirs: something they build together, a way of allowing each other a privileged view into the mundane particulars of their lives.

Lulu also starts putting some of her videos together—a collection of clips from her Flash, which, ironically, she has to pull from that dumb fan site, and then some of these.

She quickly learns that these compilations can't be too long, or they feel disjointed. What she ends up with is usually no more than a minute. The first one she's happy with starts with one of the first private videos she took, the one of her hair on the shower wall, which is mildly gross in a way she kind of likes. It ends with a Flash of Cass on New Year's Eve, catching her eye from across the party. Lulu registers *lululooks.com.* After she's made Bea tell her about a thousand times that she's not ruining her life, she posts the video as a file called WHAT I LOOKED AT WHILE YOU WERE LOOKING AT ME.

She sends it to Cass too, with a note: Thanks for helping me start to figure it out.

Cass doesn't respond directly, but the next day, she sends Lulu a picture of a pile of clothes, and Lulu recognizes the bra that's pooled on top of it, a flimsy piece of lace she remembers because it seemed so at odds with Cass's style when she first saw it on her body.

Lulu sends Cass an empty orange peel, still intact as one long, carefully peeled strip, and then an image of her lipstick-smudged pillow. She fell asleep with her makeup on last night.

She holds her breath when she sees Cass has texted her back almost immediately. It's the first sight of her skin Lulu's had in weeks: Cass's sheets caught in the curl of her fist.

Lulu takes a selfie. This is what I look like when I miss you.

Cass asks, Can I come over?

Lulu says, Of course you can.

Cass must have had time to get shy on the drive; she lingers on Lulu's doorstep like she might not be allowed to come in, one hand resting lightly against the frame, fingertips tapping out an uneven, unconscious rhythm.

Lulu stands inside, feeling slightly stranded.

"Lulu?" Deirdre calls. "Is someone there?"

"A friend," Lulu says. "We're studying."

Too late: Deirdre's spotted something she can do to make herself appear motherly, and now there's nothing Lulu can do to stop her. She clacks her way into the front hall, still in heels from her workday. "Hi!" she says. "We were just about to sit down to dinner, actually, Lu."

"Can you just put mine in the fridge? I can warm it up later."

"Maybe your friend—" Deirdre turns to Cass to supply her name.

"Cass," Cass says.

"Maybe Cass is hungry," Deirdre suggests.

"I'm fine," Cass says. "Thanks."

"Are you sure? Don't let this one make you feel bad about having an appetite." Deirdre is very fond of reminding Lulu that she doesn't diet, and Lulu is very good at not saying *That's only because you don't have to* when she does.

"I'm fine," Cass repeats.

"Well, come sit with us for a minute, at least," Deirdre says. "Lulu almost never brings friends over, and especially not to study. Do you have a test tomorrow?"

"Calc," Lulu says, inventing wildly. This is probably the least sexy thing that's happened to anyone, ever. She tries to imagine how she'll set any kind of mood if they ever get upstairs.

"Fifteen minutes," Deirdre says. "I made crispy chicken, so

it'll really be much better hot. And Olivia hasn't seen you in days, Lu."

"My little sister," Lulu supplies for Cass, who nods.

"You'll study better on a full stomach," Deirdre says decisively. "As long as we're eating, Cass, I'll make you a plate?"

Which is how Lulu ends up sitting at her family's dining room table with her stepmom and her little sister and her ex . . . whatever, who no one even knows she used to date. Her dad comes home halfway through the meal, which nixes any chance of the quick escape Lulu was hoping for. "Sorry," she whispers to Cass when she can.

"It's fine," Cass says. "It's actually kind of hilarious, to see Lulu Shapiro acting like an obedient daughter."

"I'm not *obedient*."

"I've never seen you this tame."

Lulu raises one eyebrow. Cass has the grace to blush.

"So Cass, if you go to Lowell, how did you meet Laila?" her dad asks.

"Laila?"

"God, Dad!"

"It's your name," he says, and then, to Cass: "I've always thought Lulu was silly, but she insists on it."

"We made friends at a party," Cass says.

"Cass rescued me."

"Hmmm," Cass says, not quite affirmative.

"It was a boring party."

"All parties are boring."

"I know that now."

Finally, finally, the meal ends. Lulu and Cass help clear the dishes. The two of them are alone in the kitchen. It's the first time they've been alone in a room in a while, Lulu thinks.

"We should escape," she says. "Now, before Deirdre puts on music and turns this into family kitchen cleanup time. She hasn't had all four of us around a table in years, I think. She's going to milk it for all it's worth."

"I'm down," Cass says. "Lead the way."

Lulu looks around the kitchen and realizes they're trapped. The only way to get up to her room—to any other room in the house, from here—is to go back through the dining room, which will give Deirdre another opportunity to waylay them. The *studying for a test* excuse hasn't worked so far. The only thing they can do is go out the side door into the yard, which isn't perfect, but seems like a better option than the rumble of enforced fun she can hear coming from the dining room.

She motions for Cass to follow her, and Cass does. Outside, the night is sharply cold and black, the sky lit by the city's muggy glow and a bare sliver of moon. Lulu wishes she knew if it was waxing or waning—it feels like it would mean something either way. But if the sky has signs for her, she doesn't know how to read them.

Instead she turns to Cass. "Want to see my favorite place on the property?" she says.

"The *property*," Cass says. Before Lulu can defend herself, she says, "Of course."

Lulu walks them down the hill to the orange grove. Deirdre had some gleaning organization come through last week, and the branches have been stripped of their fruit, but you can still smell the scent of them, soft sweet and sharp citrus, in the air.

"Here," Lulu says.

Cass sits on one of the benches. "I remember you telling me about this place," she says. "It surprised me then, and it's surprising me now."

"Why? What did you expect?"

"I don't think of you as an outdoors girl."

Lulu laughs. She sits next to Cass on the bench, and Cass lets her.

"I'm not," she says. "But like, my backyard is hardly the outdoors, you know?"

"What do you like about it?"

Lulu closes her eyes. She feels her answers well up in her—a mass of feeling so tangled and private she barely has words for it. "Do you remember the night we met?"

"Um," Cass says. "It was like two months ago. So yes."

"I said something stupid to you about walls."

"I don't remember that, I have to admit."

"About how I have a bad sense of direction, but I know how to navigate houses because they have walls."

"That sounds . . . vaguely familiar. And only kind of dumb."

Lulu shoves Cass with her shoulder. Cass presses back against her. Lulu doesn't move away. Neither does Cass.

"I like things I can understand, most of the time," Lulu says. "Borders. Boundaries. Rules. How to behave myself for everyone else."

"I get that."

"I like it out here too, though."

"Limited wilderness."

Lulu laughs. "Limited wilderness." She leans a little more heavily against Cass's side. "I don't know. It's not that deep, probably. Just like, it's pretty out here. And quiet. My dad doesn't hang out here. Neither does Deirdre. It's just my spot. It kind of always has been. Where I can be actually all the way alone."

"What am I doing here, then?"

"Why did you bring me to The Hotel?"

"I wanted to be alone with you," Cass says.

"Yeah. Well. Same." Lulu leans away from Cass. She wants to give her space if she needs it. "Do you still want that? Do you think?"

"I don't know."

Lulu nods. She's not sure Cass can really see her in the darkness.

Cass says, "I just. Yeah. I don't know."

"You don't have to."

"I still like you," Cass says. "I just— It's been a lot."

"It's been really a lot."

Silence falls between them. Lulu sits in it for a little while. It feels okay, being here with Cass, she thinks, not looking at her, not listening for her. Just sitting still together. Knowing that she's there.

"The thing is," Cass says at last, "I'm here. And I don't think I'm going anywhere."

"Me neither, then."

Lulu's hand finds Cass's. The weight of her, the strength, the bony squeeze of her fingers and the soft skin of her palm. Lulu knows Cass's body by touch, with the answering weight and strength of her own.

Lulu knows that Cass is going to kiss her in a minute. And she finds that she isn't afraid to close her eyes and sit in darkness before that happens. She isn't afraid to let her.

ACKNOWLEDGMENTS

THANK YOU TO Sarah Burnes for loving this little feminist book from the first draft, and Jessica Dandino Garrison, Ellen Cormier, Nancy Mercado, Lauri Hornik, Regina Castillo, and everyone else at Dial for getting it from that draft to this one.

Then Theresa Evangelista designed the (stunning!!!) cover, Cerise Steel did the gorgeous interior, and Lindsay Boggs, Elyse Marshall, Shanta Newlin, Elise Gibbs, and everyone at Penguin helped make sure people would eventually read it.

I am deeply grateful to all of you for your work in transforming this thing from a word document into an actual book.

This is the second novel I've written almost entirely at Dinosaur Coffee; thanks for the ginger tonics and all the company, dudes.

Thank you to the women of Strong Sports Gym, and even some of the men. #YALi(f)t, bro?

Mushanto: As always, mushanto.

Mom, Dad, Tiny: I love you.

My tireless, tireless friends, my extended & chosen family: I love you too.

Thank you to the people who gave me some perspective on the perspectives in this book that aren't mine: Gina Delvac, Catie Disabato, Sharifa Love, Maura Milan, and Amy Spalding.

For early reads, thank you to Amada Chicago Lewis, Miranda Popkey, and Darcy Vebber. Writing is best done in and with community, and I'm infinitely lucky to have you all as part of mine.

Karina Longworth's book *Seduction: Sex, Lies and Stardom in Howard Hughes' Hollywood* came along at exactly the moment I needed some historical perspective on how silent-era Hollywood had operated. *Beauty, Power, Danger* doesn't exist, but *You Must Remember This* does, and it's excellent.

This book was also inspired and informed by other women's tellings of the Bluebeard story, in particular Angela Carter's *The Bloody Chamber,* Helen Oyeyemi's *Mr. Fox,* and Francesca Lia Block's story "Bones," which you can read in her collection *Roses and Bones.* They helped me think through why I wanted such an old fairy tale wound through a book about Snapchat.

And last but never least: Thank you for reading it.

ABOUT THE AUTHOR

ZAN ROMANOFF was born in Los Angeles and raised in its private schools. She is the author of the novels *A Song to Take the World Apart* and *Grace and the Fever*. Her nonfiction has appeared in Buzzfeed, *Elle, GQ*, LitHub, *The Los Angeles Times, The New Republic*, and *The Washington Post*, among others. Zan lives, writes, and watches a lot of reality television in LA. Connect with her online @zanopticon.